" 'YOU CAN TELL THE PIONEERS BY THE ARROWS IN THEIR BACKS.'

"That's what my father told me, and Tom and I laughed. We all thought it was funny. Now here we are, and here comes the—what, the third? Fourth? Fifth?" Lilian sniffed, and dabbed at an eye with her sleeve, the motion barely visible in the darkness.

"We'll think of something," Kirk said. "Big mirrors to bounce it right back at them, or . . . I don't know, but we'll think of something."

"And the fleet behind that?"

"We'll take care of them too."

STAR TREK®

NEW EARTH

BOOK FOUR OF SIX
THE FLAMING ARROW

KATHY OLTION
AND
JERRY OLTION

NEW EARTH CONCEPT BY DIANE CAREY AND JOHN ORDOVER

POCKET BOOKS
New York   London   Toronto   Sydney   Singapore   Belle Terre

An *Original* Publication of POCKET BOOKS

POCKET BOOKS, a division of Simon & Schuster Inc.
1230 Avenue of the Americas, New York, NY 10020

Copyright © 2000 by Paramount Pictures. All Rights Reserved.

STAR TREK is a Registered Trademark of Paramount Pictures.

This book is published by Pocket Books, a division of Simon & Schuster Inc., under exclusive license from Paramount Pictures.

ISBN: 0-671-78562-1

First Pocket Books printing July 2000

10 9 8 7 6 5 4 3 2 1

POCKET and colophon are registered trademarks of Simon & Schuster Inc.

Printed in the U.S.A.

For Kerry and George Palko,
the best parents (and in-laws!)
a person could ask for

THE FLAMING ARROW

Chapter One

CAPTAIN KIRK was in his quarters when the Kauld ship attacked. It was late in the evening—past eleven—and he had been trying for the last hour to put down the twenty-first-century potboiler he had picked up for a little mindless entertainment before bedtime, but Ryan Hughes's tale of piracy and romance in the early Lunar colonies had proven more engaging than he'd expected. He was three-quarters of the way into it when the intercom whistled for his attention.

He pressed the reply button on the wall panel beside his bed. "Kirk here."

"Captain," Spock said. "Sensors have picked up a Kauld warship approaching the planet. It is a single vessel traveling through normal space under half-impulse power. It does not respond to our hails."

For a moment Kirk couldn't make sense of it. Kauld ships on Luna? In the twenty-first century? But then his

1

own reality reasserted itself and he remembered where he was. This was the Belle Terre system, and the Kauld had been harassing the Federation colonists ever since they had arrived here, nearly a year ago.

"Go to yellow alert," Kirk said. "Move to intercept. I'll be right there."

"Acknowledged."

Kirk looked for a bookmark, but there was nothing within reach that would work. He fingered the pages—real paper, printed especially for the colony library—then dog-eared page 248 and set the book on his bed. He would probably hear no end of grief about that from the librarian, but it was either that or lay the book facedown and risk breaking the spine. That would probably lose him his library card, one of the few pleasures this colony world, far beyond the edge of civilization, had to offer.

He was alone in the turbolift on the way to the bridge. This time of night, most of the crew were in their quarters or at their graveyard-shift duty stations. He wondered if the Kauld knew that, and if they expected it to affect the *Enterprise*'s ability to respond. If so, they would get a rude surprise. The same people who worked the day shift rotated through night duty as well; there wasn't an inexperienced crew member on board.

And few of them would regret kicking some Kauld butt in the name of defense. It wasn't professional, it wasn't Starfleet, but there it was. These sapphire-skinned, bad-tempered, antagonistic aliens had been a thorn in the *Enterprise*'s side ever since the colony convoy had entered the Sagittarian sector. What had originally been intended as a simple escort mission while on her way into deeper space had instead become an extended peacekeeping job—in part because of these alien troublemakers.

The turbolift doors opened and Kirk stepped onto the bridge. Normally at this hour, the lights would have been at half-intensity to simulate a diurnal schedule, but during a yellow alert everything went back to full operational status. He noted that Sulu was at the helm and Thomsen was at the navigation console. Thomsen was less experienced than Sulu, but she was a good navigator, and she had been gaining much more experience since Chekov had left to join the *Reliant*.

Spock was seated in the captain's chair, but he vacated it as Kirk stepped forward.

"Report," Kirk said.

Spock stepped through the gap in the railing around the captain's chair and stood by his science station. "No change. The Kauld ship is continuing on course toward the planet and refuses to respond to our warnings." He studied one of his displays for a moment, then added, "Deep-space scans do not reveal any other supporting ships. It appears that they are acting alone."

Kirk looked past the helmsman and navigator to the main viewscreen, which showed the boxy, utilitarian Kauld fighter as it sped toward its goal: the Federation colony planet Belle Terre. Was this some kind of renegade attack? Surely the Kauld crew knew they were outgunned. Besides the *Enterprise,* there were a couple of dozen other starships orbiting the planet; mostly colony freighters, but the Kauld had learned before that those ships were far from helpless.

"They usually gang up five to one," Kirk said. "This doesn't feel right."

"It is most illogical, even for Kauld," Spock agreed.

"Helm, fire a warning shot across their bow," Kirk ordered. "Let's see if that gets their attention."

"Aye, sir," said Sulu. His fingers danced on the

control console, and a bright red phaser beam lanced out just kilometers ahead of the warship.

Kirk didn't have to ask his crew for the information he needed. They reported without prompting.

"No change in velocity or trajectory, Captain," said Thomsen.

"The Kauld have activated their weapons," Spock said.

"No response to our hails, sir," said Jolley, the relief communications officer.

"They can hear us. Open a channel," Kirk ordered.

"Channel open."

"This is Captain Kirk of the *Starship Enterprise*. You are intruding in Federation space. Turn back now, or we'll be forced to interpret your actions as aggressive and act accordingly."

Cold silence answered back.

"The Kauld ship is 28,500 kilometers from the planet's atmosphere and closing rapidly," Spock said. "And there is a further anomaly in their attack strategy: I read only a skeleton crew on board."

"You think it's a kamikaze ship?" Kirk asked.

"That seems likely."

If that was the aliens' game, Kirk felt sorry for them. He didn't like the idea of firing on a poorly defended ship, but he would do it if he had to. There were sixty thousand colonists on Belle Terre who depended on him for their safety; he wouldn't risk their lives to spare a hostile intruder just because it wasn't sporting.

There was also the quasar olivium mine to consider. That, not the planet, was what the Kauld wanted so badly, and it was a prize worth fighting for. There was enough quasimatter in the core of Belle Terre's largest moon to power the entire Federation for decades. It could also power the Kauld, their rivals the Blood, the Klingon Empire, the Romulan Empire, and half a dozen other enemies as well. Kirk wasn't going to risk that out of misguided sympathy for a suicide crew. Several shipments of olivium had been intercepted by pirates on the long trip back to Federation space; if the Kauld had been behind the pirates—as Kirk suspected they were—then they already had enough to put a doomsday-type bomb on board that ship.

But since it was just one ship, there might be a chance to stop them without bloodshed. "Get a tractor beam on them," he said.

Sulu complied, but the moment the Kauld felt the effect, they fired on the *Enterprise*. Shields flared as the disruptor beam struck, and the bridge shook as the inertial dampers fought to counteract the impact.

Another disruptor shot pounded the same spot.

"Tractor beam is off-line," Sulu called out.

"Shields down to sixty percent," Thomsen said.

The Kauld had signed their own death warrant. "Lock phasers on target," Kirk said.

"Locked and ready," Sulu replied.

"Fire."

The bright red beam lanced out again, this time striking the warship directly in the port flank. Its shields flared bright as they radiated the energy, but Sulu kept the beam centered until it burned through and sliced deep into the ship's interior. Bright flame shot out of the gash, dissipating immediately in the vacuum of space . . . then an explosion ripped the ship in half and sent the two pieces tumbling in opposite directions, spewing debris from their interiors as they spun.

"Survivors?" Kirk asked.

"No life-forms register," said Spock.

"What about anomalous energy signatures? Is there a bomb on board?"

"None in evidence, but at this distance they could shield it from our sensors."

"That's what I thought. Sulu, Thomsen, target both halves. Carve them into pieces."

"Aye, sir."

The bridge crew watched as the helmsman and navigator each took a target and proceeded to reduce them to debris. They only had a few seconds before the pieces hit atmosphere, but they crisscrossed the halves of the hull with phaser fire until they fell open like blossoming flowers, then played the phasers over the exposed interiors. Power sources erupted in bright red explosions, contributing yet more destruction, but they triggered nothing resembling a true bomb.

"Cease fire," Kirk said when the first of the pieces began to strike atmosphere. They hit near the twilight band and left bright streaks of ionized air in their wakes. That would be a great light show from the ground. Some of the pieces skipped off the atmosphere and burned again farther into the daylight side of the planet.

He sat in his chair, still staring at the screen long after the last of the pieces had burned out. This had been too easy.

"Any life pods launched?" he asked.

"Negative," said Spock.

"Signals? Did they send any messages or beam anything out before we hit them?"

"No, sir," said Jolley.

"Then what exactly were they trying to accomplish here?"

Nobody spoke.

Kirk looked at the screen again, which still showed

the planet turning serenely below as the *Enterprise* slid from the night side into day. "They didn't just throw a warship away for nothing. What did they get out of it? They already know our weapons capabilities. They knew we would fire on them. What did they gain just now?"

"Allies?" suggested Thomsen.

"How so?"

"Maybe they wanted to show someone how ruthless we are."

Kirk rubbed his chin, thinking. The scratchy day's growth of whiskers felt good on his hand, which he only now realized he'd been holding clenched since he entered the bridge.

"Are there any Kauld observers in evidence? Or Blood?" he asked.

"Nothing within the planetary system," Spock said. "I detect faint energy signatures in deep space nearly five light-days out, but even they are not conclusively Kauld or Blood."

"They wouldn't want to wait five days to find out how things came down here," said Kirk. "Keep a continual scan going for warp signatures along the wave front as the light from this heads through the solar system. And listen for subspace signals from spies on the ground—or on the moons or the outer planets. They might already have put observers in place."

He leaned back in his command chair and looked out at the planet again. White clouds over blue ocean and green-brown land; it was an oasis in a vast desert of empty space far, far away from the rest of the Federation. It had taken the colonists over nine months at warp speed just to get here. They hadn't come for the olivium, but once it was discovered they had had no choice but to protect it from the aliens who wanted it for themselves. It was too powerful to allow it to fall into the wrong hands. So now the colonists were caught in a struggle for survival in a star system so far away they couldn't even see Earth's sun with a telescope. They had enough raw power to destroy every planet between here and there—but without the technical infrastructure to harness it, it was useless to them.

Still, they had become custodians of the most sought-after element in the Alpha Quadrant. Belle Terre was already becoming a crossroads, and by the time the olivium was mined out it would be a commercial hub for light-years around.

Provided it didn't fall to the Kauld first. And the only thing preventing that was the *Enterprise*.

What if Thomsen was right? If the Kauld had finally admitted that they couldn't win this battle by themselves, then they might be trying to win allies. That might be harder to do than it sounded, though. Before the human colonists had entered their midst, they had been busy trying to conquer every other race in their sector. Kirk doubted if anyone would join them without major concessions ahead of time, and after decades of war the Kauld had nothing to give.

Their only bargaining chip would be the promise of a share in the olivium if they won, but Kirk couldn't imagine anyone stupid enough to believe that the Kauld would actually keep that promise.

No, gaining allies wasn't their way. They were up to something else. But what was it?

Chapter Two

WHEN HIS communicator beeped for attention, Dr. McCoy cursed and set his mint julep on the grass. The motion nearly tipped him out of his hammock, but he regained his balance at the last moment without spilling his drink or himself on the ground.

He tugged the communicator off his belt, flipped it open, and said, "McCoy here."

"Doctor," said the thin, reedy voice of Baedrick Neville, the colony's chief surgeon. "We've got a bit of a situation here. I wonder if you could come take a look at it."

"Weeellll," McCoy drawled, "that depends on what sort of a situation it is. Have you got an outbreak of Rigelian fever?"

"No, it's—"

"A neural parasite taking over everyone's minds?"

"No, not that either. It's—"

"How 'bout a virus that accelerates aging, or radiation exposure that gives everyone synesthesia?"

"No, nothing like that. It's—"

"Then I don't see why you need me. I'm sure you're perfectly capable of handling anything else that comes along."

"Yes, but—"

"And I'm on vacation."

Dr. Neville was silent for a moment. McCoy could picture him in the hospital, his tricorder in hand, probably displaying sensor readings that revealed everything but his patient's kindergarten grade. Yet Neville insisted on getting McCoy's confirmation on anything more serious than an ingrown toenail. It was a mystery how the man had ever gotten out of medical school without a good dose of self-confidence.

He said, "I'm sorry to have bothered you, Doctor, but I thought you'd want to know. It appears to be a spaceborne pathogen."

McCoy's right eyebrow jerked upward. "Spaceborne? How do you figure?"

"The patient is a ten-year-old male who came in complaining of a headache and upset stomach. Not interesting in itself, but his story is. He says he was swimming in Lake Lytle when something fell out of the sky and nearly hit him. He thought it was a meteor and dived to retrieve it, but grew sick almost immediately."

That didn't sound like a meteor to McCoy. The park where he had been trying to relax was on a hillside to the north of town; he looked out over the red tile rooftops to the blue lake on the valley floor beyond. He could see nothing unusual from this distance, but that didn't necessarily mean anything. "Have you found the pathogen?"

"Not yet. We got some unusual readings at first, but now diagnostics reveal nothing wrong. Reynold seems to have recovered on his own, but the case was unusual enough that I wanted to check with you in case I've missed something."

The name made McCoy sit up even straighter. "Reynold? Reynold Coates? Lilian's boy?"

"That's the one."

"I'll be right there. McCoy out." He snapped his communicator shut, and with a heavy sigh rolled out of the hammock. His julep glass sat in the grass, beads of moisture grown heavy on its sides. He picked it up, took one more small sip of the sweet iced whiskey, then dropped it in the recycler on his way out of the park. He promised himself that he'd throw his communicator away next time he came here, just so he could enjoy his next mint julep to the end.

Neville had been right, though. This was one situation he wanted to see for himself.

Over the duration of this interminable mission, he'd had ample time to get acquainted with most of the colony's members, but few of them had impressed him as much as Reynold Coates and his mother. In many ways Reynold was a typical ten-year-old boy, full of curiosity and spunk, but after his father was killed in an ambush during the journey to Belle Terre, he had been forced into a much more adult role than most kids his age. Lilian possessed a true pioneer's spirit and determination, carrying on after her husband's death without complaint, but raising a son on her own was a tough job even with a boy like Reynold. Her family's dreams had been shattered during that one tragic moment in space, and McCoy wasn't about to let some errant meteor deal them any more problems.

He could see the hospital's flat roof from where he stood. Governor Pardonnet had ordered that each of the major settlements on Belle Terre should build their medical center close to the middle of town, figuring it should be near as many people as possible. There was a transporter on site, but you couldn't always count on a transporter working when you needed it, especially here. For ten hours of every thirty, a stellar phenomenon called Gamma Night disrupted the signal so badly you couldn't transport a jug of water a quarter mile. The source of the interference was a neutron star orbiting a black hole a few light-years away and spraying a beam of charged particles into the Belle Terre system with each revolution, but knowing the source didn't help shield against it.

Nor did it improve McCoy's skepticism about transporters in general. He had never liked having his body converted to energy and squirted through space, but having it done unreliably held no attraction whatsoever.

Fortunately, there were other means of transportation. Most colonists traveled by foot or bicycle, or even horseback, especially if they were homesteading in the green rolling hills. It wasn't so much because of the Gamma Night, either. The colonists' intentions had always included a simpler, more peaceful lifestyle. McCoy applauded their efforts and walked as much as he could. But just now he needed to get to the hospital faster than his feet could take him, so he opted to use one of the colony's publicly owned bicycles. They were scattered all through town, three or four of them on average in every bicycle rack. It was easy to tell which bikes were public ones by the eye-burningly bright yellow paint. Nobody in their right mind would own a bike that color, which was exactly why they had been painted that way. Despite their prevalence at every street corner, nobody ever stole them.

Nobody ever maintained them either, it seemed. He had to reject two with flat tires before he found one in good working order, and its seat was stuck in the lowest position. He shrugged and climbed aboard anyway. It was all downhill from here; as long as he was just coasting he could scrunch up.

The road followed the brook that trickled out of the foothills into the lake. McCoy loved to feel the wind in his hair and listen to the water splashing over rocks beside him as he rode into town. The vegetation on the hillsides was green again, recovering nicely from the explosion on the planet's moon that had flash-burned the entire continent shortly after the colonists arrived. The weather had settled down to the point where a person could count on it for days at a time, and people were outside enjoying it.

McCoy smiled and waved at them on his way past, and they returned his greeting with friendly "hellos" and waves of their own. He felt just like a local, and it suddenly occurred to him that he *was* a local. He'd been here just as long as anyone. The *Enterprise* had escorted the colonists out here from Earth, and ongoing problems had kept the ship attached to the colony ever since. McCoy had been treating the situation like a temporary assignment, but it had been over a year now and there was no sign that they would be leaving anytime soon. This was as much a home as he had experienced since joining Starfleet.

He found that thought both comforting and disquieting. A whole year of his career spent guarding a single colony from hostile natives. No wonder he wanted Dr. Neville to fill his own shoes as chief medical officer.

He found the doctor and his young patient in a small exam room near the back of the hospital. Even before he entered, he could hear Dr. Neville asking Reynold for more details about his swim in the lake. Reynold was a good kid, but he was still ten years old, and now that he was feeling fine again his attention span was definitely reaching its limits.

"Afternoon, Dr. Neville. Hello there, Reynold," McCoy said as he stepped into the room.

"Hi, Dr. McCoy," Reynold said. He sat on the examination bench, shirtless, his bare feet swinging back and forth. His thick dark hair, cut short enough to stay out of his eyes, stuck up at odd angles from his head, a result of his interrupted swim in the lake.

"Doctor, I'm glad you could come," Neville said as he stood to shake McCoy's hand. He was a tall, slender man, just as his voice might lead one to imagine. His hands were long and thin, but his grip was firm. A good sign that he could hold his surgical tools with fine control.

"Yes. Well, Reynold, I hear you were feeling kind of punk a little bit ago," McCoy said. He sat down on a stool in front of the boy.

"Yes, sir. I'm feeling better now, though."

McCoy waved his own tricorder across Reynold's body and studied the results. "That's what my instruments tell me, too." He smiled, then said, "Dr. Neville said you were swimming in Lake Lytle when something fell into the lake and you went after it."

"That's right."

"Did you manage to retrieve whatever it was?"

"No, sir. I didn't even get close to it before my head started hurting." Reynold looked up at the clock on the

14

wall and said, "Is it okay if I leave? Mom's expecting me to finish my chores before dinner."

"Oh no you don't," McCoy said sternly. "I notice you carefully avoided saying that you would be going straight home to do those chores. I don't want you going back to that lake until we've found what made you sick." He turned to Neville. "Anybody else, either. Is anyone down there checking it out?"

"Er . . . not yet," said Neville.

"Get someone on it. Reynold, can you show them where it landed?"

"Yes, sir!" said the boy, even more excited to be included in an official search than to do it on his own.

Dr. Neville nodded. "Very well. I called your mother when you first got here, so she should be here any minute to pick you up. I'll ask her to take you back by the lake, and I'll send a science team down to meet you there. Don't go in the water again! Understood?"

"Yes, sir." Reynold squirmed uncomfortably on the exam table, then said, "And thanks for calling my mom, but I didn't want her to get worried. Especially since I'm better now."

"I'm sure she'll want to know what happened, even so. And I didn't want you walking home alone, in case you started feeling bad again."

"Yes, sir. It's just . . . well, I don't—"

"Dr. Neville's right," Lilian Coates said. She stood in the doorway, her eyes moving from person to person in the room, assessing her son's physical well-being by the doctors' stance as well as his own appearance. Her shoulder-length blonde hair had been swept up into a ponytail held in place by a blue kerchief, and she wore a cotton workshirt and a pair of jeans, the knees of which still had rich, brown soil caked on them. She must have been working in her garden when she got the call that her son was at the hospital.

She stepped into the room and smiled at both of the men as they stood, but her first words were for Reynold. "You look fine now, but until we know what made you sick in the first place I want to keep an eye on you. Doctors? Do you have any more information than when you called?"

"I'm afraid not," said McCoy.

"But we're looking for the meteor," Neville added quickly. "That may tell us something."

"They want me to show the search team where it landed," Reynold said, his voice filled with pride.

"Is it okay for him to go back there?" she asked.

Dr. Neville looked at McCoy, but McCoy waited for him to answer. Reynold was his patient. At last Neville said, "We think so, but the cause of his sudden illness is still unknown. If you don't want him to go, that's understandable."

She ran a hand through her hair, loosening a strand from her ponytail. "Of course I don't *want* him to, but I suppose he should. The sooner we find out what happened, the better we'll all feel."

McCoy agreed wholeheartedly. There was nothing he hated quite so much as an unknown pathogen loose in a population he was supposed to keep healthy. The stream that fed Lake Lytle also provided the town's water; if something happened to that, everyone could be in trouble in a big hurry.

"Thank you," he said. "We'll check back with you tonight."

Reynold jumped off the table and headed for the door, pulling his mother behind him in his eagerness to go help the search team. As they receded down the hallway, his voice echoed off the walls: "You should've seen it, Ma. It made a splash that went halfway across the lake!"

Both men looked at the empty doorway a moment or two longer, then McCoy turned back to Neville. "Well. Don't just sit there with your teeth in your mouth. Show me the readings you got earlier from this 'space pathogen.' "

Chapter Three

DELORIC WAVED his fellow Kauld workers aside, aimed
his energy pick at the comet's surface, and drew its disruptor tip in a line down the face of the ice wall in front
of him. Chips of frozen carbon dioxide flew past him,
flashing white in the beam of his helmet light for just a
second as they shot out of the crevice, propelled by the
vaporized material in the direct path of the disruptor.
He tried to hold it steady, carving a straight line an
arm's span away from the last cut and defining a block
about the size of a coffin standing on end—a block just
like the hundreds of others he and the two others in his
mining team had already sliced free today.

Join the fleet, see the universe! He snorted at the
thought. So far, all he'd seen was the operator's end of
a lot of hand tools. He was the foreman of his team, but
that only meant he had responsibility as well as hard
work to deal with. What a joke! If he'd wanted to be a

miner, he could have stayed back home, made twice the pay, and had a comfortable bed to sleep in at the end of the day.

Instead here he was, anchored to this dirty travelling dry-ice cube, carving it up and sending the pieces off to make a chain out in the middle of empty space. There were dozens of other teams doing the same thing, enough to create a steady stream of ice blocks stretching off into infinity.

He gave the dirty white chunk before him a kick, thankful for the gravity boots that kept him from flying off into space himself, but he failed to dislodge it.

Terwolan's voice hissed in his ear through his helmet's intercom. "You missed a spot."

She was standing atop the block. He looked up, his light sliding up her legs and across her spacesuited body until he could see her arm pointing into the crack he had just cut. He peered back into the crevice. Sure enough, his pick hadn't reached deep enough to finish the job. He checked the recharge light on the handle. It was going to take another half a minute to come up to full power.

"Get the directional jets attached while we're waiting," he ordered her. She and Nialerad, the third miner in the team, moved to the task, and he took the moment to back away from the ice face and look up. There wasn't much nearby; they were five light-days away from the nearest star—forty times as distant as its farthest planet—which made the view all the more breathtaking. The velvety blackness of space was interrupted only by the glittering sprinkle of jeweled stars. This, he reminded himself, was why he had joined the fleet, not for the heroics or—

"Hey, dreamer! Wake up! Your pick's charged, let's get on with this!"

—or the drudgework. The others had finished their

job; the jets were in place, screwed directly into the carbon-dioxide ice. Deloric aimed the pick again and fired into the offending crack. It took two more passes before the block broke loose.

"Stand clear!" Terwolan called. The control unit blinked with red and blue status indicators in the palm of her gloved hand. Deloric and Nialerad backed carefully away from the slowly tumbling cube they'd created while she triggered the command that would send the ice block to join the others.

With a flash of white light from the tail ends of the jets, it oriented itself and sailed away. All three miners watched as it set out on its journey: Terwolan to be sure that she'd programmed the jets correctly, Deloric because it was the sign of a job well done—not to mention that it was a beautiful sight. He could only guess at what Nialerad thought. He wasn't the talkative sort.

They allowed themselves those few moments of rest, but their orders were explicit: keep slicing up this dirty ice ball and sending the pieces to their new coordinates until they were told to stop. Even before the block they had just released grew too small to see, Deloric said, "All right, let's get back to it."

The crew started working on the next block in line. They had already removed the comet's irregular surface, and were now peeling it a layer at a time, spiraling their way from the sunward point to the terminator. Deloric couldn't help but wonder what was going on, but he knew enough not to ask the reasons for their assignments. He might be a dreamer, but he was no fool. His job was to do what he was told, no questions asked. All the same, it was intriguing, all this activity. Though what made it even more intriguing was the added order not to go to the other side of the comet. What? Was the ice over on that side inferior? If ever there was a way to raise curiosity, it was to issue an order like that.

It was all he could do not to discuss it with his crewmates. He'd worked with them for weeks now, but he didn't know them, not like that anyway. Some people thought it subversive to speculate on the reason for any order. They might report such speculations to a higher authority, and nobody wanted that to happen. A soldier true to the cause didn't question orders. Not everyone felt that way, he hoped, but enough did to keep everyone's mouth quiet.

It wasn't enough to keep his mind from running through the possibilities while he worked at liberating the new piece of ice, and the piece after that, and the one after that. He knew this star system: it was the one that held the olivium moon mine. All of the Kauld efforts of late had been attempts to reclaim the moon from the invaders. So far all their attempts had failed, but that was something else good soldiers never discussed.

Deloric wasn't a scientist, so the finer aspects of what the olivium was good for were lost on him, but the bottom line was clear. It would give great power to whoever controlled it. That was all he needed to know in order to understand his leaders' motivation. And when they wrested the moon free from the humans, he would no doubt have a new job: mining olivium.

He needed to make a clean break. Do something heroic and get promoted, or do something stupid and get kicked out of the fleet, but this was a dead end. He had better things to do with his life than wield an energy pick. He wanted to help crew a scout ship, seeing strange new worlds and meeting exotic new aliens. He had heard stories of blue-skinned Andorians with antennae on their heads, green-skinned Orions whose women were reputed to be the most alluring in the galaxy, and other beings without even bodies in the normal sense.

He imagined himself as an ambassador to new races, learning how to cooperate rather than fight with them. That would be far more difficult than mining comets, but far more rewarding. He could see himself, Deloric the Great in his elder years, dispensing the wisdom of a long, exciting life to young new recruits about to embark on their own voyages into the vastness of space. That was the life for him!

"Twenty minutes to nighttime," Terwolan announced.

He looked up. They had worked nearly a third of the way around the comet. The relief crew would be here shortly, so that Deloric's crew could leave and get back to the bunk ship before the Blind made navigating between the comet and the ship too dangerous to attempt. He was glad that someone kept tabs on things like the time. Once he got into a job, he just kept at it until it was finished. That was no doubt why he had been made foreman, but it probably irritated his crew, who didn't seem to have his daydreams to keep their minds occupied while their bodies were providing cheap labor for the cause.

He packed up his tools and watched as the shuttle deposited the next batch of workers. The commander had forbidden any energy use that could be detected from within the star system, so all travel was to be done by rocket—chemical rockets at that!—and all communications kept to minimal power, detectable only within a few light-seconds.

He stole one more look at the space around him. He couldn't see the pearly string of comet chunks, but he knew where they were. And he knew what they were aimed at. It was just a point in space a few light-minutes to the side of the sun at the moment, but in fifteen days Belle Terre, the world around which the olivium moon orbited, would sweep through that spot.

It didn't make any sense, though. At the meager speed their chemical rockets could boost them to, the chunks of frozen carbon dioxide would be nowhere near Belle Terre in ten days. They would barely make it a few light-seconds away from the comet in that time. It would take decades for them to drift all the way in-system, and by the time they did, gravitational perturbation from the outer planets would bend their trajectories every which way.

There was no doubt, though: they were aimed at the planet. Deloric was willing to bet that the Federation colony there would be on the side facing them when it crossed through the spot they were pointing at, too. He just couldn't figure out what difference it would make.

"Hey, are you coming or not?" Terwolan asked. She was standing in the hatchway of the shuttle, her helmet light making little zigzags on the ice as she shook her head.

"Yes, Mother." He trudged toward the shuttle, thinking.

Chapter Four

CHIEF ENGINEER Montgomery Scott scowled at the toaster on the workbench before him. It was a simple, unassuming device designed to accept two slices of bread onto a spring-loaded pedestal that lowered them into a small chamber where they were exposed to radiant heat. The heaters performed the same job a conventional toaster would do with an infrared laser, giving the light, soft bread a smoothly browned surface perfect for holding melted butter and fresh preserves.

In theory, anyway. This one wouldn't heat, wouldn't raise or lower the bread platform, and wouldn't respond to any of his diagnostic probes. If he had been on board the *Enterprise* he could have scanned it and had the computer analyze it and pinpoint the problem in seconds, but he wasn't on board the ship. He was in the blacksmith's shop, trying to prevent William Thorpe from destroying a family heirloom with his horseshoe tongs and ball-peen hammer.

Thorpe was gone for the moment, but Scotty had noticed the antique bread warmer on his workbench when he'd stopped in to say hello, and he knew that the blacksmith was over at the saloon working up his courage to tackle the delicate repair job. The only way to rescue the toaster was to fix it himself and then claim he'd just been killing time until Thorpe returned.

He couldn't take it to the *Enterprise* now that he'd begun, either. Gamma Night was due any moment now, and if it caught him in midtransport, he'd be stuck in the pattern buffer until the particle storm's disruptive influence was over. It was theoretically possible to survive a lengthy stay in the buffer, but he wasn't willing to try it for anything less than a life-or-death emergency, which this was not.

Kaylene Brandon thought it was, but then it was her toaster. According to the kids who liked to gather around the blacksmith's shop—and who now stood in a semicircle around him offering helpful suggestions as he worked—she had brought it with her to Belle Terre, figuring to add a little authentic nostalgia to her family's homesteading days. Now it apparently symbolized everything about colony life for her. If it failed, so would her faith in the colony. Scotty understood how someone could develop an emotional attachment to a well-designed machine, but that seemed a bit over the top to him. If she had to fall for something, it ought to at least have an auxiliary power source.

The toaster didn't use any of the standard power supplies that Scotty was used to, but the Brandons had brought along a converter that produced alternating current from a phaser battery. Scotty knew that was working; it had burned out his tricorder when he'd connected it up directly to check the voltage. He'd forgotten how unforgiving alternating current could be to delicate electronics.

Now he was on his own, man against machine, with no technological crutches to help him. He didn't mind; he actually liked the challenge of it. This was even more fun than catching up on his technical manuals, and definitely better than helping build smelters and fabrication plants for the colony, which he had been doing earlier in the day. He had to get back to that eventually, but for now he was happy to take a little "engineers holiday" and tinker a bit.

He bent happily to the task. If the power supply worked, then the problem was probably something mechanical, a broken wire or a bent linkage. The device's internal sensors apparently couldn't detect that sort of damage, if indeed it had sensors. They were either more cleverly hidden than Scotty had ever seen before, or nonexistent.

He had decided that maybe there had to be a piece of bread on the pedestal before it would operate, so he had sent one of the children over to the bakery for a loaf. When the boy returned with it, fresh out of the oven and smelling wonderful, it turned out to be much tougher than it looked to cut it into even slices that would fit in the toaster's slots. Scotty had finally gotten two usable if a bit ragged slabs, and the children had happily eaten the evidence of his mistakes, so he made sure the power converter was switched on and set the two slices on the platforms.

"Stand back now," he admonished the kids, but there was no need to worry. Nothing happened.

"All right then, we'll try manual override," he

muttered, pushing down the plunger at the end of the toaster. The bread descended into the slots and a soft humming sound came from inside the silvery case, but when he held his hand over the slots he felt no heat.

He couldn't see past the bread, so he took the knife that he had used to carve it and slid the blade in beside one of the slices, intending to peer in and see if the characteristic red glow of radiant heat was present, but the tip of the blade must have contacted the heating element instead.

There was a loud *zzzztt!* and he jerked backward, his whole body suddenly tingling as if he'd been hit with a phaser set on stun. The children's mouths gaped open like singers in a choir, then a moment later they burst into laughter.

"Oh, so it's funny, is it?" he said, his teeth still vibrating from the alternating current.

A little girl with blonde pigtails pointed upward. "It's your hair!"

He reached up to feel the top of his head and found his hair standing on end.

"Do ye know what causes that?" he asked.

"Sticking a knife in the toaster!" the same girl said.

"Aye, that was how it happened," he admitted, "but that's not *what* happened. The electricity left a charge on the surface of my body, and some of the electrons went up to my hair where they make the strands repel each other."

"Can I try it?" asked the boy beside her.

"Uhhh . . . that's not a good idea," Scotty said. "If the frequency was just a wee bit lower, it could cook you from the inside out."

"Oh." The children backed away a step.

Scotty slicked down his hair again and grounded

himself on the workbench's metal edge, then looked at the knife he still clutched in his hand. He had burned a small notch in the tip of the blade, but it could be repaired.

The toaster was another story. He lifted the manual override lever and removed the bread, then peered inside. The heating element he'd touched was missing a good centimeter of wire, completely vaporized by the short circuit. He would have to take the whole thing apart now and reroute the wire to get enough length to splice it back together again.

He turned it over, looking for helical tensors or magnaplane fasteners, but the case was held together with Phillips-head screws. "Well," he muttered, "it looks like I'm in the right place after all," for the walls of the smithy were festooned with screwdrivers, pliers, hammers, and tongs. Scotty had a wonderful collection of similar tools in his quarters on board the ship, but he would no more use them than the captain would use one of his precious paper books to prop up a gimpy table leg. Here, though, Thorpe used his all the time. They were scratched and pitted and in some cases bent from being pressed into service as pry bars. The blacksmith wouldn't care a bit if Scotty did the same.

Whistling softly, he selected the appropriate-size screwdriver from the tool rack and set to work, but he had barely removed the first screw when Thorpe showed up, his massive shoulders, curly black hair, and thickly bearded face eclipsing the light coming in through the open doorway.

"Ah, good," he said, hardly glancing at what Scotty was doing. "I was looking for you. Something funny fell into the lake, and Dr. Neville wants us to go investigate."

"Something funny?" Scotty asked. "Funny how?"

"He didn't say, but I'd guess funny strange. Neville doesn't strike me as the kind who's interested in funny ha-ha."

That wasn't what Scotty had meant by his question, but it looked like that was all the answer he was going to get. Thorpe snatched his tricorder off its peg by the door and stepped out into the street, followed by the kids who had been watching Scotty. They had the right idea; it was either tag along or hear the story second-hand, so Scotty shut off the toaster's power supply and followed them down to the lake.

Reynold Coates and his mother were already there, standing on the end of the short pier that extended a few meters out over the water. The children all ran up to them, and Reynold pointed out over the water, then everyone shaded their eyes and looked. Scotty peered out into the lake as well, and after his eyes had adjusted to the glare of the afternoon sun on the rippling surface, he realized that a small patch of water about a stone's throw out from the pier was bubbling. It looked like some kind of gas was being released from below.

Four or five fish floated on their sides near the disturbed surface. Were they poisoned or cooked? If a hot reactor core had fallen into the water, that gas could be steam.

"What's the radiation reading?" he asked Thorpe as he strode out onto the pier.

Thorpe lifted his tricorder and pushed the power button with a calloused thumb, then laboriously poked at the sensor controls until he got a radiation scan. "Just normal background," he said. "Which is sky-high at the moment. Gamma Night's starting."

Scotty looked at the sky, but the bright blue atmosphere revealed no evidence of the energy sleeting into it from space. Not visually at least—but the effects were easy to detect in other ways. Communications would be down for the next ten hours, and the rising ionic imbalance would ultimately knock out even hand-held devices like Thorpe's tricorder. They would have to take what readings they could within the next few minutes, or wait until tomorrow.

"Chemical reading?" he asked.

"Umm, just a minute." The blacksmith prodded the controls again, then realized what the problem was and blew a thick layer of dust off the display. "Nothing unusual," he reported. "Silica, but . . ." He waved his hand through the dust cloud.

Scotty resisted the urge to take the tricorder from him and try it himself. His own tricorder lay on Thorpe's workbench, burned out through his own carelessness; he had no right to demand that someone else relinquish theirs.

He looked out at the bubbling water again. They needed to get out there and take a sample directly from the source. There was a flat-bottomed boat tied to the side of the pier; Scotty had no idea whose it was, but he didn't think they'd begrudge him the use of it to investigate something like this.

"Into the boat," he said to Thorpe.

"I want to go too!" one of the kids said, but Scotty shook his head.

"No, laddie. A great big bairn like you will swamp a wee boat like that one."

Everyone laughed, then laughed even louder when Thorpe and Scotty both climbed in. There was only a hand's width of freeboard left, and that varied considerably as the two men wobbled for balance while they unshipped the oars. They didn't bother to put them in the locks; they just paddled toward the bubbling water, Thorpe holding his oar in one massive hand while he worked the tricorder with his other.

"I'm still picking up a silica compound," he said as they drew closer. "Says here it's heavily oxygenated, molecular weight up in the thousands. That can't be right, can it?"

"It could if it were a polymer of some sort," Scotty said. "Can you get a structural reading?"

"Yeah, but it doesn't look like anything I've ever seen." He held out the tricorder for Scotty to examine. The screen showed the schematic of a huge molecule composed of mostly silicon and oxygen atoms, but it wasn't anything Scotty was familiar with either, and it changed even as he watched. Some of that was just interference from Gamma Night, but some of it was actual molecular activity. Then he noticed the warning line blinking in the corner of the screen. *Explosive gas*.

"Aha!" he said, watching the molecule grow. "Something's reacting with the lakebed. It's breaking down the sand, combining it with oxygen from the water, and bubbling off free hydrogen. Purely chemical reaction. Can you get a reading of the parent material?"

"I'll try." Thorpe leaned over the side of the boat and aimed the tricorder into the water. Scotty leaned the other way to keep them from capsizing while Thorpe waved the tricorder back and forth, but the blacksmith was unable to get a lock on anything through the meters of water. "Traces of tungsten, aluminum, magnesium, and so on," he said, sitting upright again and nearly pitching Scotty out the other side before he could compensate, "but I can't locate a parent mass. It looks like it's completely dissolved."

"Then why is the water still bubbling?" Scotty asked.

"You got me. Here, you're better at this sort of thing. You try." Thorpe handed Scotty the tricorder.

Scotty took it eagerly and began scanning for more clues. He had no more luck than Thorpe with chemical analysis or direct mass sensing, but there were a few unusual spikes in the high-frequency energy spectrum. Trouble was, they were so diffuse there was no way to tell whether they were coming from the lake or from space.

One of the dead fish floated past, so he scanned it, too. It was a rainbow trout, planted here from Earth stock. A medical tricorder would have given him more useful data, but even with Thorpe's primitive scanner and Gamma Night interfering with its beam, it was obvious that the fish had been asphyxiated. The ongoing chemical reaction had apparently pulled all the dissolved oxygen from the water before it had set to work dissociating the water molecules themselves.

The bubbles were dying down. Scotty set the tricorder's range to maximum and aimed it out over the lake. Through the rising static, he could detect low-level molecular activity all through the water. "Whatever it is, it's dissipating," he said.

"Good," Thorpe replied. Without prompting, he started paddling for shore again, and Scotty had to set the tricorder down and help so they wouldn't go around in circles. He looked back out at the lake, wishing he had better equipment, and wishing gamma night hadn't cut short what readings he had been able to get.

If wishes were fishes, he thought, looking back over his shoulder at the dead trout, then he would be back on board the *Enterprise,* pushing the engines to maximum output while the great starship streaked from star to star on a mission of galactic importance, not stuck here on some backwater planet—literally!—repairing toasters and investigating swamp gas while the last years of his career ticked slowly by. This little oddity was mildly interesting, but he was sure it would ultimately turn out to be a simple natural phenomenon, of no great concern to anyone but a hydrologist.

Chapter Five

THE BRIDGE of the *Enterprise* was eerily silent. The steady
ping of the subspace scanners had stopped. Missing also
were the various hums, bleeps, and twitters from the communications, helm, and science stations. On all sides,
snow-filled monitors hissed softly, awaiting reacquisition
of signal. Gamma Night had shut them all down, its flood
of charged particles reducing the ship's sensing ability to
the most basic system of all: the naked eye.

Captain Kirk leaned back in his command chair and
stretched his arms over his head, feeling joints pop and
muscles release all the way down into his rib cage.
Gamma Night always affected him like this. Dr. McCoy
swore that there were no physiological effects from it,
but every time the radiation storm sprayed through the
Belle Terre system and interrupted the ship's sensors,
Kirk felt as if his own body was under siege.

He hated flying blind. That attitude had been drilled

into him from his earliest days at the academy: they didn't call it "dead reckoning" for nothing. At flight speed, any random piece of debris could punch right through a ship before they even knew what hit them. The only solution was to reduce your velocity as much as possible, just drift in space and hope that nothing else was moving relative to you. It was a frustrating choice, but it was the best they could do.

Spock was experimenting with olivium-powered sensors that could cut through the interference, but he was finding the unstable quasimatter much trickier to work with than he had anticipated. Instead of simply extending an instrument's range, the new power source seemed to affect its very nature, giving the sensors new and unpredictable side effects. Kirk was confident that his science officer would eventually figure it out, but in the meantime, Gamma Night still shut them down for ten hours out of every thirty.

As a stopgap measure, Spock had rigged up a low-frequency radar unit using the forward deflector, but a wavelength long enough to penetrate the particle storm was practically useless for detecting anything smaller than a battle cruiser. Nonetheless, the Vulcan kept his eye on the fuzzy green monitor as its refresh line swept around and around in a slow circle. Sulu and Thomsen directed their attention to the main viewscreen, while Jolley coordinated lookouts on observation decks throughout the ship. If anyone spotted anything moving against the stellar background, Jolley would put it on the main screen under high magnification, and Thomsen would calculate its course manually.

It was a hell of a way to run a starship, Kirk thought as he stood up and paced once around the bridge. He might as well paint concentric red rings around the top of the saucer section.

"Captain," Spock said as he started a second lap, "may I remind you that your presence is required in—"

"I know."

Spock turned back to his sensor screen, his already green face practically fluorescent in the monitor's phosphor glow. Kirk knew he was stalling, but it was hard to leave the bridge when his ship was so exposed to danger.

Besides, he had an ulterior motive. He knew that Governor Pardonnet was waiting in the *Enterprise*'s conference room, cooling his heels and making small talk with Shucorion, the former alien spymaster turned ally. The young governing head of the Belle Terre colony would not be happy with the wait, nor with the company, but Kirk wanted to make a point. He'd invited the governor to this meeting days ago to discuss the need for a stronger defensive system for the planet, and Pardonnet's own schedule had determined the meeting time. He had insisted on putting it at the end of his workday, symbolically giving it the lowest status of his many appointments and no doubt hoping that Kirk would cancel it because of the on-board hour.

A small smile tugged at Kirk's lips as he strode into the turbolift. No chance of that. He couldn't have planned it better himself. Timing was everything, after all.

"You have the bridge," he said to Spock, then the turbolift doors slid closed and he rode it down to deck 7 and the briefing room where Pardonnet waited.

The door had barely opened before Pardonnet said, "Captain, I am a busy man. I don't have the time to sit around this ship waiting for you—"

"It's good to see you too, Governor," Kirk said. "You're looking well." In reality, the usually calm, well-dressed young man appeared somewhat rumpled, as though he'd spent all of Saturday night in his Sunday best.

Kirk looked at the stocky, blue-skinned alien sitting two seats to Pardonnet's right. "Shucorion, thank you for joining us."

The alien bowed his head in the traditional greeting of the Blood, as his people called themselves. "At your service," he replied.

At your service. Sure. *Only so far as that service furthered his own goals of supremacy for the Blood over their longtime enemies, the Kauld,* Kirk thought, but he merely nodded and took his seat across from the two leaders. They had chosen to sit with their backs to the viewport, ignoring the sight of Belle Terre floating serenely in space only thirty thousand kilometers away. Was it the frontier mentality of never putting your back to a door, or were they both tired of looking at the source of all their troubles?

Kirk didn't mind. This was his ship, and a planet seen from geosynchronous orbit was beautiful no matter how much trouble it was.

"Captain, can we get on with this?" Pardonnet asked.

"Of course. My apologies for being late, but we were securing the bridge for Gamma Night."

"What?" Pardonnet checked his wrist chronometer. "For the love of . . . I can't be stuck here for the next ten hours!"

"I'm afraid you have no choice. Not to worry though. You can have access to the recreation areas when we're finished, or if you prefer, I'm sure we have a free room where you can rest."

A look of resignation slid over Pardonnet's face. "We'll worry about that later. Let's get started."

"Very well, Governor, I'll cut right to the heart of the matter. We have to start building up our defenses again. The Eau Clair flood wiped out over half of your ground-based shuttle fleet." He pointedly used the official name for the river valley, rather than the colonists' own term for it: the Big Muddy.

Pardonnet opened his mouth to speak, but Kirk kept going without pause. "You've decommissioned three of the remaining space freighters just in the last week. I know it was in the original mission plan to use the cargo ships for raw materials once we arrived here, but the situation is different now. We're sitting on top of a gold mine, and everybody wants a piece of it. Even if we can keep the prospectors at bay, the Blood and the Kauld could resume hostilities at any moment, and if they do, we'll find ourselves in the middle of it within hours."

Shucorion didn't even blink, which by itself told Kirk he'd hit uncomfortably close to the mark. The Blood leader had allied his people with the Federation for one reason only: protection from their enemies, and everyone knew it. Neither race was native to Belle Terre—their star system was light-years distant—but ever since the discovery of quasar olivium deep inside Belle Terre's moon, they had conspired as much to keep each another away from the new resource as to gain it for themselves. If the Kauld ever gained a toehold in the Belle Terre system, there would be some "regrettable incident" that would spark a battle, and Shucorion would scream for military assistance from Kirk and the Belle Terre colony until they were driven away.

Kirk looked back to Pardonnet. "We need to refit all of our spaceworthy ships with phasers and beef up their shields. Likewise, the colonists should all be trained to handle a ground invasion. I don't know if it'll be human or Kauld or somebody we haven't even heard of, but it's only a matter of time before somebody tries to pick your plum, and we've got to be ready for them."

Pardonnet steepled his fingers in front of him on the tabletop. "Captain, I appreciate your concern, and if I've learned anything from you in our . . . shall we say 'tempestuous' past, it's not to underestimate your assessment of a military situation. However, I don't really think this *is* a military situation."

"We just shot down another hostile ship less than an hour ago," Kirk reminded him.

"I heard. It was a single ship, wasn't it? A few overeager privateers now and then hardly comprise a significant threat. Besides, even that will soon stop now that we've begun mining olivium and selling it to the highest bidder. Our prices are high, and the risk of piracy en route to the developed sectors of the galaxy no doubt makes the price even higher by the time it reaches the open market, but surely it can't cost as much to simply *buy* the product as it would cost to fight a prolonged battle over interstellar distances for it."

Kirk admired his reasoning. If everyone looked at the universe the way he did, there would be no need for a military buildup. Unfortunately, not everyone was quite so logical in their thinking.

"You're being libertarian again," he said. "It would be a fine system if everyone was a nice guy, but some people like taking things without paying for them. The only way to stop people like that from doing what they want is to make it physically impossible. Maybe if we make a big enough show of our preparations, they'll see it's impossible before they try, but either way we've got to make our military presence strong enough that we can win the battle whether it happens or not."

"Spoken like a true soldier," Pardonnet said.

Kirk felt those words strike home. He didn't want to be a soldier, and Pardonnet knew it. Nothing would please Kirk more than taking the *Enterprise* out into unexplored territory again, to search for strange new worlds instead of babysitting a bunch of colonists who had gotten in over their heads. Given a choice, he would do just that; but he didn't have a choice, and Pardonnet knew that, too. They were stuck with each other until the situation changed, and like an old married couple they simply enjoyed pushing each other's hot buttons once in a while.

Kirk resisted the urge to return fire. He merely stated the obvious. "At the moment, a soldier is what you need. Believe me, the instant my presence is no longer necessary, I'm warp nine for deep space, but until that time I'm your guardian angel."

Shucorion coughed politely. "The Blood would gladly augment your defense force with more ships of our own."

Kirk suppressed a sardonic grin. "I'm sure you would. Unfortunately, that would precipitate the very conflict with the Kauld that we're trying to avoid. We need our own ships, staffed from the colony."

"What?" Pardonnet said indignantly. "You want my people, too? We're already shorthanded everywhere!"

Shucorion ignored his outburst. "Or you need a neutral third party," said the alien. "Fourth, in this case."

"Hire peacekeepers?" Kirk asked. The idea had never even occurred to him. "Where?"

"There are many other races in this sector."

"And what's to keep them from taking the olivium for themselves if we let them in here with warships?"

"We are. The Blood, the Federation, and yes, even the Kauld. If none of us can win on our own, we will work together to ensure that no one else does, either."

40

Kirk thought it over for all of two seconds. "No. That sort of thing has been tried before all through human history, but it always falls apart. The different sides make temporary alliances and gang up on each other until everybody's at war with everybody else. We need one very powerful force here, not half a dozen small ones."

"And who guarantees the loyalty of the force?" asked Pardonnet.

"I do," Kirk said flatly.

Pardonnet nodded. "Your word is as good as the deed. So is your first officer's. In fact, I believe I could trust nearly every member of your crew to uphold the principles of the Federation against the greatest temptation. But what happens if this ship is destroyed? Suppose a spy gets on board with an antimatter bomb?" His eyes flicked momentarily to Shucorion, then back to Kirk. "Or suppose some errant asteroid smashes you out of orbit during Gamma Night. What then? Who takes your role, and what is their agenda?"

"We'll establish a chain of command."

"Which will only be as strong as its weakest link. No, Captain. I much prefer a society without arms at all to a society where everyone holds a phaser to his neighbor's head."

"People have tried that, too," Kirk reminded him. "Remember Nantes III? Providence Prime? Felicity Alpha?"

Pardonnet narrowed his eyes. "No."

"Not surprising," Kirk said. "They don't exist anymore. The first hostile force that came along wiped out every colony."

Shucorion stared at both men in open astonishment. "You left colonies undefended?"

Kirk snorted. "Many times. Humanity has more than its share of idiots." He looked quickly at Pardonnet.

"And no, Governor, that was not a barb at you. But those who forget history are doomed to repeat it."

Pardonnet nodded. "I understand the need for security, and I agree with you in principle. I'm just trying to balance that against the colony's need for resources. Our forests all went up in smoke during the Burn, the chaotic weather wipes out any crops we don't keep under cover, and we lost entire communities during the flood. We've got nothing to rebuild with except brick and whatever we can scrounge from the cargo ships. If we turn them all into gunships, I'm afraid there won't be a colony to protect."

"We're getting smelters on-line," Kirk reminded him. "It won't be long before they'll outpace any salvage operation."

" 'Not long' to you is an eternity to someone living in a tent," Pardonnet pointed out.

Kirk looked out the viewport at the planet below. From here it looked like paradise. He wouldn't mind staying in a tent on one of the far-side islands that had missed the brunt of the blast when the olivium moon had exploded, but doing it in a refugee camp would be another story. Pardonnet definitely had a point, but dammit, so did he. They could both have what they wanted if they could just wait a while, but neither could afford to do that.

He looked over to Shucorion. "How about a different kind of assistance besides military?" he asked.

Shucorion cocked his head to the side, a trace of amusement sparkling in his eyes. "You would accept emergency housing from us?"

"I don't see why not," Kirk said, glancing from him to Pardonnet, who had already opened his mouth to protest. "It would be a good chance for the colony to use some of its newfound wealth, and the influx of olivium into your economy would do you a world of good, too. Plus the shipments of building material would allow us to demonstrate your ability to field a fleet on short notice, but would do it without threatening the Kauld. We would all win."

"Indeed," said Shucorion. He seemed quite pleased, as well he should. There were far more subtle implications to the deal than a simple trade. Shucorion's people had started out opposed to the Federation presence on Belle Terre. They had later become allies, but uneasy ones, still unsure how they would fare in dealing with a power that spanned hundreds of stars. By asking this simple favor, the colony would be taking the first step toward making them true confederates, not just the weaker partners in a marriage of convenience.

Of course there would be complications.

"Captain," Pardonnet said. "No offense to Shucorion, but have you seen what the Blood consider housing?"

"No," Kirk said. He'd been too busy with the colony to look at anything outside the Belle Terre system. "But it's got to be better than tents."

"That's a matter of opinion," the governor said.

Shucorion laughed. "Don't worry. Mud huts don't travel well. We will bring prefabricated plasteel panels that you can assemble as you wish."

"At what price?"

Shucorion yawned. "I'm afraid I don't deal directly in such trivialities, but I can assure you that the price will not be exorbitant. I will have my people call your people and work out the details."

Pardonnet blushed slightly, and Kirk suppressed a smile. One of the hardest things for a leader to learn was how to delegate the details.

"Good," Kirk said, laying his hands flat on the table.

"That's solved. You'll get your building materials, and we'll keep the colony ships in orbit for defense. Now let's talk about training ground troops."

Pardonnet looked again at his wristchron. "Must we?"

"You're stuck here until gamma night's over," Kirk said. "We might as well take advantage of the opportunity."

Pardonnet leaned toward Shucorion. " 'Opportunity,' he calls it. Very well, then, lay on, Macduff."

"Okay, here's what I was thinking. . . ." Kirk began, but as he settled in for a long round of negotiations, his mind was already thinking ahead to the next problem he had to solve. He'd been so worried about the Kauld and about profiteers from back home that he had completely ignored the threat from other quarters, but Shucorion's innocent suggestion had shown him his oversight. Even if he didn't hire peacekeepers from among the locals, he needed to learn who was out there and how they felt about the Federation presence on Belle Terre.

He would have to part with at least one starship for a survey of local space. And that ship would need a crew. Who should he send on the mission?

Chapter Six

"YOU'RE KIDDING, RIGHT?" Dr. McCoy rubbed the sleep from his eyes and regarded Kirk's face in the viewscreen, but he could detect no sign of a joke in his captain's features. In fact, Kirk looked a bit haggard, as if he had been up all night. That would explain the dawn call—it was already midmorning up there, and Kirk had probably decided if he couldn't sleep, nobody else would either. Good thing Gamma Night had disrupted communications through the night or he would surely have called even earlier.

"No, I'm not kidding, Bones," said Kirk. "I need someone who can assess a situation quickly with whatever data they've got on hand, instead of waiting for every detail before they make a decision."

"I'm not sure if I take that as a compliment," McCoy drawled. "Shootin' from the hip is a good way to get people killed."

Kirk shook his head. "This is a scouting mission, not an in-depth study. I just want to know who's out there, and I want the information to come from *my* crew members, not Shucorion. We can send out another expedition to investigate anything interesting you turn up, but this is just a first glance."

"What you're saying is, you want me to perform triage on the entire Sagittarian sector."

"Right."

McCoy drummed his fingers on the edge of the communications console. "Who are you sending with me?"

"Scotty."

That was a relief. At least they would *get* there, wherever "there" was. "And who else?" he asked.

"That's it. We're sending you out in a refitted cargo tug. It's all engines and very little living space, but it's fast, and there's more than enough room for two."

"I guess I should be thankful you didn't bottle me up with that pointy-eared computer," McCoy muttered as he stood up and reached for his clothing.

Then he heard a bleep from the subspace scanners and realized Kirk was on the bridge. "No offense intended, Spock," he said, turning around to draw on his pants.

"None taken, Doctor," the Vulcan said from off screen. "I assure you, I am similarly relieved."

He pulled on his green turtleneck, buckled his pants, and turned around again. "When do we leave?"

"As soon as Scotty gets everything on line. He says he can't possibly do it in less than two days."

"So I should expect him to be ready sometime this afternoon," McCoy asserted.

Kirk smiled. "At the latest."

"I'll pack my bags."

"Good. Kirk out."

After the screen winked off, McCoy sat down on the edge of the bed and rubbed his face again. It was a hospital bed in one of the unused rooms on the second floor, a place to bunk down for the night and little more, but it had become a home-away-from-home during his extended "shore leave." He had grown used to the quiet peacefulness of it after hours, the view of rolling hills out the window during the day, and the convenience of living in the midst of the colony's largest city.

The food was about as good as cafeteria food anywhere, but it beat the rations he and Scotty would be eating on board their converted cargo tug. He sighed and headed down the hall into the 'fresher, then went on down to breakfast. Might as well have one last real egg before he left.

He found Lilian Coates there, delivering fresh produce from her garden on the way to the school, where she was both the librarian and the chief administrator. Everyone wore multiple hats in the colony, but McCoy wondered how she balanced two careers and still had time for gardening.

"Good morning," he said as they met in the doorway. "Here, let me help you with that." He took one of the two baskets she was carrying, admiring the ripe tomatoes that filled it to the brim. Her basket was equally full of firm green peppers.

"Thank you, Doctor," she said.

He couldn't help admiring her as well, as she stepped past him. She looked radiant in the early morning light streaming in through the windows. Her light blonde hair glowed like a halo around her, and her smooth skin and slender face gave her a delicate, almost fragile appearance.

"How's, uh, how's Reynold this morning?"

"He seems fine. I made him go to school today, but I'm going to tell his teacher to keep an eye on him just in case."

"That's a good idea. We couldn't find anything wrong yesterday, but *something* made him feel bad."

"I just hope it's not contagious. I don't want everyone in the entire school coming down with the flu."

"They won't," McCoy assured her. "But even if they did, I'm sure Dr. Neville could handle it."

She nodded. "I'm sure he can, but I have to say I'm glad to have Starfleet's best medical officer in town as well."

"What?" McCoy said in mock surprise. "Is he here, too? This town's got more doctors than a golf course on Wednesday. Good thing I'm headed into space again soon, or next thing you know there'll be lawyers."

His joke didn't have quite the effect he'd hoped for. Lilian dropped her basket, scattering peppers all across the floor. "You're leaving?" she asked.

There were maybe a dozen people seated at various tables, and two servers in white aprons behind the counter across the room. They all looked up at the noise, then looked away as McCoy set down his basket and began to gather up the peppers. "Not the whole ship," he said. "Just me, and only for a few . . . well, I don't know how long it'll be, actually. Probably a few weeks."

She bent down next to him. "A few weeks. Where are you going?" She didn't sound all that relieved at the news.

"Just a little scouting mission," he said airily. "The captain thinks it's time we called on our neighbors and checked 'em out up close."

"I see." They stacked the peppers back in her basket,

and he helped her to her feet again. She held onto his hand a moment longer than necessary. "Be careful."

"Well, now," he said, "I always am."

"Good." She turned toward the serving line, where she set the peppers on the counter. "I'm sorry," she said to the servers, "but they'll have to be washed again."

"That's all right, honey," said the older of the two women. She narrowed her eyes and added, "You look like you've seen a ghost."

"I have," she said, turning away.

McCoy set his basket on the counter beside hers and followed her to the door. "I'm sorry. I brought back bad memories."

She shook her head. "It's not your fault. You'd think after this much time I'd be able to get over it."

They walked down the corridor to the front door, and he followed her outside. "You don't just 'get over' the loss of a husband. It can take years to even accept it. You're coping quite well under the circumstances."

"Am I?" She stopped and looked up at the eastern hillsides, still in shadow this early in the morning. The sun shone directly into her face, but she didn't even blink. "I sometimes still feel Tom's arms around me at night. When I'm in a noisy room, I hear his voice among the others. When Reynold pops around a corner, I see Tom's face first. Is that normal?"

"For you, it apparently is. Everybody handles grief differently."

She turned her face toward him, and for a moment her pupils were tiny pinpricks before they opened up. "If this is 'handling it,' then I'd hate to watch somebody fall apart."

Her words hung between them like thick fog in the morning air. McCoy cursed himself for a fool. He should have seen this coming, but he had been so impressed by her fortitude that he had completely missed the warning signs. She wasn't working through her grief; she was overworking herself to the point of exhaustion so she could forget.

"You should take some time off," he said. "Go visit one of the other settlements, or—"

"I don't—"

"Or just stay at home and read if you'd rather. But you should set aside some time for yourself. You haven't had a spare moment since you got here."

"I don't want a spare moment."

"Tell me what you want, then."

She started walking toward the school again.

"I'm serious," he said, keeping pace with her. "You know better than anyone else what would do you the most good. Think about it. What do you want?"

She stopped so quickly he nearly ran into her. She took a deep breath, then said, "I want to go home. Coming here was a mistake, and staying here is an even bigger one. This place isn't just dangerous; it's deadly. It's one big natural disaster after another, from the olivium in the moon to the weather. I'm tired of watching everyone I care about die one by one. I want to go home."

"That . . . could be arranged," he said slowly. "If that's what you truly think best. It wouldn't be a comfortable trip, but you could probably hitch a ride on an olivium freighter."

"And be attacked by pirates the moment we crossed into unguarded space? No, thank you. I've had my fill of that." She ran a hand through her hair and said, "I guess what I really want is to already *be* there. Or better yet, to have never come here in the first place—as long as I'm asking the impossible."

"Going home isn't impossible," he said as they started walking again. "But you should think it over carefully before you make a decision one way or the other. Make sure it's what you really want to do. Make sure you're going toward something and not just running away."

"Doctor, I've been going toward something all my life. I wanted to be there by now, but that something keeps changing, keeps moving out of my grasp. The irony is that I had what I wanted all along and didn't realize it. Now part of what I had is permanently lost." She crossed her arms and hugged herself in the chilly morning air. "I'm sorry to have unloaded on you like this, but you *did* ask."

"Yes, I did," McCoy admitted. "I won't badger you about it, but I want you to think about this while I'm away. When I get back we can talk some more. In the meantime, why don't you give yourself a break? Take a few days away from the school and find something that you like to do and haven't done in a long time. Relax and enjoy yourself."

She gave him a look that said, "Easy for you to say," but before she could protest, he said, "Uh-uh. Those are doctor's orders."

"Yes, Doctor," she said. Her face softened and she added, "I'll look forward to your return. Maybe you can have dinner with us?"

"I'd be delighted."

She turned away from him and walked toward the low, brick schoolhouse. Several children were playing tag on the hard-packed playground, their laughter and squeals piercing the morning air.

McCoy watched until she disappeared into the school. The gnawing in his gut was partially the effect of having one of those difficult discussions that doesn't seem to have any good solution, and partially from anxiety over his upcoming mission with Scotty, but there was a third component he could not only identify but cure fairly easily: he was downright hungry. As he returned to the cafeteria, he wondered what his chances were of sweet-talking one of the cooks into making an omelette with some of those fresh tomatoes and peppers.

Chapter Seven

IT WAS AMAZING how quickly a mine could change the look of a place. Even more so when the whole place was a mine. Deloric sat by the tiny window of the shuttle and watched the devastated landscape of the comet slide by. They'd been slicing away at the seemingly endless carbon-dioxide ice for at least four days. Now, he could see that the constant work by hundreds of miners had carved away one whole face of the comet.

Halfway through, he thought. Four more days of cutting, and then what? He still had no clue what this was all about.

Terwolan sat behind him, her booted foot pushing against the back of his seat in a constant rhythm. He found it both annoying and comforting. Annoying that he had to put up with that kind of distraction and comforting that someone he knew was close by. She had no more clue to what was going on than he did. Somehow that helped soothe his irritation. At least he wasn't the only one in the dark here.

The shuttle landed with a thud as its gravity skids locked onto the ice. Deloric could see the workers from the previous shift gathering to board the shuttle once his shift cleared the airlock. There was something different about the way they stood, waiting to get on board, but he couldn't put a finger on what it was.

With heavy sighs of resignation, the miners inside the shuttle rubbed their eyes and adjusted their ears one last time before latching down their suit helmets for the duration of the shift. Deloric found that while he didn't like not being able to touch his head for hours at a stretch, the suit had benefits other than the obvious one of keeping him alive in the vacuum of space. For one thing, he only had to smell his own recycled air. For the duration of his shift, he was free of the stink that occurred when too many hardworking bodies lived for too long in too small a ship.

He switched on the suit's power pack and tested the lamp and comm units. All working. He was ready to fling more ice into space.

But as he descended the shuttle's ramp and headed toward the tool locker to get his energy pick, the project overseer stepped up to the group. "Never mind the picks and jets," she said over the common frequency. "The last of the ice got sent off about midshift. Team leaders, go to channel two."

Deloric reached over to the control pad on his left wrist and keyed his radio to the private channel. A dozen others did the same. Terwolan and Nialerad stood there beside him, waiting for him to relay their orders. He wondered what they thought he learned about the project during these beginning-of-shift briefings, and whether they would be amused or alarmed to learn that he was just as ignorant as they.

When the team leaders had switched over, the overseer said, "The rough work is done. We're installing the disruptor now." She gestured over her right shoulder toward the center of the comet's flat face. Deloric could see a hole carved there, one big enough for ten or fifteen people to huddle in if they didn't mind working close together. In the middle of the hole stood a turret gun from a Kauld battleship. What were they going to do with that, defend the universe's biggest snow fort? From whom? Who would want it?

He itched to ask, but instead waited for more instructions.

The overseer said, "Teams one through thirty will make a topographic survey of the exposed face, finding the lowest spot in each sector. Teams thirty-one through fifty-five will sink pylons into the ice inside the central crater and fuse them in place while teams fifty-six through sixty attach the disruptor to those pylons, mounting it so that it can be raised and lowered as well as rotated all the way around. We're going to slice a thin layer off the face at a level just below the lowest point. We want those pylons *solid,* and we want the disruptor absolutely stable when it makes the cut. We want the exposed face to be perfectly flat when you're done."

Deloric looked out at the ice. It extended for three or four *rho,* far enough for a person on the opposite edge to be a mere speck. The miners had followed survey lines as they removed the carbon dioxide blocks, but they had still left behind a rough surface crisscrossed with gouges and cuts. There were knee-deep valleys where overeager crews had dug deeper than their neighbors, and there were voids where pockets of methane ice had boiled off from the heat of the mining activity. He spoke up. "If we cut deep enough we can take care of the surface irregularities, but what about the voids? We've been hitting those all the way through. There are bound to be some at whatever level we make the cut."

The overseer said, "Fill those in with waste material from the part we cut away, then make one final pass to polish it flat. We're talking optically flat here. Deviation of half a wavelength of light or less."

"Half a wavelength?" he said softly, awed at the idea of smoothing something this big that precisely. "What for?"

"You don't need to know." Her tone of voice made it clear he shouldn't have even asked.

"Right. Sorry. We'll make it flat."

"Good."

She reached out to her arm and clicked her radio control back over to the common channel. He did the same. "All right, people, get to work."

Deloric's team was number twenty-three. He switched his radio to the team's private channel and said, "We're surveyors today, marking low spots. Terwolan, you take the rod. Nialerad, you set points and record their elevation. I'll run the level."

"Oh, sure, you take the cushy job," Terwolan said.

He knew she was just kidding, but he didn't know how to answer her except with the truth. "I take the job with the most responsibility. That way if we mess up, they only shout at me. You want to swap places and get into the loop?"

She snorted. "Hah. They don't pay me enough to be responsible."

The three of them walked over to the tool locker,

their footsteps slow and deliberate with only the gravity boots to hold them to the ice. They had taken their turn as surveyors before, so they already knew what to do without further instruction. Edging around a stack of paint drums that hadn't been there yesterday—silver, Deloric noted—he picked out a level from the shelves of equipment, looking for one that had less dings and wear-and-tear than some of its neighbors. Nialerad and Terwolan didn't seem to care as much about the condition of their tools. They just grabbed for stuff—a mallet, a bag of stakes, a datapad, and a graduated range pole. He was about to tell Terwolan to get a different rod since the one she snatched was bowed, but attitude or not, she was an observant worker. She sighted down its length before heading out, quickly saw the flaw, and replaced it.

Deloric conferred with the other team leaders, and they decided to divide the surface of the comet into thirty pie-shaped wedges, one for each crew. Everyone headed out to the middle to start, kicking off and drifting over the ice rather than trudging along its surface. They traveled in a close pack, always within reach of someone else in case someone drifted too far from the ice to reach it with a gravity boot.

As they approached the crater with the disruptor in it, Deloric realized just how big the gun was. The business end was as wide as his body, and the accumulator was easily three times his length. This was a heavy assault weapon, designed to overload an enemy starship's shields and slice all the way through the hull beneath. Carbon-dioxide ice would be as thin as smoke as far as that gun was concerned. Even at low power, it would slice off the face of the comet without a whisper of resistance.

Was this the only tool they had for the job? That

seemed unlikely. If they had access to this kind of weapon, they had access to tactical beams as well. And given the heavy losses that the fleet had taken in their battles with Federation, no commander would sacrifice even a single big gun without a very good reason.

They needed this one right where it was. That meant they expected to use it for more than just leveling the comet's face. He looked upward, toward the star five light-days away. He wouldn't be able to spot a hostile ship until it disengaged its dynadrive right over their heads, but he couldn't help wondering if he should be expecting company.

Not on this shift, he decided, or the overseers would be working everyone harder.

He stretched out and touched his toe to the ice behind him, letting his boots' angled gravity field provide enough drag to slow him to a stop just short of the crater. The others skidded to a stop around him, except for Nialerad, who misjudged and skidded out over the edge. Without a word, he whirled around and got his hands in front of him in time to bounce off the disruptor barrel, then pushed himself back beside his crew.

"Good reflexes," Deloric told him, well aware that everyone else was laughing on their own private channels.

"Boot caught a void," Nialerad said.

"Ah." Deloric led the way around to the point of the section they'd be surveying and set up his level while Terwolan and Nialerad trudged out a few hundred paces. He enjoyed surveying. It wasn't rocket science, but it made more use of his brain than pick work. He sighted in on three of the reference beacons set around the perimeter of the comet's face, establishing the same datum as everyone else, then focused on the graduated rod that Terwolan held in a shallow depression. "Seven point six two," he said, reading the marks off the scale. Nialerad entered the elevation into his datapad, then marked it with a stake while Terwolan walked on toward the next low spot.

They quickly learned that Deloric could see the depressions much more easily from a distance than the other two could when they were right over them. He began directing them from spot to spot, zigzagging them back and forth in an ever-broadening pattern as their pie-wedge opened out before them.

The first dozen stakes went quickly, but they soon realized their part of the comet was riddled with small voids. The crew who'd mined here must have been cursing their bad luck while trying to get an acceptable piece of ice to ship off. Deloric's crew quickly began to curse theirs too, because they repeatedly had to make judgment calls as to which ones could be filled and which ones should be undercut.

As the crews expanded outward and the team leaders reported back their lowest readings, the job became easier and easier. Since the whole purpose of what they were doing was to find the level at which the disruptor would make its slice, there was no point in marking anything that wasn't lower than what someone had already found, so they quickly switched into a competitive rush to break the current record. It became a game, with people shouting their results over the common frequency and people betting on the final winner.

Over it all, the turret gun hunched menacingly at the center of all their antics, like a grim ruler overseeing his loyal but ignorant serfs as they toiled for his secret mission. Whatever that mission was, it continued to elude Deloric. He examined the mount, admiring the way the emitter could swing through a complete circle in every direction. It had been designed to go on the tip of a warship's fin, where it would be able to defend the most area around the vessel. Here it would punch holes clear through what was left of the comet if it fired downward—a definite surprise for anyone on the other side!—but Deloric doubted if that was its purpose. They wouldn't have needed to cut away so much ice just to do that.

No, whatever the disruptor was supposed to shoot at after it leveled the comet's face, it would be on this side. Except that there was only one thing within range: the long stream of carbon dioxide ice they had been sending in-system.

The disruptor beam would vaporize that in an instant. He could see no good reason to do that. It wasn't like it would explode or anything; it would just become an expanding column of carbon dioxide vapor.

Aimed right at the Federation colony planet.

With an optically flat surface at one end.

An ugly suspicion began to grow in his mind. He'd seen the barrels of silver paint waiting beside the tool locker. He was willing to bet that their next job would be to spray the face of the comet with it.

"Hey," Terwolan said. "I'm standing here."

"Hmm?" He looked down, disoriented.

"You want to call out the shot?"

The shot. Holy father of terror, the shot.

Chapter Eight

"GET READY, DOCTOR," Scotty said as he reached for the tug's warp controls. "This may be a wee bit rougher than you're used to."

"How rough?" McCoy asked, his eyes narrowing and wrinkles appearing in his forehead. He was seated in the copilot's chair before the wraparound control board, but he was studiously avoiding contact with anything vital. Scotty was happy to see that; after all the modifications he'd done to this pile of scrap, piloting it was going to be tricky enough without conflicting commands from an inexperienced copilot.

"I'd lean back in my chair if I were you," he said. "At least until the inertial dampers adapt to the engines' new performance figures."

McCoy didn't look happy about that. He apparently knew enough about engineering to know what could happen if the inertial dampers were off by more than a few hundredths of a percent when a ship went into warp. Even his superb medical skills couldn't help a person who was smeared into strawberry jam against the rear bulkhead.

"Wait a minute," the doctor said. "I think I forgot my razor back on the *Enterprise*. Why don't I go get it while you make a test flight or two?"

Scotty looked at him askance. "You can borrow mine. Hang on, here we go." He shoved the lever forward, feeling the electrical contacts connect with the smooth *swish* of copper sliding on copper.

Hard wiring, he thought. *What have I gotten myself into?* All the same, he felt a thrill as the tug responded and leaped into warp. True to his warning, the little ship shimmied and bucked like a targ on a tether. He glanced up at the viewscreen and saw not the normal smooth, straight streaks of hyperspace shooting past them, but an insane jumble of bright zigzags. The small control cabin creaked and groaned as engines designed to haul huge cargo containers from star to star poured all their power into just the tug.

That alone would have made for a bumpy ride, since Scotty had stripped the tug down to the bare minimum, leaving practically no inertial mass to smooth things out when spatial anomalies influenced the warp field; but he had made one other modification to the craft that affected it even more. The engines normally ran on antimatter, but antimatter was in short supply this far from civilization. There was, however, a lot of quantum olivium just waiting for a good home, and that was even more powerful than antimatter. Where antimatter merely released its energy by annihilation with normal matter, quantum olivium catalyzed the annihilation of space itself. It was like having a miniature Big Bang continually erupting inside your containment field.

He hoped it would stay inside the containment field. That was the tricky part.

Squinting to read the blurry displays, he adjusted the Schofield converters to route more power into the field generating coils.

After the longest eight seconds in history, the inertial dampers' active logic matrix finally adapted to the new thrust parameters, and with a last swift kick in the rear as the new program took effect, the buffeting settled down. Scotty called up the status monitors and double checked the ship's major systems. Navigation, communications, shields, and what weapons arrays they had were all optimal. The external sensors needed calibration, and the autogalley had gone off-line during the ride, but other than that they were in the green.

"Hah! Not bad for a derelict old can of bolts, don't ye think, Doctor? Doctor?"

He turned to see Dr. McCoy taking deep breaths and slowly releasing his grip, finger by finger, from the worn armrests of the copilot's chair. His eyes were wide, and his eyebrows were knotted together over the bridge of his nose. "Not bad? I just saw my whole life flash before my eyes."

"Really?" Scotty made a show of checking the readouts. "Must ha' been a leak in the chroniton flux generators."

McCoy eyed him stonily. "There's no such thing."

"Ah. Well, then, that explains it." Scotty looked at the navigation display for real. "We're doing warp eleven point eight," he reported happily. "At this pace, we'll reach our first target star in less than a day."

"What's the name of it?"

"BTS 453."

"That's not a name."

"It's all we've got. It stands for 'Belle Terre Survey' object number 453. Spock's been doing deep space scans when Gamma Night lets up, and this star apparently has evidence of a technological civilization on one of its planets."

McCoy flexed his hands. "Spock. I should have known. 'BTS 453' is exactly the sort of fond, endearing name he'd give a star with people living around it."

"We could give it our own name, I suppose," Scotty said.

McCoy thought it over, then shook his head. "No point in it. We'll learn what the natives call it soon enough."

That was certainly true, Scotty thought with pride, but from his tone of voice, McCoy didn't seem to appreciate just how fast they were going. At her normal cruising speed, it would have taken the *Enterprise* five days to cover the distance they would be covering in one. The *Enterprise* couldn't even reach warp 11.8 without risking severe damage; to maintain that speed for more than a few minutes would be suicidal. This converted tug however, with its souped-up engines and tight, form-fitting little warp field, could keep it up indefinitely.

A sudden thought made him cock his head and say, "I'll tell you what else could use a name, though."

"What?"

"This ship."

"Didn't it come with one?"

"It was called the *Selenite* when it was in service, but the nameplate was on a hull section we left behind, to cut down on mass. At the moment we're just BTR 23."

"Let me guess. Belle Terre Reserve?"

"Registry."

"Ah." McCoy rubbed his chin and stared out at the white streaks that space debris made as it swept past them in hyperspace. "Well, it's fast, so why don't we just make a play off the initials and call it *Beater?*"

Scotty snorted.

"What?" asked McCoy, frowning.

"You, ah, weren't into garage mechanics when you were young, were you?"

"No."

"A 'beater' is what you call something that's worn out, held together with wire and prayers, and is generally a hazard to navigation."

"Weeell, then," McCoy drawled, "it's perfect. You just called this a 'derelict old can of bolts,' and I don't know about you but I was certainly praying just a minute ago."

Scotty patted the bulkhead at his side. "Aye, but I was just bein' affectionate. We don't want to—"

An alarm drowned him out in midsentence. He looked to the control board, saw that the plasma-flow couplings were starting to overheat, and adjusted the thermal dampers to compensate; but that overloaded the power transducer, which in turn sent a ripple of overloads through the accumulator buffers, the Heisenberg baffles, and the phase-control monitors. Half of the controls were manual; Scotty busied himself with adjusting things back into operating range, but the computer kept overcompensating with the systems it still controlled, and the values began to oscillate back and forth as he struggled to outguess it.

The ride grew bumpy again. "Now what?" McCoy demanded, but Scotty ignored him. He needed all his concentration on the controls. But even that wasn't enough. The oscillations grew wilder and wilder until finally, just before the olivium reaction went critical, he slapped the emergency abort switch and yanked back on the T-handle.

There was a stomach-wrenching twist as they tumbled back into normal space, then the buzzing alarms quieted one by one until the cockpit was silent.

"On second thought," Scotty said, "I think *Beater* suits it just fine." He stood up and squeezed past McCoy's chair to the access door into the tiny crew quarters and the engine room beyond. "Come on, Doctor. Let's go see what we need to wire back into place."

Chapter Nine

VELLYNGAITH, the commander of the All Kauld fleet, paused in the speech he was giving to the room full of his warship captains. They had come here at his orders, though some were less than enthusiastic about the meeting. He knew many of them were disillusioned with the way the war with the humans had gone. Several had sustained major damage to their ships and lost many fine members of their crews. But he could see that despite themselves, they were very interested in what he'd been saying. By Kurzot, they should be.

These Federation vermin were proving tougher to dispatch than Vellyngaith had estimated. By all rights, it should have been as easy as a steeth taking out a sick zagette that had strayed too far from the herd. Obviously, this particular zagette wasn't as lame as he had thought, but there had to be a limit. He suspected it was well below the power he was bringing to bear this time.

The last major offensive had nearly worked, but Kirk had managed to turn the tide of battle at the last moment. The Kauld fleet had sustained tremendous damage and had ultimately been forced to withdraw, but not before seeing the colony and their Starfleet protectors suffer as well. Even so, Kirk still controlled the olivium mines on the colony planet's moon. Every time he thought of that travesty, Vellyngaith's blood churned and he ground his jaws in anger.

He looked about the room and realized that every other Kauld here felt the same way. Many of those in this audience had crossed paths with that annoying human, and none of them had come away any more victorious than Vellyngaith. Kirk seemed blessed by fate, favored by the gods, and luckier than chance itself. That alone would make him an obvious target for anyone with a sense of proportion, but he also had an ego the size of the galaxy. He was just *begging* to be knocked down. Even if he didn't control the most valuable prize in this sector of space—the Kauld's sector at that—he would attract the attention of every warship commander in this room.

He would continue to win, too, unless a radical new battle tactic were employed. One like Vellyngaith was about to unveil.

"The humans," he spat the word as though it tasted foul, "have had luck on their side. But it is they who are in the wrong here. It is they who have taken what is not theirs to take. It is our moral obligation to make a stand and take back what is rightfully ours."

The assembled captains cheered his words. He basked in their response to his pep talk. What he'd said so far was nothing that any of them hadn't thought of on their own. Perhaps that was why they cheered, because someone of his level had underscored their own feelings. Well, the best part was still to come.

He clasped his hands together behind his back and leaned forward. "I need not tell you how the humans have humiliated us, time and again. But I tell you now, their time has run out."

"What makes you so sure?" The voice was deep, resonant, and full of scorn.

Vellyngaith spotted the heckler in the crowd. Gongalen, captain of the *Sharf,* sat, arms crossed and waiting for an answer. Vellyngaith recognized him as a tough Kauld with a sharp mind and a sharper tongue that often brought him more than his share of trouble, but his battle record spoke for itself. *And his timing is perfect,* Vellyngaith thought.

"My sources inform me that the humans have sustained heavy losses due to severe weather on the planet. They underestimated how badly the climate was affected when the explosion on the olivium moon flash-burned the planet's one main supercontinent. Ever since they landed, they have struggled for mere survival, but they are slowly losing the battle. For instance, they apparently parked most of their ground-to-orbit craft on low ground. Several settlements, including one of the four largest, were also in the same valley. All were completely wiped out by a flood."

He advanced the wall screen's display to show reconnaissance photos of the devastation. The explosion on the moon had blown huge chunks of regolith free, some of which had impacted the planet below, creating craters that had filled with water during the torrential rains that followed. Those crater walls were highly unstable, and one had finally given way, flooding the entire valley below it within minutes.

"This is only the latest of many natural disasters to befall them. And with every such setback, the colonists have concentrated on rebuilding their settlements rather than their defenses. We, on the other hand, have kept a low profile after our last near-win, thus adding to their false sense of security." He paused again, letting the crowd's anticipation grow just to the edge of annoyance before flipping the wall screen to the next sequence.

"During this time, not only have we repaired our ships and trained new recruits, we have built another fleet." He timed his announcement to coincide with a display of several shiny new Kauld warships.

The commanders erupted in bedlam at the sight of such an array of ships, but a loud, grating voice cut through the others like a knife through unarmored flesh. "This is a simulation. Such a fleet would take years to build. By the time they are finished, we will have already won." It was Yanorada, whose own plan of attack had just been triggered a few days earlier.

Vellyngaith acknowledged his statement with a slight bow. "So we thought, which was why we approved your plan. But then we realized the flaw in our thinking. We don't need to build a fleet of ships from scratch. We need only to fortify that which is already available to us. In reality, only three ships will see their maiden voyage. The rest are either exploration vessels, cargo transports, or mining barges that have been refitted with armor and weapons, using the newest technology available. And I do mean the newest *olivium* technology."

The murmur rose from the assembly as they digested this new piece of information. It was the reaction Vellyngaith expected. If all went well with the rest of his presentation, there would be many similar reactions from the audience. By the end of the session, he planned to have each and every one of these captains believing that he was the greatest tactician his people had ever known.

He wasn't there yet. Gongalen spoke up again. "Technology is only part of a successful battle. The finest ships alone cannot win if the enemy is clever. It is the Kauld behind the controls that makes the difference. The captain of a cargo ship may do his job well, but that doesn't mean he can win a battle." Some captains nodded, while others whispered in their neighbor's ear.

"I can't agree with you more," Vellyngaith said, regaining the floor. "Which is another reason you are all here. It will be with your input that I will issue the new promotions and assignments."

More murmurs and whisperings rose from the audience. This could affect them directly. Someone had to fly those pretty new ships!

"And then there is our secret weapon." He pressed the control that would advance the display again, at the same time saying, "Yanorada's plan will destroy the planet's atmosphere, but it will take time. Time we don't have. My plan will destroy the atmosphere, wipe out the human colony, and burn the surface down to bedrock—in seconds."

The screen showed the planet resting serenely in space, swirls of cloud scattered across its day side, the terminator drawing a dark curve around its bulging flank. Then, without warning, the scene turned brilliant blue, and the clouds were ripped away like leaves in a hurricane. The entire atmosphere churned, slid sideways, and streamed out into space, while the continents beneath were charred black and the exposed oceans began to boil.

He let it go for a few more seconds, then froze the image. "None of you need to know how this will be accomplished. All you need to know is that it will happen. My weapon will wipe out the colony once and for all."

This time the entire room erupted in shouted questions and accusations, but Vellyngaith merely let them go on for a few seconds, then said loudly, "I stake my future upon this. It will work. But I will not risk a leak from any source, not until the . . . device . . . has already been triggered." The room settled down, if only so people could hear him.

He didn't answer their questions, merely went on with his presentation. "As I said, I will wipe out the colony, and I will do it without the loss of a single Kauld ship. Unfortunately, that cannot be said of the final phase of the attack."

He flicked the screen to the next simulation. The *Enterprise* leaped toward the assembled captains, drawing a strangled cry of dismay from a few and growls of anger from the rest. Behind the *Enterprise,* dozens more Federation ships swooped into view, their shields shimmering around them.

"Given enough time, our secret weapon can also burn through a starship's shields. We may be lucky enough to kill one or two before they scurry for cover, but as I noted earlier, luck seems to favor the Federation. Therefore we will not rely on luck. We will rely on our own skill and our newly augmented fleet to finish them in ship-to-ship combat." The simulation showed the All Kauld warships swooping around the Federation ships, whittling away at their defenses until a final barrage of disruptor fire blew them apart one by one, like the grand finale in a fireworks display. He let it run until the last ship was an expanding cloud of debris, then shut off the screen.

"We have ten days to prepare. On day eleven, Belle Terre and its olivium moon will be ours."

Chapter Ten

CAPTAIN KIRK paused at the door to the library. Through the window he could see half a dozen school children crowded around the front desk, where Lilian Coates was reading aloud to them from a picture book. They were young, maybe seven or eight years old, though Kirk was not good at judging children's age.

This didn't seem a good time to interrupt, but as he turned away from the window he saw Lilian turn the book around so the kids could look at the pictures, and he saw that she only had three or four more pages to go. She was reading them *Archie Echidna Goes to Arcturus,* a book that had been popular when Kirk was a boy. He smiled as he remembered the spiny marsupial's adventures among the vegetable people, and how Archie had fallen in love with a sea urchin.

He looked at his own book while Lilian read the next page of hers and showed her audience the pictures.

He'd smoothed out the dog-eared page and finished reading it, but his mind hadn't really been on the story. He'd been running through contingency plans for defending the colony under any conceivable attack scenario, trying to tally the numbers of available ships and potential crews.

He leaned against the wall next to the door. The faint noises of school activity echoed down from the classrooms along either side of the hallway, while thoughts of training a citizen's defense network mingled with thoughts on the tactics of gaining Governor Pardonnet's support for the program. Both men had the colony's best interests at heart, but they disagreed on what posed the biggest threat to its well-being. They were both trying to predict the future, but there were only a limited number of resources to go around, and neither man wanted to waste them on the wrong project.

One aspect of the future of which Kirk was certain: they had not seen the end of trouble from the Kauld. This lull in activity only meant they were regrouping for more aggression to come, and the longer they waited the bigger that trouble would be. The suicidal run of the lone Kauld ship nearly a week ago still bothered him, too. That was a radical departure from their normal tactics. It hadn't worked, but he couldn't help wondering what else they might try. What other unexpected approaches should he expect?

"Holding up the wall, Captain?" Lilian asked. She had opened the door so softly he hadn't even noticed. She was smiling mischievously, her light skin and blonde hair aglow in the overhead light.

"I, ah, was just checking for gravitational anomalies," he said as he straightened up. He decided that sounded lame the moment he said it, but she smiled anyway.

"Always nice to know you're looking out for us."

"Actually, I saw you reading to the kids and didn't want to interrupt."

"Ah. That was very thoughtful of you. We're done now." She held the door open for him.

"I was just bringing back a book," he said, handing it to her, but he followed her inside as she walked toward her desk. By virtue of its age, the library didn't smell like others that Kirk had visited. The books were all too new to have that dusty, closed-in smell. Instead, he imagined that this was more like what a late twentieth-century Earth bookstore or print shop might have smelled like. Fresh paper, wet ink, and bindery glue.

She set the book on the polished wooden top along with dozens of others to be checked back in, but she didn't go around behind the desk. She leaned back against the rounded edge, her hands resting there beside her hips, and said, "I heard that Shucorion's people are going to help the flood survivors with emergency building materials."

"That's right," he said, proud of that little bit of negotiation.

"Any chance of tacking on a couple hundred desks and chairs to that order?"

"I . . . hadn't thought of that. Are you short that many?"

"We're not, since not many of the refugees came this far, but most of the schools between here and there are donating equipment to resupply what they lost, and I'm coordinating the effort. I've asked Bill Thorpe about building new furniture, but he says most of the good

lumber trees were destroyed in the Burn, so we don't have a lot of spare wood to build replacements with."

"Furniture," Kirk said, shaking his head. "Every time I think I've got a handle on the extent of things, something new pops up that I've forgotten."

"You can't think of everything," Lilian said. "It's not your responsibility anyway. I should have put in my request through normal channels."

"No, no, that's all right," he said. "I'll look into it. It'll probably amuse Shucorion to be asked for something so mundane."

"The mundane can seem pretty important when you have to do without it." She crossed her arms in front of her chest. "I feel so bad for all the people along the Big Muddy. I wish there was more I could do for them."

"So do I."

"I've seen pictures, but I don't really know what it's like for the survivors."

Kirk thought it over for a moment before he said, "I'm going out there for a look at their defense situation. I'm taking an airplane so I can get a feel for the territory. Would you like to come along? Maybe it'll give you a better idea of what they need, too."

She was already saying, "Oh, I couldn't possibly," when she stopped herself, frowning, then said, "All right. They can do without me for a while here. Let me tell the principal where I'm going."

She went around to the other side of her desk and pressed an intercom button on the recessed communications panel. "Paul, it's Lilian. I'm taking the afternoon off."

By the sound of his voice, Paul seemed nearly as surprised as Kirk had been. "You are? That's—that's great! Have fun."

"It's not for fun," she said. "I'm going on a tour of the Big Muddy with Captain Kirk." Then she looked up at Kirk, realizing how that sounded, and blushed. "I didn't mean it that way."

Kirk smiled and said, "That's okay. I know what you mean. Besides, once we get to Big Muddy, I suspect there won't be too much to enjoy. But the trip to and from can be quite pleasant, and it looks like it should be a nice day for flying."

Lilian glanced over her shoulder at the small window behind her desk. Kirk followed her gaze. Bright rays of early afternoon sunlight sparkled against the small ripples and irregularities in the glass.

"It's been a lovely week. Such a relief from the rainy season," she said. She turned back to her desk and tucked in her chair. "Well, shall we go? Or did you want to check out another book?"

He looked longingly at the shelves of books, their spines all straight and even with each other. "Later, maybe. I have too many other things on my mind at the moment to be able to read for pleasure."

They left the building and started walking the several blocks to the airstrip. It seemed only fitting that a pioneer town like Buena Vista would have something as quaint as an airstrip. The colonies had had a fleet of shuttles when they first arrived, but due to poor planning most of them had been lost in the Big Muddy flood. Kirk thought of the incident as the All Your Eggs In One Basket Disaster, but thanks to Sulu's ingenuity the colonies still had a quick means of transportation between towns, using his propeller-driven airplanes.

"Have you ever been in one of the colony's planes?" Kirk asked Lilian.

She looked at him and said, "Not yet. But I have

flown before. My Uncle Lee had a pilot's license back when I was just a kid. He'd show up at family gatherings and take whoever wanted to go on plane rides." She smiled at the memory. "He could only take one at a time, so all my siblings and cousins would argue about who'd get to go first."

"Must have been a small plane."

"Very small. It was a replica of an old gasoline-powered model. A something-or-other Kitten, or maybe it was a Cub. Some little animal name, anyway. It had an electric engine, of course, but I remember the propeller still made a lot of noise."

"So I've heard," Kirk agreed.

"There were just two seats, one in front and one behind." Her eyes went all dreamy, recalling her childhood. "The first time he took me for a ride, I must have been about eight, not much older than those children I was reading to. It was late autumn, and he made me put on this heavy denim overall because he said it'd get cold up there. He helped me roll up the sleeves and the legs, and then boosted me into the front seat of the plane. My first thought was, 'He's going to let me drive!'"

"Not, 'I don't know how'?" Kirk asked, grinning.

"That was my next thought." She laughed and said, "Before I could embarrass myself, Uncle Lee told me that he always flew from the back seat. I still remember the feeling I had then, relief and disappointment all at once. But that all went away when we took off and I saw what our town looked like from the air. All the leaves on the trees were turning color, and I could see my school and our house. It was pure magic."

"It sounds like it."

She nodded. "My mother would get all nervous about us flying in that plane, because Uncle Lee had built it himself and the shell was just canvas stretched around the frame. She was sure it was a deathtrap. But she let us go anyway. My brothers and I thought she was such a worrywart, but I look back on it now and think she was a brave woman."

They turned off the main road and walked toward the airstrip, where a bright orange wind sock extended at a shallow angle out to the west from a high pole beside the grass runway, and a boxy gray airplane waited on the ground outside a metal hangar. Its angular fuselage and straight wings had been riveted together from pieces of old cargo containers, and its windshield was made of two flat panes of glass set at an angle. The whole works only stood a little taller than a person, even counting its three spindly legs. The single propeller in front looked far too small to pull even such a tiny vehicle through the air, but these planes had already proven themselves time and time again long before the flood wiped out the regular shuttle fleet.

The pilot was walking slowly around the plane, examining the control surfaces and their linkages. Kirk was glad to see him doing that, since there were no automatic diagnostics and no way to make in-flight repairs if something went wrong.

The pilot saw Kirk and Lilian walking up to the plane and straightened up to say "Hi," but he forgot he was standing under the wing and his head hit the hollow surface with a loud *bong!*

"Oh, are you all right?" Lilian said, rushing up to him.

He blushed red as a brick. "I'm fine, thanks. Name's Herman. I'll be your pilot."

"Here, let me see," Lilian said, standing on tiptoe to look at the top of his head.

While she fussed over the pilot, Kirk looked up at the

wing. Herman was a tall, stocky man; if anything had been harmed, that would be where the damage was.

There were no obvious dents in the wing, and apparently none in his scalp either. He finally succeeded in fending off Lilian's attentions and coaxing her and Kirk into the plane.

There were two seats in back and two in front. Kirk helped Lilian into the back seat behind the pilot's chair, then took the copilot's seat for himself. He pulled the wide shoulder belts down from either side of the seat back, crossed them over his chest, and buckled them into sockets at either side of his hips. A third belt went across his lap, tying him down securely. He looked back to make sure Lilian was belted in as well, and she flashed him a thumbs-up.

He looked back at the control panel in front of him. There was a dual set of everything, but he had no intention of touching any of it, except in an emergency. The U-shaped steering yoke moved in all three dimensions, there were control pedals for his feet as well, and enough dials and gauges on the panel in front of him to give a starship navigator a nervous breakdown.

"Have you flown before, Captain?" asked Herman as he climbed into the seat next to him. The entire plane shifted under his weight. It couldn't mass more than a couple hundred kilograms—probably less than the combined mass of its passengers.

"Not one of these," Kirk admitted.

From behind him, Lilian said, "I thought you had done this before!"

"I've flown planes," Kirk said. "And shuttles and fighters and starships. I flew a planet once. But never a plane quite like this."

"It's a kick in the pants," Herman said as he pressed

the start switch and the propeller started spinning. "Once I get 'er in the air, I'll show you how."

Kirk felt the same electric tingle of anticipation that he'd felt the first time he commanded a starship out of space dock, but as the plane shook in the propeller's backwash, he also felt for the communicator on his hip. In an emergency, he could always call for a beam-out. Then he remembered why he'd scheduled the plane ride when he had: Gamma Night was just about to hit. He had decided to get something useful done during the blackout for a change. The *Enterprise* would be safe enough with Spock in command, and the colony's airplanes were primitive enough that they weren't affected by the particle storm, so it made sense to use the time for flying.

It had made sense while he was on board the *Enterprise,* at least. Now that he sat in the cobbled-together contraption and contemplated riding it into the sky, it didn't seem quite so bright an idea, but he wasn't about to back out now.

Herman shoved the control yoke all the way forward, pulled it all the way back, and rotated it from side to side, watching the ailerons and elevator respond out on the wings. The controls on Kirk's side mimicked his motion, momentarily giving him the uncomfortable feeling that a ghost was sitting on his lap.

Then Herman released the parking brake and let the plane roll forward, bouncing gently over the irregularities in the ground until they reached the runway. He looked to the right—the direction the orange wind sock on its high pole was blowing—then to the left, and when he was satisfied that the air was clear, he turned right and taxied down to the end of the runway. As he maneuvered the plane around, Kirk could see bumps and low spots down the strip. Though he knew the ground had been rolled flat and the grass mowed short when the airstrip was built, it didn't look like anyone had smoothed the surface since the last rainstorm.

Before he could point this out to Herman, the pilot pushed on the right foot pedal and ramped up the engine, spinning the tiny plane around in a tight half-circle until they were pointed back down the runway. Then he shoved the throttle all the way forward for takeoff. The noise from the props was as loud as Lilian had described, and Kirk could see that Herman was concentrating on the job at hand.

The little plane bounced down the runway, gaining speed. Kirk's teeth rattled and he was glad for the seat belt that kept him from banging his head against the rippling metal roof. He glanced back at Lilian, worried that she'd be upset by all the jouncing, but she was peering out the window, watching with a broad smile on her delicate face as the landscape rushed by.

Just when Kirk was sure the contraption was going to shake itself to pieces, Herman pulled back on the yoke to bring the plane's nose skyward, and the rest of it followed. As soon as the wheels left the ground the shaking stopped, and the plane's engine sounded smooth and strong. The horizon took on a less-than-horizontal angle as they climbed.

Herman banked the plane and blue sky filled most of the view from Kirk's side, while Lilian's side of the plane got a breathtaking view of the countryside below. He could see her studying the features of the land; then she looked up at him all excited.

She pointed at the ground and said something, but the drone of the engine and propeller drowned her words. He couldn't quite read her lips, either. Was she saying, 'a bee tattoo!'?

His confusion must have been evident. She loosened her harness and scooted close enough that he could smell the minty scent of her hair. She said into his ear, "I can see the school!"

"Oh!" he shouted back.

She didn't wait for him to say more. With a smile befitting an excited eight-year-old, she pressed her nose back to the window.

Chapter Eleven

McCoy PEERED past Scotty's shoulders, trying to see what the engineer was doing inside the cramped access panel. From the curses and thumps emanating from within, it sounded like Scotty was battling an infestation of Gorsonian zools, but he swore he was merely recalibrating the thermal dampers on the plasma-flow couplings.

It might as well have been zools for all McCoy knew. In fact, if it *had* been zools, he might actually have been able to help. As it was, he'd been stuck holding the light while Scotty crawled in up to his waist inside the engines and battled entropy on his own.

The engine room was the size of a cargo bay, but there was barely room enough for two people to stand abreast anywhere in it. Huge hulks of gray, humming machinery loomed out from all sides, and more receded into the darkness beneath the wire mesh catwalk on which McCoy stood. Pipes and cables connected them all together in a jumble worse than any nervous system he had ever seen, and the air smelled of hot metal where something had burned. There had once been lights overhead, but only two of them still worked, both on the far side of the cavernous room. A parallelogram of light spilled off to the side from the open doorway into the crew quarters, just forward of the engine room, but it shone at the wrong angle to help either McCoy or Scotty see what they were doing.

The place had all the atmosphere of a cemetery on a muggy night. McCoy would have sworn he heard something moving back there among the reactors and the generators, but he knew there couldn't be. Scotty and his engineering team had practically rebuilt the ship from the viewscreen back; they would have spotted anything bigger than a mouse.

"Could ye hold the light a wee bit more to the left?" Scotty said for maybe the tenth time in as many minutes.

McCoy obligingly shifted the beam, but the access hatch was too small for him to move it more than a couple of centimeters before the light was shining on the outside of the engine housing instead of the inner workings. "That's as far as it'll go."

"Try the other side, then," Scotty said. "I've got a loose helical coupling and I can't see to get the torque amplifier on it."

McCoy shifted the light again and held it steady while he tried to parse out the engineer's words. Helical couplings and torque amplifiers sounded so techy, but he was a scientist; he should be able to figure them out. He tried to imagine what they would be. A helix would be like a DNA molecule, and a coupling would be something that joined two other things together. And a torque amplifier. . . .

"Wait a minute," he said. "You're talking about a bolt and a wrench."

Scotty snorted. "Aye, that I am, but a helical coupling bears about as much resemblance to a simple bolt as a subdermal hematoma does to an 'owie.' "

"A subdermal hematoma generally *is* an 'owie,' " McCoy said. "Except when it's idiopathic."

Scotty considered that a moment. "What's 'idiopathic?' "

"It's a fancy word for 'we don't know what causes it.' What's a torque amplifier?"

"It's a fancy wrench." Scotty wriggled sideways, shoved his right hand out the hatch, and waved the long, slender instrument he held in his fingers. It was about thirty centimeters long, tapered to a blunt point on one end, and had at least a dozen thumb switches along the handle. A glowing display beneath the switches registered 0 Newtons.

"When I touch it to a helical coupling, it reads the torque specifications from the coupling's embedded microchip and adjusts its force field to the proper range, then either loosens or tightens it as necessary. Which is why I don't want t' be fooling around with it in the dark. If I accidentally remove an engine mount, we could wind up with a serious problem next time we call for thrust."

"Oh," said McCoy, holding the light a little steadier while Scotty pulled the tool back inside the engine compartment with him. "Why don't they put a light on the end of the wrench?"

Scotty laughed softly. "If they did, there'd be nothing for assistants to do."

McCoy looked nervously over his shoulder. "I could

go looking for whatever's making that clicking sound back there."

"It's just the Heisenberg baffles resetting themselves," Scotty said. "Nothing to worry about."

"That's easy for you to say," McCoy muttered. The hair on the back of his neck was standing straight out, and even though he knew it was ridiculous, his subconscious mind kept waiting for some alien monster to swing down out of the darkness and bite his head off in one gulp. He longed to shine the flashlight out there, but the thought of Scotty unscrewing the wrong 'helical coupling' kept him aiming it into the tight workspace instead.

"There," Scotty said. "Hold it right . . . there . . . got it. One down. Only four more t' go."

Four more? They'd been at this at least two lifetimes already. McCoy used his free hand to rub the small of his back, but he stopped in midrub when he heard a screeching sound near his feet. He jerked the light downward just as he realized that it was Scotty whistling.

"Doctor?" Scotty said patiently. "The light?"

"Sorry. You startled me." He aimed the light back where Scotty was working.

"I dinna think *Loch Lomond* was all that spooky a song."

McCoy ignored his sarcasm. "How can you whistle when we're stuck out here in the middle of nowhere with a broken engine?"

"Same way I whistle any other time. A little higher, please. Thank you." He banged on something solid, and even the metallic ring it made sounded somehow cheery.

"You're having the time of your life, aren't you?" McCoy asked him.

"Well now, I'm not sure I'd go that far," Scotty said, "but I have had worse assignments. And after all the time we've been spending on the ground lately, any excuse to get back into space for a while is fine by me."

McCoy wished he could say the same. He'd joined Starfleet to get away from a bad marriage and a bitter divorce, not because he had any burning desire to see the galaxy. He had eventually come to enjoy the "strange new worlds" part of the fleet charter, but he had never cared for the "boldly going" bit. As far as he was concerned, the only thing worse than wrapping a spaceship inside a hyperspace bubble and squirting it through the ether was tearing a body apart molecule by molecule and beaming it through a transporter. He would much rather ride a bicycle wherever he needed to go, or use his own two feet.

He knew better than to tell that to Scotty. The *Enterprise*'s chief engineer had started fights over less. The two of them had to live practically in each other's laps for who knew how long; there was no sense irritating him.

Something made a soft thud off in the darkness. McCoy twitched, but he forced himself to ignore it. No doubt one of the phlogiston deframmulators had merely changed polarity.

He forced his own lips into a circle and whistled softly, not sure he liked the echoes of his own noise any more than the random sounds of the ship.

Then he felt the creature brush his leg. He cried out "Yeow!" and leaped backward, swinging the light around in an arc designed to either illuminate or eliminate whatever it was, he wasn't sure which.

Metal rang again from inside the engine compartment as Scotty twitched in reflexive reaction, but McCoy swept the light down the catwalk as a gray and white blur streaked off into the darkness again.

"Doctor McCoy," Scotty said, scooting out of the

access hole and rubbing his bruised head, "I really have to—"

"There's a cat in here!" McCoy said.

"A cat?"

"Felis domesticus. Small, slender, long tail. . . ."

"I know what a cat is."

"Well one just rubbed up against my leg."

"Did he, now?" Scotty looked into the distance, where McCoy's flashlight beam cast deep shadows in which anything could be hiding. "Are you sure?"

"It was either that or a damned hairy ghost." McCoy shined the light down on his leg, where three or four silvery hairs, each a couple of centimeters long, clung to his pants.

Scotty nodded slowly. "Well, that would explain my missing field-strength meter." He held up his right hand and wiggled his little finger, on which an oversized ring sported a circular gauge. "I lost it two days ago, and it turned up this morning right in the middle of the pilot's chair. I didn't think I'd dropped it there."

"How long since this ship's regular crew left?" McCoy asked.

"A week, at least," Scotty said.

"The poor thing must be starving." McCoy knelt down and reached out toward the darkness. "Here kitty. Kitty, kitty, kitty."

"After that shriek o' yours, I doubt if he'll be very eager to come back."

"I didn't shriek."

Scotty rubbed the back of his head. "Dinna shriek? My God, man, I thought you'd been eaten alive."

"Well, for a second there I thought the same thing. Here, kitty, kitty."

"You should try offering it some food. And don't aim

the light in its face. Aim it at yourself so it can see you, instead."

"Now there's an idea," McCoy said. "Here." He handed Scotty the flashlight, then stood up and went into the living quarters. The bright overhead light nearly blinded him after the dark engine room, but he found the autogalley—still off-line—and rummaged through the emergency supplies stored beneath it until he found a foil pouch of dried meat. The fine print identified it as emu strips, vacuum-sealed and preserved by irradiation over six years earlier. He scanned it with his tricorder, which reported no toxins, so he took it back into the engine room and tore open the package.

The aroma was as strong as the live emu. He pulled out a rubbery finger-sized strip of meat and held it in front of him, saying, "He ought to have no problem smelling this. Here kitty, kitty."

They didn't have to wait long. Within a minute, the cat stuck its head around the side of a pipe, its eyes glowing green in the dim light. It shunned the corrugated metal catwalk, tiptoeing gracefully along a wiring conduit and leaping from machine to machine until it stood partially obscured by a finned heat radiator just out of reach. Its short fur was mostly gray, with faint black stripes on its sides and tail and white under its chin and along its belly.

"Come on," McCoy urged it. "Just a little closer." He set the bag down by his feet so his left hand was free.

"You're not going to try to grab it are ye?" Scotty asked.

"No, I'm not going to grab it," McCoy answered. "I do know something about cats."

He held the meat out. The cat clearly wanted him to reach out to where it waited, but he held his hand steady, and at last the cat leaned forward and jumped to the metal grating in front of him, then stepped cautiously closer. It sniffed the strip of meat, then licked at it.

"Must not be as hungry as we thought," Scotty said softly.

"Cats are careful," McCoy whispered back. "It just wants to know what I've got before it eats it."

Satisfied that the smelly stuff was edible, the cat took it in its teeth and backed away. McCoy kept hold of his end, but the cat growled and kept tugging, so he let it go. The cat backed away a few steps and hunkered down to eat, its fangs making short work of the meat strip.

McCoy was ready with a second one when the first was done. The cat came right up to him this time and took it from his hands without sniffing it first, then backed off and finished it just as quickly. McCoy held onto the third one and made the cat let him pet it before he let go, then he backed up and led it into the living quarters before he would feed it again.

The cat hesitated at the door, sniffing cautiously, but its hunger finally overpowered its fear of the new people on board its ship and it stepped on through, tail high. Scotty came in behind it and closed the door.

"Now what?" he asked.

McCoy looked for a collar, but there was none. He scratched the cat between the ears and said, "I guess we give it a name."

Chapter Twelve

DELORIC'S BUNK had long ago lost its springiness. When he lay down on it, it creaked and groaned. When he got up from it, *he* creaked and groaned. Even sitting on the edge of it like he was now caused his hips to ache.

Had he been the sole user of the bed, the problem wouldn't exist. His mother had described him as small-boned. His father said he was a runt. His first girlfriend, Shayla, said he was built the way a Kauld should be built. Not too skinny, and certainly not overly muscled. He missed Shayla. In fact, if Shayla were here, then there *would* be a good reason for his bunk's broken springs. He smiled at the thought, but it was short-lived.

The real reason his bed was in such sad shape was because Kertenold used it while Deloric toiled away on the comet's surface. To be fair, Kertenold probably felt the same sense of ownership of the bed and that it was Deloric who slept soundly while he worked hard. But

Kertenold stood a head taller than Deloric and weighed half again what he did: he was bound to wear things out faster. At least he didn't sleep in the bunk above. It would ruin Deloric's night to have someone Kertenold's size *and* their bunk land on top of him.

The thought of hot-bedding with someone else originally disgusted him. He was a fastidious sort, and he'd been certain that whoever used the bed before him would contaminate it. The first few nights on board he had changed the bedding before crawling in, but once the work on the comet started he was too tired to care. Some sleep shifts, he was so exhausted that he would probably not have noticed if anyone else, male or female, was still in the bed.

Tonight would be different. He'd been thinking so hard since the last work shift he was sure his brain would melt. When he had nights like this back home, sleep would sometimes elude him for days.

About half his shiftmates were still up, milling around the cramped ship. In the lounge, some of the crewmembers were rolling hexies in a game of chance, betting the hard, dry cakes that served as dessert from dinner. The winner didn't have to eat them. In the far corner, three or four others were swapping dirty jokes. Deloric had already heard them, or some variation, and grew weary of the laughter.

He thought maybe a glass of warm yeerid milk would allow him to sleep, but the cafeteria had already closed and the dispenser in the lounge was empty. Clearly, the universe was against him tonight. But as he turned to leave, he heard someone quietly playing a bantar and singing an old folksong. The young woman sat near the lounge door and started in on the second verse. It took a moment, but Deloric finally realized she was singing "Teeth of the Tajar," an antigovernment anthem from four or five generations back. The only way she could get away with singing such a song was because it was against the old government, which the current government had overthrown.

The singer's voice was soft, but certain of the notes she hit. Deloric admired anyone who could make music. He'd tried three or four different instruments, only to give up on them within days, and his singing voice would scare a rock. Hers was pretty, even if the words she sang were harsh. He listened to her sing about greed and the lust for power and the evil it led to. The song made just as much sense today as it had the day it was written. It was just as true—and just as damning. He wondered if the singer had chosen it on purpose, if it was her way of telling the rest of them that she had figured out what their hard work over the last week would ultimately be used for.

She wouldn't look up. She couldn't afford to let a glance confirm his suspicion, for anyone could be a spy, even him. She was taking a risk just playing the song. He was just as glad that she didn't look at him, for he knew he couldn't hide his feelings from her, either. He lingered by the door and listened to three more verses, then headed for his bunk, humming quietly.

There was no single moment when it became clear what he had to do. He only knew he had to do something. The lights were already dimmed in the bunk room, so he shuffled his way down the aisle of beds, but instead of removing his clothing, he just pulled back the covers, crawled in, and waited until he heard the room fill with the sounds of sleep. Kertenold would kill him if he ever found out, but Deloric was beyond caring.

He thought about destroying the giant mirror he had helped build, but the only way he could think of to do that was to crash the bunkship into it, killing everyone including the crew out there at work on it now. He couldn't bring himself to do that. He thought about breaking radio silence and warning the human colony five light-days away, but they were in the Blind. His message would be buried in the wave of charged particles streaking toward the planet, and they would never detect it. Besides, that would be treason, and no matter what he thought of the project, he couldn't bring himself to betray his own people.

That left only one choice. When the last of the gamers turned out the lights, he eased from his bunk, took his small flashlight from the tiny personal locker at his feet, and headed for the door. He was two-thirds of the way there when someone in an upper bunk snorted awake and grabbed his shoulder.

"Hey! Hey! Is it time to get up already?" came the sleep-thickened voice. It sounded a little like Nialerad.

"No, it's okay. Go back to sleep," Deloric whispered.

"Where you going?"

"Shhh. To the little miner's room."

"The what?"

"I got to use the toilet. Too much yeerid milk," he lied.

"But they're at the other end of the room."

What was this guy? The self-appointed hall monitor? "Someone got sick in there. I'm going to use the ones in the next dorm."

"Oh . . . that's good." The guy's voice sounded muffled, like he was talking through a pillow and his words were slurred together.

"Now go back to sleep," Deloric whispered. Heavy, steady breathing was the response he got. People were so weird when they were almost asleep. He slid out from under the man's heavy hand and cautiously resumed his mission.

The hallways were dimly lit and deserted. The bunkship was small compared to the Kauld warships, but bunkships were much more efficient in this sort of off-world mining situation. They were designed to serve as a satellite hotel rather than a ship, since they spent the majority of their time in orbit around the mine.

That worked to Deloric's advantage in a couple of ways. As small as the bunkship was, it wouldn't take him very long to get to the shuttle bay, and he wouldn't have time to back out of his plan.

Instead of taking the lift, he opted for the stairs, thinking that his chances of running into anyone else would be practically nil. But he regretted that choice almost instantly. A single lamp illuminated each landing, and the garish light cast odd shadows through the metallic mesh of the stairs, sending chills up his spine at every turn. Worse, each step he took echoed like thunder, no matter how gingerly he moved.

He tiptoed up the two flights to the shuttle deck, then eased the heavy door shut and leaned against the wall, feeling the cool, smooth metal against his head, hands, and back. His heart was beating hard and fast, and he was surprised at how ragged his breathing had become, even though he had done nothing strenuous. But within a few moments he gained control over his body again and moved cautiously down the hall. The bay itself was at the far end of the now darkened hallway and back behind the suit lockers.

The silvery suits hung in rows on metal hooks. He was already reaching for his out of habit when he realized he probably wouldn't need it where he was going.

He grasped the empty gloves, taking a moment to say goodbye to his former life, then he turned toward the shuttle bay and was about to step through the doorway when something made him stop. His skin tingled as though someone had tickled his back with a feather.

Down a different hallway and around a corner to his right, the lift doors slid open with a barely perceptible whoosh. Careful footsteps padded his way. Who else could be roaming around up here at this time of the sleep cycle?

What if it was a guard, coming to get him? His heartbeat shot up and his skin broke into a sweat, but he forced himself to calm down. He hadn't done anything wrong. Not yet. This wasn't a prison ship, though at first glance there wasn't that much to distinguish it from one. He had as much right as anyone to wander the halls at night.

So did whoever had just arrived. It was probably someone who couldn't sleep, out perambulating, trying to relax while they had the chance. But the image of a prison wouldn't leave his mind. The other person's steps slowed the closer they got to the intersection of the halls. It wasn't the gait of someone on a casual stroll around the ship. That person was sneaking!

Deloric cautiously sidled up to the wall so that he would be behind the corner as the intruder came around. He felt woefully unarmed, with just his palm-sized flashlight to use as a club. His only other advantage would be surprise. Maybe.

The other's footfalls stopped just short of turning the corner. Deloric's body tensed like a bandar string about to break. Any moment . . . any moment. . . .

A female Kauld stepped out from the shadows and Deloric sprang in front of her, shining his light at its brightest setting smack in her face.

She yelped, high-pitched and short. And in return, his pent-up nerves made him jump back and shout, "Yaaa!"

Then he regained his senses enough to recognize his intruder: Terwolan. He quickly clamped his free hand over her mouth and urged her to "shhhhh!"

She didn't shhhhh. She twisted her head and tried to bite his fingers, while simultaneously swinging a fist at him and kicking out with her right foot. Deloric dodged back, but not before she'd clipped him on the shoulder.

"Hey, it's me!" he hissed. "Stop it!" He grabbed her arm before she could hit him again.

Terwolan kept struggling, and he finally realized that the light in her eyes kept her from seeing who he was. He turned his flashlight toward his own face, then aimed it at the ceiling. There was a moment of startled recognition on her part, marked by her wide eyes, then he felt her relax.

"What are you doing here?" she whispered when he let her go.

"I could ask the same question of you," he whispered back.

"I couldn't sleep," she said, her voice full of defiance.

"Me either." That was true enough.

They stared at one another for a moment, sizing each other up in a way they never had in their weeks of working side-by-side. Terwolan looked tired, but there was something else in her expression, an oppressive weight that hadn't been there before. Deloric finally said, "You figured out what we're building out there, didn't you?"

Her eyes shifted to the shuttle bay door, then back to him. She swallowed and said, "Maybe."

"So have I."

They stared at one another again, Deloric feeling the first glimmer of hope he'd had all night. He didn't believe Terwolan was a spy, but how could he know for sure? And how could he convince her he wasn't one himself?

"The way I see it," he said carefully, "A person who didn't like it would have two choices: treason or exile."

"I notice you didn't give him the option to just go back to bed and forget about it," she pointed out.

"I . . . um . . . don't think he could do that." He looked into her eyes, desperately searching for confirmation there, but he just couldn't tell. "They're going to fire it tonight."

That got a reaction. Her eyes widened, and her expression darkened. "How do you know?"

"We're five light-days out. The human colony will be in direct line with the carbon dioxide stream in five days. And it's the middle of the Blind time, both here and there. Nobody will be able to detect the energy release."

She nodded slowly. "That makes sense. So what are we going to do?"

He relaxed just a little. She had said "we." His flashlight was growing heavy; he shifted it from his right hand to his left and said, "I can't bring myself to commit treason, but I can't be part of this any more either. I was going to take one of the long-range shuttles and head for deep space."

She smiled. To Deloric it was like the sun coming up. "Great minds think alike," she said. "Let's go."

She took her spacesuit. Deloric revised his plan and did the same. You never knew when you might need to do an EVA. They didn't put them on, just hung them inside the shuttle's airlock as they entered. They hurried on through the small passenger/cargo bay and into the control room, lights automatically turning on ahead of them as they went.

"Do you know how to fly one of these?" Terwolan asked him as they sat in the control chairs before the instrument panel.

"Not this particular kind, but I've flown shuttles before," he told her. "How about you?"

"I've flown this model before."

"You're the pilot, then."

She nodded and got to work bringing the engines online. Deloric switched on the navigation computer and scrolled through the list of preprogrammed destinations, looking for anything that might offer safe refuge to a couple of deserters. He hated thinking of himself in those terms, but that's what it would look like to anyone else.

The Blood homeworld slid by, highlighted orange. It was interdicted, of course. No contact was allowed with the Blood Many except under direct orders from the High Command. Deloric didn't want to run to the Kauld's oldest enemies anyway. He just wanted out of this whole militaristic mess.

"Launch in ten," Terwolan said.

He looked out through the viewport. The hangar doors were opening. This was it. Alarms would already be sounding in the communication center. Books and games and mugs of skath would be flying as bored controllers leaped up from their midshift diversions to see what was going on.

He thought about trying to bluff their way clear, but he knew he'd never be able to pull it off. He had no reason to be leaving the bunkship at this hour, especially not in a long-range shuttle. Besides, intership communications wouldn't work beyond the shuttle bay anyway, not during the Blind. He left the communications panel switched off and peered out at the widening swath of starry space, figuring he could help spot trouble by eye if there was any.

Terwolan took them out fast, banking hard just beyond the doors and accelerating away in case anyone tried to fire on them. The comet was a pale half-circle sweeping across their field of view, growing more full as they swung around behind it. Now Deloric could see what he had been forbidden to look at before: a tall tower stuck out the back side, circular coils ringing it all the way up from the base to the tip. It was an accelerator of some sort, and it was aimed straight through the comet's central hole.

"Uh-oh," Terwolan said. Deloric glanced over at her, saw that she wasn't even looking at the comet, and followed her gaze upward to the immense Kauld battleship keeping station just a few *rho* away.

His breath caught in his throat. The battleship was too far away for him to see its gun turrets, but he could imagine them well enough, all swiveling around to track the tiny shuttle.

"Evasive maneuvers!" he said.

"It's Blind time," she reminded him. "They couldn't hit another battleship at this distance without their tracking sensors." Nonetheless, she swung the shuttle through another arc and fed more power to the engines.

She was just in time. A bright red disruptor bolt sizzled through the space where they had just been. Another drew a ragged line between them and the ball of ice. Either the gunners were getting lucky, or they were better shots than Terwolan had thought.

"Duck behind the comet," he urged.

"Good idea." She banked them around until its

bumpy surface eclipsed the warship, then aimed straight out into space and held their acceleration at maximum. In the rear-facing viewscreen, the comet shrank precipitously behind them, shrinking from a wall of ice to a snowball to a pebble. The warship edged out from behind it, but Terwolan cut the engines, effectively reducing their visibility to nothing before the gunners could take aim. She used the steering jets to alter their course a few more degrees, but that wasn't even necessary. The warship didn't fire again, and after a tense couple of minutes, its nose swiveled back to point down the line of carbon dioxide ice stretching in-system.

"They're not even chasing us?" Deloric asked in disbelief.

"They must have bigger things on their mind," Terwolan said. She rotated the ship around so they could see the comet straight on. They were way off to the side now, and receding fast. The battleship was almost as distant on the opposite side. The bunkships were much closer, but also out of the line of fire. The string of ice that the miners had launched into space should have been invisible, but it suddenly flared bright red, like a thin knife blade slashing open the fabric of space for as far as the eye could see.

"They fired the disruptor at the core," he said. "That vaporized the carbon dioxide."

An instant later, the back side of the comet glowed white. The whole thing lit up from inside, but that was nothing compared to the brilliance of the light beam that shone through the central core and down the long column of vaporized ice. It was so intense Deloric threw his hands over his eyes for protection, but even then it was too bright. The flesh of his hands wasn't enough to block it; only the bones did that. He turned away, eyelids slammed shut even against the reflections inside the shuttle, but he felt the back of his head grow hot in the glare.

"Get us out of here!" he shouted.

Terwolan groped blindly for the control board. The shuttle turned slowly, the swath of intense light sliding up the back wall as it did. They could actually hear its progress by the sizzling of plastic controls and trim panels, and they could feel the heat of it burning their skin.

And this was just the *leakage* from the laser beam.

"I can't find the warp controls!" Terwolan shouted. "I'm blind!"

Deloric peered through the slit between two fingers, wincing in pain. He couldn't see anything but brilliant white, either, but after another few seconds the ship rotated around so its bulk cut off the worst of the light. He blinked, stuck his face right next to the control board, and peered at the labels until he found the "engage" button. There was no course set yet, but he didn't care. He mashed the button with his entire fist, then fell back into his chair as the engines wrapped the ship in their magnetic embrace and threw them into darkness.

Chapter Thirteen

SPOCK WAS hunched over the conglomeration of electronics parts he'd cobbled together in the science lab, examining his connections with an inductive logic probe. Something was wired improperly, but this was his second pass through the system and so far he had been unable to find the problem.

It had to be a connection. Everything else was working as it should. The signal generators in the deflector dish at the front of the ship's secondary hull had been modified to accept greater output from the olivium power source, the data processors checked out when he ran a self-test, and everything worked individually. It was only when he hooked it all together and tried to run his modified radar unit at full power that the system malfunctioned.

Gamma Night had once more reduced the ship's sensor range to uselessness. Crew members with binoculars outperformed even his low-frequency radar, which was the only electronic scanning device that worked at all under the onslaught of charged particles from out-system. And both systems were limited to the speed of light. Anything could sneak up under warp power, and nobody would know until it had dropped into normal space right on top of them.

The *Enterprise* desperately needed subspace scanning capability during Gamma Night. Spock didn't normally consider brute force an acceptable alternative to elegance, but in this case brute force seemed the only possible answer to the problem. He needed sensors powerful enough to cut through the interference and return a clear signal, even when they were being inundated by noise.

Gaining the requisite power was not the issue; olivium-enhanced emitters provided more than enough. The problem lay in processing the reflected signals when they returned. *If* they returned. Energy was pouring into subspace—at least, it was if the power indications could be believed—but precious little of it was returning. At the power level he was using, his signal should have been bouncing off everything, including the tiny gravity wells around individual hydrogen atoms. The receivers should have been overloaded with echoes even if the signal was only reflecting off the gravity wells around the planets; instead, they registered only 2 percent above background, even when the whole system was running wide open.

There had to be a data error somewhere. That much energy couldn't just disappear. Spock was pumping the equivalent of a small sun's output into space—it had to be going somewhere. He suspected it was, and he suspected it was coming back to the detectors, too. They just weren't programmed to handle the intense signal in addition to the intense background noise. They were apparently cutting out when the incoming data grew too complex to process.

Trouble was, he could find no instruction in their programs that would make them do that. Logic probes made while the system was running showed no sign of overload. The system behaved as though it simply wasn't getting a signal back.

Spock set the probe down on the bench beside the breadboard circuitry and rubbed his eyes. He'd been at this for hours. He should be asleep, but Gamma Night didn't arrive on a convenient schedule, and he didn't want to wait for another cycle to test his modifications.

He took a few deep breaths to oxygenate his blood. There was no problem with the connections. He had to believe the evidence: energy was pouring out into subspace but not coming back. How could that be?

It had to be the olivium. Every time he had tried to power something with it, he had had unexpected problems. Mr. Scott had succeeded in overdriving warp engines with it, but the material's space-time altering nature merely enhanced what a warp engine was supposed to do anyway. Sensors were supposed to do the opposite, and therein lay the problem. Sensors were supposed to bounce signals off the subspace manifestations of whatever real-space objects were out there and read the reflections, all without actually altering whatever they were reading. The Vulcan P'tar—and Heisenberg on Earth—had proved that every act of measurement altered the experiment, but normally the effect was of no consequence on a large scale. Long-range subspace scans didn't run afoul of the uncertainty principle.

With quantum olivium in the circuit, however, that wasn't necessarily true. Spock suspected that the emitted signal was doing something he hadn't anticipated. Its power wasn't just disappearing.

Where was it going, though? Anything that absorbed that much energy should shine like a beacon, in both normal space and subspace.

There was only one logical answer: He wasn't using the right detector. Low-frequency gravity-wave detectors obviously weren't picking up anything, even though that was what he was broadcasting. Electromagnetic waves weren't any more useful. There was just as obviously nothing returning to the ship in visual wavelengths, or the spotters posted at the observation ports would have reported it. That left ultraviolet and even higher-frequency ranges.

The ultraviolet and X-ray bands were easy to check, and just as easy to dismiss. There was nothing there. And beyond that there wasn't an electromagnetic spectrum. At ultra-high frequencies, the boundary between energy and matter started to break down. He might as well start looking for exotic particles—quarks and the like.

He could, of course. The range of detectable frequencies went all the way up to matter waves. He just hadn't believed that it was possible for a signal to be transformed that far from its initial form. But now it was the next logical thing to check.

It was the work of a moment to adjust the detectors. He slowly raised the frequency, and with it the energy content of the particles he was searching for, through the elemental quarks, into the lepton range, searching for electrons, positrons, neutrinos. . . .

There was a flash of light, a loud *bang,* and the entire breadboard circuit on the workbench erupted in flame. Spock grabbed the extinguisher from the wall beside the bench and efficiently smothered the fire, then silenced the alarm and called an "all clear" to security.

The acrid smell of burnt plastic and electronics quickly dissipated through the ship's ventilation, but a hint of it remained on Spock's hands. He could detect it as he settled back into a chair and steepled his fingers before his nose in a pose he often took when concentrating on a puzzle.

The theory was simple: the outgoing signal travels from the emitter, encounters either matter itself or its subspatial distortion, then bounces off and returns to the detectors as a signal that the data processors turn into meaningful information. The exploding circuit indicated an overload, proving to Spock that a signal was indeed being detected and that the amplification stage of the detectors was functioning correctly. That the overload occurred while he was scanning the ultra-high frequencies would lend credence to the theory that the signal was being transformed. On the other hand, it could simply mean that he had detected an extraordinarily large, naturally occurring neutrino burst.

Either way, he had some work to do. He picked up the scorched circuit board and studied it. There was enough damage that he would have to build another. It would not take long to reconstruct, but he wanted to determine that the original design of the board was sound.

He checked the time. There were still a few more hours of Gamma Night left. If he worked quickly, he might be able to make another test run before it ended. He rubbed his eyes again and set to work.

Chapter Fourteen

STARLIGHT FILTERED thinly in through the forward view-port of the darkened observation deck as the battleship *Tonclin* took its position. Vellyngaith stood front and center, admiring the sculpted comet and all that it represented. He stood alone, a man with his thoughts only a few minutes from the firing of the laser. It was the pinnacle of his career so far, and he wanted time to relish that accomplishment.

The rest of the All Kauld fleet were in an uninhabited star system nearby, running drills and testing out their newly refitted ships for the big battle that would take place in five days time. He'd laid down the master plan of attack and left the details to the captains themselves to work out—and fight over. They were the ones, after all, who knew their own strengths. Those who were taking over the refitted ships that had started out as nonmilitary had the biggest task ahead of them. They had to learn how these ships handled under their new drives, and what kind of limitations they might have.

The captains of the three new warships had been like children given agrav 'cycles for their birthdays when all they had asked for were sleds. The reports they'd sent back to Vellyngaith had all been positive so far, and tinged with a sense of awe. Not since the Tholians' gift of dynadrive had the Kauld seen this kind of leap in abilities. And this time, the Kauld had developed it themselves, using the olivium they had liberated from the human mining operation.

And it was a small amount of olivium they had managed to take back from the humans, at that. By rights it should have all belonged to the Kauld. Then there was that traitor, Shucorion. Not that Vellyngaith had expected any better of him. In fact, he'd proven mildly helpful to a point. Even so, once the humans were gone, Vellyngaith would turn his full attention toward Shucorion and the rest of his sorry race.

The door into the observation deck opened quietly. The light from the corridor reflected on the forward viewport, and Vellyngaith saw the silhouette of his attendant, Celerneth. Without turning around Vellyngaith said, "What is it?"

"The viewing party is getting restless, sir. They would like to know when they can enter."

Vellyngaith suppressed a sigh. This moment of quiet contemplation would be over too quickly as it was. He glanced over his right shoulder toward the silhouette and said, "Soon, soon. Break out the katanga liquor if you think they need a diversion; I will signal when it is time."

"Very good," Celerneth said and closed the door.

Vellyngaith looked back toward what was left of the comet. It was a magnificent piece of work. The carved face shone, its highly polished surface aimed down the light-minutes-long column of ice. The last of the work crews had been picked up from the comet's surface and brought aboard the *Tonclin,* where they would be housed until they could be reassigned.

Beyond the comet, several *rho* away, sat the bunkships. They hadn't been removed yet, and wouldn't be immediately. Once the battle was over, they would continue to serve their purpose while the Kauld mined the rest of the olivium from the moon, then as the last of the deposits were recovered from the planet's surface.

No, reverse that, he thought. Mine the planet first, before Yanorada's plan made it too difficult—unless there was some way to reverse it now that it had been triggered. But Yanorada had sworn it couldn't be stopped.

Just like Vellyngaith's plan.

He was ready now. He checked his wristchron. It was time. He stepped to the wall and pressed the intercom button. "Celerneth, you may now escort my guests to the observation deck." He didn't wait to hear Celerneth's response before he turned back to the viewports.

An unexpected motion caught Vellyngaith's eye. A Kauld long-range shuttle popped into view from around the restructured comet. The view shifted as the *Tonclin* responded to orders from the bridge, no doubt from his second-in-command, Tenoweth. He watched as the shuttle took evasive measures and managed to escape the disruptor beams fired at it. He frowned. His gunners should have hit it at this range, even with the Blind muddling their targeting computers. Perhaps Tenoweth had ordered a warning shot, since communications were out as well.

The shuttle slid behind the comet, and Vellyngaith didn't see it reemerge. He wondered what it was doing out in this remote part of space during the Blind, and then realized that it probably came from one of the bunkships.

Was something wrong with the laser? The very possibility infuriated him. There couldn't be. Not now. Everything depended on perfect timing. And everything was ready. The carbon dioxide stream was extended to the optimal length, the exciter beam was ready, and the target would be in position momentarily. All systems were go.

Could someone be trying to sabotage it? He snorted in derision. Let them try. The weapon was ready to fire. Even a direct hit on the accelerator would only set it off, and once that happened, there would be no stopping it.

Besides, it would be faster to simply fire it now rather than chase off after the trespasser. Vellyngaith reached for the intercom button on the wall beside the viewport, but before he could call his second-in-command and tell him to let the shuttle go, the view out the 'port slid back to where it had been before. He smiled in satisfaction. It comforted him that his second had reacted in the same manner as he would have himself.

He made a mental note to check with the bunkships and see who was missing a shuttle and a worker or two. If the fool survived his joyride, he'd wish he hadn't when he learned what his punishment would be.

The doors opened, and his guests entered the observation deck. He went to the control panel on the wall to his left and turned on the lights to a dim glow to allow enough visibility so that people wouldn't trip over the few chairs and tables in the room, but not enough to compete with the view outside. The observers were few but very influential, mostly dignitaries who would be able to go back to the homeworld after the show today and report to the masses the magnificent feat their own Vellyngaith had performed for their welfare. Vellyngaith wanted to be sure they saw every detail of his genius.

"Welcome," he said. "Please, come forward and behold our victory over Federation."

Gasps and other sounds of appreciation escaped from the people as their brains registered what they were seeing. One decorated old warrior, aged but far from feeble, approached Vellyngaith and said, "This is your doing?" He pointed a crooked finger at the comet, and held a stern look in his brown eyes.

"I gave the order to build it, yes." Vellyngaith held his elder's gaze, eye to eye.

A long moment passed before the old man cracked a smile and said, "I knew we could count on you!"

"Then let's not waste any more time. We have endured the usurpers' presence long enough." There was no point in speechifying. Nothing he could say would match the weapon itself. Vellyngaith pressed the intercom button on the wall beside him and said the only word that was necessary: "Fire!"

Another collective gasp arose from the small gathering as a beautiful bright red light momentarily illuminated the column of frozen carbon dioxide. It glittered brilliantly, like a string of rubies across the black drape of space.

The cheering and applause had already begun when the accelerator on the comet's back side luminesced white, the glow shooting through the core and down the now-vaporized trail of ice. The light from the core grew bright to the point of being painful, then continued to blaze.

Vellyngaith squinted against the glare. It was magnificent! The raw power of it all—and he commanded it!

The others in the observation deck no longer made

sounds of inspired approval. The gasps turned into moans and cries. Most of his guests now shielded their faces with their hands and arms. One had dropped to the floor and used the bulkhead to hide from the intense light. The room grew noticeably hotter with each passing second.

At last, Vellyngaith admitted to himself that the leakage from the laser was too much. "Polarize the viewports!" he ordered into his intercom.

The windows responded so quickly that he suspected the helmsman had his finger poised on the control, anticipating the order. The brilliance from his creation dimmed, but not enough.

"More polarization," he ordered.

"Sir, we're already at full."

Vellyngaith laughed. These viewports could block out the light of a sun from within its own corona. His laser was more powerful than a sun—from the *side!*

He opened his eyes a sliver. The pain! And the heat. He could hear the whine of the room coolers working in vain. Hah! These aristocrats would have a story to tell when they returned home.

But he wanted them impressed, not blinded. Reluctantly, he said, "Lower the blast shields."

A heavy panel slid down from overhead, its hardened composite hull material doing what simple polarizers could not. Darkness swept across the ceiling as it lowered into place, but it stopped three-quarters of the way down.

"All the way," Vellyngaith ordered.

"It's stuck, sir." He heard the panic in the helmsman's voice. The shield rose partway, then lowered again, but it didn't gain any ground. "The tracks must be warped from the heat, sir. The entire port side of the ship is overheating."

"Roll us sideways," he ordered. "Now!"

He felt his ship lurch into motion. The brilliant swath of light swept upward, narrowed to a thin line, then disappeared as if a switch had been thrown. The bulk of the ship shadowed them now.

It was pitch-black inside the observation room. Vellyngaith found the light controls by feel and turned them up all the way, wincing as the touch panel burned his fingers. It was still barely enough to see by after the intensity of a moment before, but it soothed his guests' panic. They were rubbing their eyes, tears streaming down their faces. But the Kauld were a tough species. There would be no complaining from them, especially in light, as it were, of their success.

"I apologize for your discomfort," he said. "The weapon is obviously more powerful than even I had expected. What we felt was just the glare from it, but imagine what will happen when the beam itself strikes the human colony. The entire planet will feel more than mere discomfort."

They seemed little mollified, but he didn't care. He had more important things to worry about. The ship was still moving, even though he had only ordered a roll. What was going on up there on the bridge? Were those fools actually backing off? A hot streak of anger ran through him. His orders had been to maintain their position during the unveiling and firing of his laser.

He motioned to Celerneth and instructed him to aid his guests and return them to their cabins to rest; then, hands clenched into fists, he stormed toward the door into the corridor, but it wouldn't open more than a hand's width apart. He jammed his fingers into the crack to pull it open, only to find the metal too hot to touch.

He jerked his hands free, sticking his fingers in his mouth to cool them, then shoved his booted foot into the crack and pushed. The doors squealed and lurched apart, and he stalked down the corridor to the lift.

"What's the meaning of this?" he hissed into the intercom the moment he stepped into the lift car.

"Sir," his second-in-command replied, "the ship sustained heavy damage down the port flank, and the starboard side was starting to go as well after we rolled." Vellyngaith could barely hear him over the alarms going off on the bridge. "We had to move or be cooked."

Damage? To his ship? The spell the laser had cast over him finally began to lift. He'd been so enthralled with the sheer enormity of his accomplishment that he'd allowed his vanity to overcome his sense.

"If you wish, I'll hand you my resignation when you return to the bridge."

"What?"

"I did break a direct order," Tenoweth pointed out.

True enough. But to what degree? Tenoweth had kept the ship stationed until it was too dangerous to remain. Everyone had seen enough to understand what was in store for the humans. And his prompt action might have saved the ship.

"We'll discuss that when the time is right," Vellyngaith said. A moment later the lift deposited him on the bridge. Tenoweth stood at attention, arms folded behind his back.

"What's our status?" Vellyngaith growled.

"Decks 3 through 10 are reporting hull damage along the port side, almost all external sensors were overloaded, and the crew lounge is on fire. I've ordered it vented to space as soon as everyone is out."

"Injuries?"

117

"A few, mostly burns on those who were working close to the hull."

Vellyngaith's own fingers throbbed. He'd take care of that later. "Get crews moving on the repairs as soon as we're at a safe distance." He looked around the bridge, saw everyone busy taking care of their own stations, and relaxed slightly. He'd made a mistake, but it hadn't been deadly.

"The Blind is still knocking out communications," Tenoweth said. "It will be some time yet before we can contact the bunkships and see what kind of damage they've sustained. We may have to take on their crews."

Vellyngaith paused to think, then said, "Run the visual recordings we took of the firing sequence."

The image of the comet appeared on the forward viewscreen just as Vellyngaith remembered it. He studied it now for other details. The bunkships could be seen on the other side, then the runaway shuttle, the ship's disruptor beam chasing it. No other trace of it as it swooped behind the comet. He studied the image when the bunkships were visible again and felt a knot twist his gut. They were stationed closer to the laser than the *Tonclin* had been. They wouldn't have been able to get their engines on-line fast enough to escape the heatwave that poured from the laser. Those bunkers were gone.

He didn't need to continue the recording, but he did. The red flash, then the white hot light reached out and—there was no more. The recording device had obviously been destroyed at that point.

Vellyngaith's enthusiasm, though a bit dampened by the unexpected loss of the work crews, emerged once again at the sight of such raw power. He already had a way to use the total destruction of the bunkships in his favor. One of the biggest problems with his plan was that there would be no martyrs for the common people back home to honor and sing songs about; well, now they had plenty.

A sudden thought made him pause. "How far away are we?" he asked.

"Five light-minutes. I didn't want to go farther during the Blind."

Vellyngaith looked at his wristchron. Five minutes, eh?

"Carry on. Get those repairs underway and report when the Blind is over."

"Yes, sir."

He walked through the bridge and took the private lift to his cabin, just overhead. It was a mess inside; paintings scorched brown by the heat, papers actually burned, plastic melted. He ignored it all and climbed up the stairs to his private observation bubble, a full-circle dome on the ship's forward point that gave him a better view—though unenhanced—than he could get from the bridge itself.

He turned once around, watching, not sure what he would see from this distance, nor just when the light would catch up to the ship. But when it came it was unmistakable. A bright point blossomed among the stars, then a white streak lanced out across the night, extending for as far as the eye could see.

Not quite. Way down the line, at a place so distant it almost looked like the vanishing point, the beam faded away. That would be the last of the carbon dioxide column. Beyond that was empty space, and as anyone who had fought a laser battle knew, a pure light beam—even one as powerful as this—was invisible in a vacuum.

He smiled and rubbed his palms together, despite the pain. The humans would never know what hit them.

Chapter Fifteen

THE BIG MUDDY RIVER was living up to its name. Kirk and Lilian and their pilot had visited five town sites along its banks, and every one of them had been knee-deep in sticky brown muck flushed downriver by the flood. The sixth was proving impossible to find a landing site near, though a few low passes overhead made Kirk wonder what the point would be even if they did. There was practically nothing left here to salvage, and certainly nothing to defend from interstellar marauders.

Nonetheless, people were down there sifting through the wreckage, scavenging what they could. A few gray tents rippled in the breeze on a bank above the high-water mark; the people down there weren't going to let themselves get caught by the same disaster a second time.

They looked up and waved as the plane flew over. The pilot, Herman, waved back with the wings, tilting them left and right, then he straightened out and climbed higher above the valley floor. "Do you want to make another pass?" he asked Kirk, shouting to be heard over the noise of the propeller.

"No," Kirk said, shaking his head in exaggerated motions in case the pilot couldn't hear him. He'd seen enough. In fact, he'd seen enough of the whole valley—enough to know that Governor Pardonnet hadn't overstated the problem when he'd described the reconstruction effort.

He twisted around in his seat to look at Lilian. "Ready to call it a day?" he asked.

She nodded. She certainly looked like she was. Her childlike eagerness to go flying had been smothered under the ache of sympathy for all the destruction they'd seen today. Kirk almost wished he hadn't offered to bring her along, but they had had fun on the flight out, and besides, as the school administrator she needed to see the situation first-hand.

Herman took the plane up and over the ridge to the north, then turned west toward Buena Vista. Green mountainsides and steep canyons replaced the gray floodplain, reminding everyone that only one river valley had flooded. Kirk took special encouragement in the realization that the rest of the continent looked this good less than a year after the Burn. It meant the Big Muddy would recover as well.

Herman must have been thinking similar thoughts. "Hey," he said, "you want to see something that'll put a smile back on your faces?"

"How far out of the way is it?" Kirk asked.

"Not far. Ten, fifteen minutes at most."

"Okay."

Herman banked the plane farther north again, aiming for a snow-capped mountain peak in the heart of the range. Shadows from the late afternoon sun accentuated every ridge and cirque on its glacier-carved flanks, but Herman swung wide to the east of it and descended into a deep valley beyond.

It was mostly in shadow. It took Kirk a few seconds for his eyes to adapt, but when they did, it was as if someone had withdrawn a curtain from a mural. Huge trees rose up out of the valley, reaching straight and true into the air above a canopy of dense foliage. Hundreds of birds took wing as the airplane approached, wheeling around in tight formation and diving for cover. Out Kirk's side, a waterfall tumbled off a high cliff and turned to mist before it reached the ground. The recovering vegetation elsewhere had been pretty, but this little patch of greenery was obviously the forest primeval.

"How did this survive the Burn?" Kirk asked.

"Orographic cloud cover," Herman said. "The peak makes its own weather. Most days there's a permanent cloud bank here. It must have been raining cats and dogs the day the moon blew, and that protected it."

He circled around so Kirk and Lilian could get another look, then climbed back out of the valley and headed on toward home. Kirk felt his mood lifting with the plane, and when he looked back at Lilian she was smiling again.

"Want to try flying it again?" Herman asked Kirk.

"That's all right," he said. On the way out he had proved to everyone's satisfaction why he was a starship captain and not a bush pilot. He had no doubt that he could master the skills required if he needed to, but he saw no need to subject Lilian to another bumpy ride.

She had ideas of her own, though. She leaned forward from the back seat and said, "Could, um, could I try it?"

Herman looked over at Kirk. Kirk would have to

trade seats with her if she was going to take the controls.

"I . . . sure, why not?" he said, unbuckling his harness.

They had to squeeze past one another in the narrow confines of the cockpit. The shifting weight made the plane pitch and roll, and even though Herman tried to compensate for it, they wound up thrown together half a dozen times before they managed to exchange places. Kirk strapped himself into the seat behind Lilian, figuring the plane would balance better with his weight on that side.

She had to scoot the seat forward to reach the pedals. Herman went over the controls with her, giving her the same explanation he had given Kirk, then let her grasp the yoke, taking his hands off the one on his side.

The plane bounced upward and banked to the right. She overcorrected, but brought it back to level after that, then tried a few banks and turns on purpose.

"Remember the rudder," Herman told her.

The plane suddenly yawed to the right, then to the left. "Yow!" she yelled. "It's touchy!"

"Yep," he said, grinning. That was just what Kirk had said, too.

She did a few S-turns, then banked the plane hard right, nosed down a few degrees, and did a slow spiral. While the world swirled around them, she asked, "Will it loop if I pull back hard enough?"

"Yeah, but—"

"Can I?"

Herman looked back at Kirk. "Captain?"

Oh sure, Kirk thought. *Drop it on me.* But obviously it was safe or Herman would have just said "No." He looked out the window just to make sure that they had plenty of air below them, then nodded and said, "Go for it."

"Here goes!" Lilian dropped the nose another few degrees, straightened out their bank, then pulled back on the yoke. The view out the windscreen rolled downward, the horizon flashed past, then it was sky . . . sky . . . sky while they grew lighter and lighter. Kirk felt himself falling into his harness, but it only lasted a second before the plane nosed over and centripetal force pressed him back into the seat.

"Wahoo!" Lilian yelled. The propeller revved higher as they fell down the back side of the loop, and the horizon swept past again, this time upside-down. For a moment they were looking straight down at the rough terrain, then the horizon came around again and she leveled the plane out.

All three of them cheered, though Kirk noticed Herman carefully checking the instruments as well.

"I always wanted to do that in my uncle Lee's plane," Lilian said, "but Mom would have had a heart attack."

"Now it'll be your kids having the heart attack if you tell them what you did," Herman said. Then he laughed. "Actually, if Reynold finds out about this he'll be pestering me to let him do it, too."

"It'll be our secret." She turned part-way around toward Kirk. "Captain? No fair telling on me."

"I wouldn't dream of it," he said, grinning just as wide as she. Her smile was contagious. He felt lighter now, as if he had left half his worries behind in the loop.

They flew the rest of the way back in relative silence, watching the landscape slide past beneath them and the sun sink into the distant clouds. The horizon was turning pink by the time they landed. They endured the bone-rattling deceleration on the grass runway, then taxied to the hangar and switched off the motor. The propeller freewheeled to a stop, leaving them in a silence so profound that Kirk couldn't be sure if his ears even worked anymore.

Then Lilian unbuckled her harness, the click filling the tiny cabin, and Herman popped open his door. "Home sweet home," he said as he climbed out.

Kirk waited for Lilian to step down to the ground, then clambered out past her seat and stood beside her, stretching his arms out and feeling his joints pop.

"Thanks for the ride," he told Herman. "And thank you, too," he said to Lilian.

"Any time," she said. To Herman she added, "I mean that. Any time you need a copilot, let me know. That was fun."

He nodded. "I may take you up on that."

Lilian held out her hand to Kirk. "I suppose we should get back to town and see if everything fell apart in our absence."

He took her hand in his, and they walked back down the access road. "You seem to be a natural pilot," he said. "Adventurous, too."

She laughed. "For a librarian."

"I didn't say that."

"But you were thinking it."

He looked at her for a moment, enjoying her smile. "I was thinking how wonderful you looked at the controls, with the plane upside down and the whole world at your fingertips."

"Hmm," she said. "It's been a long time since I felt 'wonderful,' much less looked it."

"You still do," he said.

She didn't say anything to that. She might have

blushed a bit, or it might have been the deepening red glow of sunset.

They walked to the edge of town in silence, just enjoying each other's company, but as they passed the first houses, Lilian said, "So what's on your agenda for the rest of the evening, Captain?"

He looked up into the sky. "I suppose I should get back to the ship and make my report."

She laughed softly. "That's going to be a little hard to do for the next few hours, isn't it? Gamma Night won't be over until almost midnight."

Gamma Night. In the excitement, he'd completely forgotten. The *Enterprise* was on its own, and so was he. He'd made a few preliminary plans this morning, but he hadn't finalized any of them. "Maybe I can catch the Governor at home and talk with him about the rebuilding effort," he said.

"You could. Or you could catch the school administrator at home and talk with her about all the things you saw today. If you do, she might even ask you to stay for dinner."

"She might, might she?" Kirk squeezed her hand. "I bet she's a better cook than Pardonnet."

She shrugged. "I wouldn't know about that, but she hasn't poisoned anybody yet."

"Well then, I think I'd like that."

They walked on into town a few more blocks, then Lilian led the way down a side street full of single-story brick houses with stone walkways flanked by flowerbeds leading from the street to their front doors. A few had white picket fences, but most defined their boundaries with thick green hedges.

After all the devastation he had seen today, Kirk was glad for a little suburban tranquility. It felt good to see the colony as it was meant to be. The hedges and flower gardens were still young, and there wasn't a tree taller than himself, but the place looked like it had a future.

Lilian turned in at a house with bright yellow sunflowers in front of it. Kirk glimpsed a vegetable garden in back with corn growing taller than the trees next to it. Tomatoes and squash provided splashes of color. He knew the colonists grew most of their own food in just such plots, but it hadn't occurred to him that the gardens would be pretty as well as functional.

The inside of Lilian's house was a bit less tidy than the outside. Perhaps having a ten-year-old boy had something to do with that. Just inside the door there was a living room filled with books, artwork, and toys; to the left a hallway led toward the back of the house, and an archway in the back wall of the living room led to the kitchen. Reynold called out from the room at the end of the hallway as soon as he heard the door open. "Mom, can I go over to Nathan's house tonight? We've got to finish our science project."

"We have a dinner guest," she told him.

"Oh." He stuck his head around the door jamb. "Oh! Hello, Captain."

"Hello," Kirk said. "What kind of science project are you working on?"

"It's really bril," Reynold said, and Kirk made a mental note to ask Lilian later if "bril" meant what he thought it did. "We're putting a hologram projector and a force field generator side by side, and we're going to see if we can use the force field to make a holographic image feel like it's solid."

"That's . . . an ambitious project," Kirk told him. "What do you intend to do with it if you get it to work?"

"Make movies!" Reynold said. "Wouldn't it be just overly toom if you could actually walk around inside the scenes and feel what's going on?"

Kirk imagined it would be toom indeed, whatever "toom" was. In fact, the more he thought about it, the more staggering the implications became. If it actually worked, Starfleet could use something like that for hand-to-hand combat training, or simulated first contact situations, or even recreation on long voyages.

"That sounds interesting," he said. "Let me know how it goes."

"I will. Can I go, Mom? It's due tomorrow."

"Did you finish your—"

"Yes."

"All right, then. Be careful."

"We will." He disappeared into his room again, then reappeared with a box full of electronic parts. Kirk held the front door open, then closed it softly behind him.

"That really is an interesting idea," he told Lilian as he followed her into the kitchen.

She laughed. "Oh, he's never at a loss for those. Getting him to stick with anything for more than a day is the trick." She stepped into the kitchen. "Come on, let's see what we can find in the pantry."

Chapter Sixteen

SCOTTY SAT in the pilot's chair and turned the small ionic-exchange sensor over in his hands, examining the few parts of the component that could go wrong. It was a metal tube about two centimeters thick and ten long, and it operated the temperature circuit in the forward environmental controls. It was supposed to, at any rate, but for the last several hours the temperature had been rising, and nothing Scotty did had been able to stop it.

He checked the socket at the base of the sensor, tracing the data line from the connector through the port to the actual Maxwell exchange filter, but he wasn't finding the problem he expected. The housing looked sound, he didn't see any wear on the delicate connections, and the filtration sieve appeared to be rotating to specs. So why wasn't it working?

He set the sensor aside and stretched his arms high over his head, only to have them smack into the ceiling

129

panel. He'd forgotten he'd left it hanging open like that when he'd sat down, expecting a fast job tuning and re-installing the errant sensor. He would have whacked his head a good one if he'd stood up too quickly.

He checked the time and realized that he should have awakened Doctor McCoy half an hour ago. They were taking turns sleeping and minding the *Beater* while she limped her way toward BTS 453. They'd been moving by leaps and stalls for a little over a day, but right now the engines purred like their stowaway cat when he scratched her behind the ears, and he was pretty sure they would stay fixed for a time. Then he checked the ship's course and realized they didn't need to. They were nearly there.

He dropped them out of warp and did a sensor sweep for other ships. Nothing. They were still light-hours out from the planet, farther than Jupiter was from Earth. That was far enough away to avoid being spotted by any of the locals' defense sensors, and close enough to monitor their communications and get an idea of just how advanced their spacefaring abilities were. Plus they needed to learn where these folks stood in relation to either the Kauld or the Blood.

Scotty eased up out of the chair and swung the ceiling panel closed, then walked back to the dark crew quarters where he could hear snoring coming from McCoy's bed. They'd left the doors open in the living spaces of the little ship in hopes that the air would circulate and give them a more comfortable temperature throughout. "Doctor?" he said, giving the door jamb a rap.

McCoy jolted awake. "What is it? Someone hurt?"

"No. 'Tis time to get up. We've arrived at the planet."

"Oh. Right." McCoy yawned. "You wouldn't have managed to get the autogalley back on-line yet, by any chance? I could sure use a cup of coffee."

"No. Sorry. We still have plenty of rations, and I thought we might want to be able to work in the control cabin without having to strip down to our skivvies."

"Oh, so you got the temperature regulator fixed?"

"Doctor, could you just once ask me a question that I could answer positively?"

"Sorry." McCoy tossed back his blanket and sat up, then stopped, a puzzled look crossing his face. "Here's one. Do you know why I can't move my legs?"

"Aye, that I do. The cat is sleeping on them."

"She is?" McCoy pulled the blanket up again and there, stretched out across his legs, lay the gray-and-white cat. She yowled at McCoy, clearly cussing him out for awakening her so rudely; then she stood up and stretched so hard her whole body shook, jumped down from the bed, and stomped away in a huff.

"How can a three-kilogram cat be such an immovable object?" McCoy asked. He swung his feet to the floor and rubbed his eyes.

"Dinna you know? Cats generate their own gravity fields. That's how we learned to make such fool-proof gravity generators on our starships—by studying cats."

McCoy gave him a peeved look. "Don't blow smoke at me this early in the morning."

"Aye, Doctor." Scotty left to let him dress with some privacy.

They were still calling their stowaway "Kitty," but after observing her for a day or so they were getting closer to a name. They had both noticed a pattern to her behavior, at least. She'd be curled up on one of the bunks in the crew quarters taking a tongue-bath, or even sleeping peacefully in a quiet corner, then she'd suddenly burst into action and run full tilt through the galley into the control room. She'd be moving so fast that when she came to the backs of the pilot's and copilot's chairs she'd jump from the floor and hit a chair back with all four feet, twist in mid-rebound, and land with her feet already scrabbling for purchase to send her back the way she came. If she approached either man while in one of these high-energy states, she'd skid so that she stood sideways to him, back arched, ears back and tail twitching. The little toe dance she did would probably scare a mouse senseless, and Scotty discovered that she would stand her ground even if he mimicked her sideways attack and advanced upon her.

Then just as quickly as it started, her energy level would drop back to normal and she'd resume her nap like nothing had ever happened. Scotty had suggested they call her Electron, because of her ability to jump to a higher energy state, but McCoy had said it would be damned silly going around calling, "Here Electron, Electron, Electron."

As the Doctor emerged from the bunkroom, Scotty resumed the argument. "We could call her Ellie for short."

McCoy staggered toward the autogalley, fumbling for his precious morning coffee. "We could call her The Queen of England and it probably wouldn't matter to *her*." He stared at the inert galley for a moment, then took his dirty mug from the countertop, filled it with fresh water from the tap, and stuck it into the molecular heating field. "Cats have an innate ability to ignore anything that doesn't suit them," he said while he waited for his water to heat.

"Aye," Scotty said, " 'tis true enough. But we canna go around just calling her 'Kitty' all the time. Where's the imagination in that?"

McCoy pulled his mug out of the heat field, poured instant coffee powder into it straight from the ration pack, and stirred it with the same spoon he had used yesterday. "Weellll, I do like the idea of changing energy states."

"So it would seem."

The doctor slurped at his coffee. A little shudder went through him, then he sucked in a deep breath and continued as if nothing had happened. "So we're there, eh? What do you know so far?"

"Nothing. We just arrived."

McCoy stepped past him into the control cabin, his mug in his hand. He looked out the viewscreen at the small green-and-white marble ahead of them, then sat down in the copilot's chair. "Woo-ee, it's like a Georgia summer in here, isn't it?" He tugged at his shirt collar, then took another sip of hot coffee. "Feels like home. What do we do first?"

Scotty looked at him in wonder for a moment before sitting down himself. Zero to warp ten in thirty seconds. Was that a doctor trick, or was it just McCoy?

"Let's check for energy usage and communications," Scotty said, setting to work at the sensors.

"Right. I'll take communications." McCoy put the universal translator's earpiece in his left ear and bent over his console, slowly tuning through the electromagnetic spectrum. Scotty brought the long-range scanners on line and began sifting for power sources. There were thousands of them on the ground, and quite a few in orbit as well. It looked like the locals were technologically advanced enough to have a network of communication satellites. A quick survey of the companion moons showed outposts there as well, so they were also advanced enough to have gained at least some space travel capabilities.

"So what else does that quantum shift thing?" McCoy asked.

Scotty looked up. "What?"

"Electrons. Cats. What else changes energy states like that?"

Doctors, Scotty thought, but he held his tongue. A bead of sweat rolled down his forehead, reminding him of the stubborn Maxwell filter, so he said, "Ions." The heat sent his thoughts back to the Brandons' heirloom toaster. He winced, remembering that it still sat unusable in a cabinet back on the *Enterprise.* At least it wasn't in the blacksmith shop with old Thorpe tempted to try his hand at fixing it.

He turned back to his scanners, but he kept thinking about McCoy's question. What other name would capture the spirit of their little stowaway? Heating element? And the doctor'd thought Electron was a mouthful! Toaster? Not bloody likely. . . .

"It'd be nice if we could find something . . . celestial," McCoy said. "You know, since we found her while we were in space."

"We could call her 'Quasar.' "

"Nope."

"Wormhole."

"No!"

"Pulsar."

"Uh-uh. How about 'Supernova'? No, wait, just 'Nova.' "

Anything if it lets us get back to work, Scotty thought, but he had to admit that "Nova" was better than anything they'd come up with so far. And by the twinkle in McCoy's eye, Scotty knew that the doctor was pretty pleased with the name, and with himself for thinking of it.

"Nova," he said. "Hmmm. Well it surely passes the 'here Nova, Nova, Nova' test." The more Scotty rolled the name off his tongue, the better he liked it. And naming her after a flaring star worked, too. "Sure. Nova it is."

He looked back into the crew quarters, but she was nowhere in sight.

They set back to work at the sensors, and a few minutes later Scotty had at least an idea of what kind of place they had found. BTS 453 was approximately half land, half water, with roughly two-thirds of the land mass occupying the southern hemisphere. There were rudimentary ice caps at the poles, and the atmosphere's content was similar to Earth's. Weatherwise it was also similar to Earth, with cyclonic disturbances and evidence of jetstreams and areas of high and low air pressure. There was also a bit of an industrial pollution problem, from the looks of things.

The heaviest population densities appeared to be located not along the coasts, as it was on most inhabited planets, but near the center of each continent. Upon closer inspection, he found why that was. Most of the continents had a central network of large lakes connected by rivers.

He detected a lot of life in the oceans as well, but not of the type he found in the obviously urban areas of the planet. The oceanic life-forms were either much larger or much smaller than those he suspected were the technologically adept life-forms on the ground.

Scotty then turned his attention to the three moons. The closest was small, about three hundred kilometers in diameter. His sensors picked up two manned stations, one in either hemisphere. The second moon sat farther out and had one manned outpost. The distance to the third and largest moon was an order of magnitude farther than that of the inner ones, and he didn't detect any signs of life there at all.

He set the sensors for a subspace scan, already knowing he would find nothing there, and leaned back in his chair.

"Any luck, Doctor?"

"Terrific, if you call cataloging 417 channels of apparent entertainment and 123 supposed news broadcasts lucky. The lower end of the spectrum seems to be reserved for transportation comms. Airplane controls and taxi service and the like." McCoy took the translator earpiece out and gave his ear a good rubbing, then took a drink from his mug, draining it. "The highlights I garnered from the news centered mostly around land boundary conflicts, ecological disasters, and political elections. Not a word about Kauld or Blood or olivium."

"Anything about interplanetary relations?"

"Only that one of the stations on the closest moon, the one they call 'Ulu,' is due for a change of personnel. Apparently it's a science station and there are no permanent residents, no one's trying to colonize it. Oh, and by the way, the natives call their planet 'Casail.' Let's be sure to tell Spock."

Scotty sighed. "It sounds like we've found a prewarp society here."

"I'd agree to that. What did you discover?"

Scotty related the information he had gathered, then when he saw McCoy's glazed expression he said, "My God, man. That sounded just like an encyclopedia entry, didn't it?"

McCoy laughed. "Yes, but you left out the gross national product."

"No, no. I have that, too. Just didn't think ye'd be interested."

"Well, if it'll make you feel any better, I'm sure this information probably *will* be included in the next encyclopedia."

Scotty shook his head. "I'm so glad I've been assigned to an exploration ship rather than to a survey team." He got up and stretched his legs. "I mean, reading sensors all the time, just cataloging data, not getting to really *see* what you've found. That's not the life for me."

McCoy chuckled. "I think I know what you're saying. But there is a certain appeal to the other side of exploration. It'd give a man a chance to think, to ponder his place in the universe. To reflect on his own choices in life."

"My, aren't we getting a wee bit philosophical so early in the morning?"

"It's hardly morning any more. It's time for some lunch." McCoy got up and squeezed past Scotty to the store of rations. Over his shoulder he said, "I think it's obvious that we're not going to find help or allies here."

Scotty joined him, both men sorting through the stack of rectangular self-heating food containers, looking at the labels.

"Interesting that they've escaped notice by the Kauld," McCoy said. "Chicken à la king. That'll do."

"This place isn't exactly on the way to anywhere," Scotty reminded him, "and they're technologically far enough behind the Kauld or even the Blood that neither o' them scoundrels would bother with them. Yet."

"You're not going to eat another packet of *that* stuff, are you?" McCoy asked.

"What's wrong with Vulcan latica? It reminds me of haggis."

"I rest my case."

"Ha. Well then, it just means more for me."

Within seconds of opening the containers, the cat appeared, sniffing the air, leaning on their legs and reaching high with her front paws.

"Not if *she* has anything to do with it," McCoy laughed. He was already fishing out bits of chicken from his meal and putting them on a small access panel that they used for feeding her.

"Dinna ye mother teach ye better than to beg?" Scotty asked the cat as he held a chunk of latica out for her. "By the way, we've named you 'Nova.' "

If the cat cared, she didn't show it.

"I'm assuming our job here is done," McCoy said. "Where do we go next?"

Scotty wiped the corner of his mouth and said, "The next likely planet is two light-years away, according to the data that Mr. Spock supplied us with."

"How many more 'likely planets' does he have listed?"

"Let me check." Scotty moved back to the control panel. "He gave us thirty-seven."

"Thirty-seven! By the time we get through all those, Belle Terre will be a thriving crossroads. There's got to be a better way to get the information we need."

Scotty agreed. He pulled up more of the data that Spock had supplied them with and studied the maps. There were several isolated places listed, but he figured that the isolation would increase the chances of those worlds being like Casail: populated with people just taking their first few steps out of the cradle. McCoy came up behind him and looked over the information, too.

Scotty said, "I think we'll have better luck if we keep to these areas here. In fact," he said, pausing to take a closer look at a section where a lot of space travel was likely, "I think we should set our heading for right here." He pointed out the coordinates to McCoy.

"Why?" McCoy asked, one eyebrow rising to punctuate the question.

"To an old space-dog like me, Doctor, that looks like an oasis. It's central to several active planets, but it isn't a planet itself. I'll bet it's some sort of outpost. That's where we'll find what we need. We can sit tight and let the warp-capable civilizations come to us."

"Sounds fine by me."

Scotty programmed the coordinates into the ship's navigational computer and set it on a fast pace toward their next destination. "Now, if you'll excuse me," he said after the warp field had settled down and subspace was streaking past outside, "I'm going to take myself a wee bit of a nap."

"Hey!" McCoy said. "What about the heat in here? It's stifling."

"Aye, you're right." Scotty picked up the Maxwell exchange filter and handed it to McCoy. "All ye need to do is find out why this isn't working, then just plug it in." He pointed to the ceiling panel above the pilot's chair, then turned away toward the crew quarters.

Chapter Seventeen

THE SHUTTLE had been badly damaged. Deloric and Terwolan floated in their spacesuits beside it, making a visual inspection to see just how bad it was. All around them the stars were tiny points of silvery light, but in their soft glow the shuttle showed what too much light could do. Every surface that had been exposed to the laser's fury had either melted or charred. Access hatches had welded themselves to the hull; thruster ports were clogged, and most of the sensors were unrecognizable lumps.

Deloric and Terwolan weren't in much better shape themselves. They had both been burned on their faces and arms so badly that the skin was blistering. Their hair was coming off in crisp chunks. They could see again, but every time he blinked, Deloric could still see the laser beam slicing across his field of vision. It had been torture putting on his spacesuit, but they needed to know how badly the shuttle had been damaged.

Their blind jump had taken them a few light-hours away. They were still on the edge of the same star system they had been in, but they had gone far enough to be outside the Blind. Deloric was glad of that. The Blind was theoretically not dangerous to a properly protected person, but he had taken about all the radiation damage he was willing to endure for a while.

"You know anything about warp engines?" Terwolan asked him, pointing at the partially melted bulge on the shuttle's underside.

"No," he said, "but I know it's working or we wouldn't be here."

"The control panel doesn't even acknowledge its existence," she pointed out.

"It's got to be just a sensor glitch. We know it's getting commands."

"It's going to be mighty hard piloting this thing without feedback."

"Yeah." He looked at the reaction engines at the back. The bell-shaped nozzles were okay—after all, they were designed to withstand far more heat than they had received today—but the fuel lines leading to them were partially melted. "It's going to be hard doing it without normal-space engines, too, but I think we'd better try. If those fuel lines rupture, we're dead."

Terwolan pulled herself around back for a closer look. "It's just the left engine. The right side is okay."

"So we can go in spirals. That's good news."

"We can shift the center of gravity to the right as much as possible by moving things around inside. And the forward steering jets are still good, so I can compensate with those, too. It'll be enough to get us into port somewhere."

So long as they didn't try to land on a planet, but that went without saying.

"We're not going to get much in trade for it when we get wherever we're going," he said.

"Trade?" She looked over at him, her head tilted to the side inside her helmet.

"I don't know about you, but I'm not exactly rich at the moment, and we're not going to be able to access our payroll unless we want to trip every security alert in the sector. We'll have to sell the shuttle for room and board until we can find work and set up new lives. And anyone we could sell it to will know it's stolen, so they won't be generous."

She was silent for a moment, then she let out a long sigh. "I hadn't thought that far ahead, but you're right. We're criminals now. We'll have to start over from the beginning with new identities, new friends, the whole works. I won't be able to see my family again."

"It may not be that bad," he said, trying to reassure her, "but we do have to be careful."

They moved forward again, pulling themselves along using the partially melted handholds set in the hull. Deloric inspected the frames around the front windows and decided they would probably hold against air pressure from inside for as long as they needed to, and Terwolan checked the landing skids to make sure they wouldn't buckle under the shuttle's weight in a gravity field.

After they had seen all they needed to, they went back inside. The airlock door lurched closed behind them, sticking twice before sealing tight enough to allow the lock to be pressurized. When they stepped through into the shuttle, Deloric closed the inner door behind them as well, just as a safety precaution.

Removing their suits was agonizing. When Deloric

bumped his burned nose on his helmet's neck ring, he thought he would pass out from the pain. He gritted his teeth and peeled off the rest of his suit, then went to the medical locker and found a burn ointment with a topical anesthetic in it. He and Terwolan slathered it over their hands, forearms, and faces, then sat down at the control panel and went over their options.

Deloric called up the list of preprogrammed destinations. Whether or not the autopilot could fly the ship without feedback from the engines was anybody's guess, but it would certainly help to know the course to follow even if the ship couldn't do it on its own. Most of the choices were military bases and supply depots, but there were a few neutral worlds and commercial ports of call. He looked for something nearby; nearby and busy. If they had to blend in with the crowd, it would help to have a crowd to blend in with.

Terwolan was looking over her shoulder. "How about Hingal IV?" she asked. "It's a major commercial center."

He had been there once, and still remembered the customs procedure. They had inventoried everything—including his teeth!—to make sure he wasn't trying to smuggle anything in or out. "Too much security," he said. "How about the Fenorik Ring? It's a moon-sized space station. People come and go there all the time."

"It's also the home base for the Arecta syndicate. I may be a criminal, but I don't want to deal with them."

"Good point." They scrolled on through the list. There were hundreds of possible worlds and space stations to choose from, but it was alarming how quickly most of them could be eliminated. The end of the list was scrolling onto the screen when he finally saw it.

"Naresidan Cluster," he said, just as Terwolan pointed at the same entry and said, "There!"

It was perfect. The original Naresidan was an old slowboat, a cylindrical canister a dozen *rho* across that had carried a thousand Naresi colonists across ten light-years of space over the course of generations. It was so primitive it actually rotated for gravity, but it was built to last, and it was so much a home to the colonists by the time they arrived at their prospective colony world that only thirty of them even attempted to live on the planet. The fifteen survivors returned to the ship within a year, and the Naresi had lived in orbit ever since. They added to their living space from time to time, at first mining the asteroids for more raw materials but later buying old cargo ships from neighboring star systems after they had been discovered by dynadrive-propelled travellers. The resulting conglomeration of habitat modules and ships looked more like an industrial accident than a space station, but it was a free port, and its owners accepted anybody who wanted to join them, no questions asked.

The shuttle wouldn't even *exist* a day after they got there. Anything salvageable would be sold to pay for their cubic, and the rest would be melted down and used to build more living space.

"Let's do it," Deloric said.

Terwolan reached for the controls.

Chapter Eighteen

WHAT THEY FOUND in the pantry turned into a gourmet meal, as far as Kirk was concerned. With a generous serving from her stash of semolina flour and a few eggs from the neighbor's hens, Lilian made fresh pasta, then sent Kirk out to the garden with a reed basket to collect whatever vegetables looked ready to pick. He found a double handful of cherry tomatoes, a green pepper, something akin to a head of broccoli, and some peas practically bursting from their pods.

Lilian joined him and began picking leaves of lettuce and endive. "It's odd," she said, pushing foliage aside in search of a ripe salad tomato, "how the mineral content in soil will affect the way a vegetable will grow."

"How do you mean?" Kirk asked. He laid the greens on top of the other vegetables he'd put in the basket.

She plucked a good-size tomato from the vine and

handed it to him. It was smooth and solid in his hand. A strong, pungent smell wafted from the tomato's leaves.

"Take a look at the bottom," she said.

"Looks good to me."

"That's not an accident. The first tomatoes I grew here were all misshapen. The plants were spindly and the fruit would rot from the bottom up. When I talked to our botanist, she said the Burn left the soil too acidic. All the ash, I guess."

"What did you do?"

"When I planted these seedlings, I added some lime to the soil. The difference is like night and day." She stood and offered him her hand. He took it as he got up and followed her back into the kitchen, where he took the vegetables out of the basket and rinsed them in the sink.

"What is that wonderful smell?" he asked.

Lilian was at the stove, stirring a pale yellow sauce in a gleaming pot. "This?" she asked, taking the pot from the heat and holding it under his nose.

Light steam rose from the pot, and it brought with it a tangy aroma that made his mouth water. "Oh yes. That."

She smiled and resumed her stirring. "It's the lemon brundel sauce for the pasta primavera."

"Brundel?" he asked as he sliced tomatoes for their salad.

"It's an herb that tastes like lemon. It's easier to grow than lemons are, doesn't need the warm tropical climate real lemons do. Are you done shelling the peas?"

"Coming up."

The meal went together quickly, complete with crusty rolls and a dessert of rhubarb crunch. They sat across from each other at the dinner table.

"More pasta?" Lilian asked after they had slowed down a bit.

"Yes, please. This is delicious!"

"I didn't realize how hungry I was," she said. She loaded more onto his plate and took another scoop for herself.

"It takes a lot of energy to be a pilot," Kirk said. "Besides, it was a busy afternoon on the ground, too."

She nodded. "My heart goes out to those poor people. I think I'd be more useful to them if I went out and helped shovel muck than I am sitting here and ordering furniture for them."

"But they'll need that just as much," Kirk said.

They ate dessert as they watched the brilliant colors of the sunset through the window. As the room fell into twilight, Lilian lit two white candles and placed them on the table.

"Nice," Kirk said. He gazed at Lilian's delicate face in the soft glow of the candles. He liked the way the flickering flame made her eyes sparkle. "I haven't dined by candlelight in a long time."

"You haven't been on the surface much, then," she said with a laugh. "We decided to go with a central power supply instead of independent home units, thinking it'd be much more efficient, but now with all the wind and rain taking out our transmission lines, we're seeing the downside of the idea."

"There seems to be a downside to a lot of good ideas," Kirk said.

"Such as?"

He looked into the candle flame. "Well, the governor can find a whole host of good reasons to dismiss most of my suggestions."

Lilian chased the last of the crumbs from her dessert

across her plate with her fork. "And you can find equally good reasons to dismiss his plans too?" she asked, looking up from her plate.

"Touché. I'm afraid it's true. It sounds like what we envision for Belle Terre's future is mutually exclusive, but I can't believe it is." He folded his napkin and placed it beside his empty plate. "After all, we both want the colony to succeed."

"What sort of plans are you clashing over? Or is this a confidential subject?"

Kirk smiled. "Not all that confidential, really. What it all boils down to is that I think Belle Terre is still in danger from the Kauld. I don't want to scare you, but they want that olivium and I can't believe they've given up on it."

"But Pardonnet feels that the threat is over?"

"He feels that the Kauld are *my* problem. He has too many problems of his own. And he does. You saw what a disaster the Big Muddy area is. The cleanup job alone will take a huge effort, and the rebuilding will take even more. The problem is, we both need more manpower than we've got."

Kirk fell silent. He cursed himself for letting business interfere with what had started out as such a pleasant evening. Maybe it wasn't too late to steer the conversation away from the Kauld and Pardonnet. "I'm sorry. I don't need to bother you with these kinds of things."

"It's quite all right. I have my own issues with the governor and some of the decisions he's made in the past." She stood and gathered the dishes from the table. Kirk wondered if she had issues with some of his own decisions as well. He stood also and started to help, but she said, "I'll finish this. Why don't you have a seat in the living room, and I'll bring us a glass of wine."

"That sounds good."

The living room was lined with books. Kirk turned on the pole lamp closest to the shelves to see what kind of books a librarian chose to own, and the answer became quickly obvious. This one, anyway, read . . . everything. The top three shelves held fiction, from the Greek classics to Charles Dickens and Ernest Hemingway to the latest murder mysteries from Mars. The next shelf had histories of humans, Vulcans, and Romulans, and even a thin volume of Klingon history bound in what looked to be targhide. That must have been a hard book to come across.

The "how-to" books filled another three shelves, covering subjects like her beloved garden, bicycle repair, beer- and winemaking, and carpentry. She even had a copy of Jayne's Guide to Non-Federation Ships.

The bottom shelf of every bookcase was littered with children's books. Unlike the others, which showed careful handling and little if any wear, these books had been well loved. The covers were tattered and some of the spines were broken. He could see pages sticking out at odd angles, no longer bound with the rest. Some little boy had spent a lot of time with these colorful friends.

He was just thumbing out a crumbling copy of nursery rhymes when Lilian returned with two crystal glasses of dark red wine.

"You like books, too, don't you, Captain?" she said, as she handed him a glass.

"Please call me Jim. And yes, I do. I appreciate being able to use the colony library."

"I'm glad you do. If kids see someone like you coming to check out books, they'll be more likely to do the same."

"I didn't know I had that much influence."

"You do, and not just with the children." She turned on the lamp on the end table and set her wine glass down. She picked up a box of rocks and a jacket from the couch and sat down, patting the cushion beside her. "I had to fight for the cargo space to bring real books here, you know."

He took the hint and settled in next to her. "I didn't realize . . . is that one of the issues you have with the governor?"

"It was. Once word got around that he thought we should only bring duotronic memory modules, I started a campaign to convince him that was a bad idea. What if the electronic readers couldn't function properly out here? All that information would be useless, irretrievable." She took a sip of her wine.

He sat quietly for a moment, contemplating a world without any kind of written word. The *Enterprise* didn't have the room to hold a paper communal library, but the computer stored millions of works electronically. If the computer malfunctioned, the loss of literature would be the least of their worries. Still, Kirk kept a few "real" books, as he thought of them, in his quarters.

"As long as we're stationed here, I'll be happy to set an example for the locals." He smiled and reached for his wine.

The lights suddenly winked out. Kirk instantly snatched his communicator from his belt, then he realized it was still Gamma Night and stuck it back in place.

He started to stand up, but Lilian reached out and found his arm in the dark. "It's all right," she said. "This happens a lot during Gamma Night. We're not under attack."

"It's certainly . . . startling," he said, sitting back down.

"You get used to it."

The only light was from the candles in the dining room, and what little starlight filtered in through the windows. Lilian still held onto his arm. After a moment she said, "I should bring the candles in here."

Kirk's eyes were already adapting to the darkness. He turned toward her and saw the faint halo around the edge of her hair and the twin sparkles of her eyes. "I have a better idea," he said, leaning forward to kiss her.

There was an awkward moment when he thought he had misread her, but then her lips met his and her hand slid up his arm to cradle the back of his neck. "I do like your ideas," she murmured. "Got any others?"

Chapter Nineteen

THEY WERE almost two-thirds of the way to the outpost when the alarm sounded. McCoy jumped up from his seat in the galley, scattering Nova off his lap, and rushed for the control cabin. The status monitor in the middle of the console blinked a warning: *subspace activity detected.*

"Well I'll be damned," he muttered. Nothing like tripping over what you were looking for on the way to the flashlight.

He checked the direction it was coming from. Not ahead of them. It was in a star system off to the side half a light-year and already receding. He slowed the *Beater*'s speed down to warp four and scanned for more information, smiling when he saw the number of warp signatures. Fifty-five ships! That had to be an entire civilization.

"A bird in hand is worth two in the bush," he said, turning the shuttle toward the source and running the

speed back to warp ten. He kept the scanners on maximum as he approached, looking to see where the ships
were travelling to and from, but the warp signatures
were all confined within a tiny area of space around
one of the outer planets. All fifty-five ships were making tiny jumps, warping in and out and looping around
one another like a hive full of angry bees.

"What the heck?" he muttered. He watched the solar
system draw closer on the navigation display, then
dropped out of warp while he was still a light-day out.

There was nothing visible in the optical; just a star
and its planets, with no evidence of activity around any
of them. Even at high magnification, there was nothing
to see. Whatever was going on in there had started less
than a day ago, and it had come from out-system.

The subspace sensors were full of activity. McCoy
worked with the controls, cursing his rusty skills with
this sort of thing. Where was Spock when you needed
him, anyway? Irritating as the Vulcan could be at times,
there was no denying his skill with a sensor sweep.
McCoy thought about waking Scotty, but he decided to
give it another few minutes before he did that. He at
least wanted to be able to say what he'd found.

The computer began piecing together an image as
more data came in. The individual ships were just
points of light milling around, but tiny barbs of energy
lanced back and forth between them, and every few
seconds a brilliant flare would burst out.

"Uh-oh," he whispered. He had seen this sort of thing
before. Many times before, both in simulation and in
real life. Somebody was fighting a major space battle.

He gauged the distance and decided to risk a closer
look. They were so intent on each other, he didn't think
they would see a momentary jump from his angle.

He took the shuttle into warp again, held it for five seconds, then dropped back into normal space. That still put him a few light-hours away, but the subspace signals were much stronger now. He could actually see the ships in the high-intensity scan. Sure enough, they were fighting, though nobody seemed to be doing much damage. There were a lot of direct hits, but nothing strong enough to penetrate shields. It looked like they were running battle drills.

He squinted, trying to see the ships' outlines in the false-color image. They looked familiar.

He broke into a sweat that had nothing to do with the malfunctioning environmental controls. Good God, those were Kauld warships.

"Scotty!" he yelled. He heard a scrabbling sound and turned around in his chair, but it was just the cat. Nova had been about to jump into his lap again, but she tore off into the darkened crew quarters, and a moment later Scotty yelled, "Hey! Ow!"

Nova came barreling back into the galley, the engineer right behind her.

"We've got trouble," McCoy said.

"Aye, I'll show you trouble," Scotty said, holding up his right hand, where a red streak across the knuckles dripped blood. "That little creature got me with her claws."

"The Kauld are going to get Belle Terre with more than that," McCoy said. "Have a look."

Scotty looked over his shoulder at the displays, then he sank slowly into the pilot's chair. "Have ye warned the *Enterprise* yet?"

"I just now discovered it."

Scotty tapped at the control board, dumping the video buffer into permanent storage. "Let's give it another few minutes, then back away to a safe distance and send this to 'em."

"Good idea."

They watched in silence as the mock battle progressed. Some of the ships were slow and boxy, obviously pressed into duty from civilian use, but well over half of them were the familiar Kauld warships. Three were brand new, and represented a complete departure from the others. They were fast, sleek, and deadly.

Scotty frowned as he watched them in action. He zoomed in as much as he could, tapping his fingers nervously on the control board as he collected the information, then finally he said, "Let's not press our luck. Time to warn the Captain." He swirled the shuttle around and engaged the warp engines, throwing them back into interstellar space.

While he piloted them away from the Kauld fleet, McCoy powered up the subspace communications equipment and adjusted it for a narrow-beam transmission, triply encoded, to the Belle Terre system. "McCoy to *Enterprise*," he said. "Come in *Enterprise*."

He waited for a response, but got nothing even after two more hails. Then he checked the time.

"Hell, it's the middle of Gamma Night back there."

"Oh," said Scotty. "Sure it is."

"Should we head back?"

Scotty rubbed his hand, scratching absently at the dried blood from Nova's claw marks. "No," he said finally. "Gamma night will be over before we could get there, so a subspace radio message would still beat us home. And we haven't learned much we didn't already know, really. The Captain already guessed the Kauld were building up another fleet. He's sure to order us on with our mission, if for no other reason than to see if we can find out whether that's all of them or if this is part of something even bigger."

"Do we still want to head for that outpost?"

"I think so." Scotty checked the navigation display. "It's less than two hours away at top speed. If we're quick about it, we can check it out and report what we find there, too, when Gamma Night's over."

McCoy stared at the blank viewscreen. Light-years away from home with bad news and no way to report it; he hadn't felt quite so isolated in years. Suddenly the trip had lost what little charm it had possessed.

He was still fretting when they arrived at the outpost. From communications traffic as they approached, they learned that it was called Naresidan. McCoy thought "Scrap Pile" would have been a more descriptive term, but maybe that's what "Naresidan" meant in the owners' native tongue. The place looked like an architect's nightmare. Starships of all sizes and styles were docked to booms sticking out haphazardly in all directions. Most of the ships were blocked from moving by the ones parked next to them, and it wasn't until he checked at high magnification that he realized that most of the blocked ones were welded in place. The inner ones were barely recognizable as spacecraft; they had been modified, added to, joined together, and in some cases split open like clam shells and welded to the outer surfaces of still larger ships.

At the center of it all, nearly obscured by the others, rested a cylindrical drum at least five miles across and twice as long. It rotated slowly, no doubt providing gravity on its inner surface by centrifugal force. It was a primitive trick, but it worked. And so did everything else in the outpost, it seemed. The place was a frenzy of activity, with ships coming and going almost continually. No two were alike, either.

"I guess we found what we were looking for," McCoy said softly.

"Aye, that we have," Scotty agreed. "Now if we can just figure where to park without becoming a permanent part o' all that."

McCoy got on the comm and requested permission to land, and the controller talked them into a berth inside one of the long spines. As they edged into a landing bay and nestled down between two bulky cargo freighters, McCoy muttered, "I feel like a bug crawling into the Statue of Liberty."

Scotty brought them in with hardly a bump. The external sensors registered atmosphere inside the bay. McCoy checked it for toxicity, but while there were plenty of organic compounds, it looked breathable enough.

"Well, let's go take the tour," he said, getting up and heading for the airlock.

He opened both doors at once, and was just stepping out when a gray streak darted between his legs and Nova bounded down the ramp.

"Hey, come back here!" he shouted, but the cat didn't even slow down.

"Nova!" He ran down the ramp after her, but that just urged her on. She ducked around one of the freighters and disappeared.

"Dammit!" he said. "Nova, come back here." He rounded the corner after her, but she was nowhere in sight. There was a crew busy unloading wooden crates from the back of one of the freighters. They were of three different species, all of them rippling with muscle. They looked at McCoy for a moment, then went back to work.

"Did you see which way she went?" he asked.

One of them, a fanged, blunt-nosed fruit bat sort of creature, said, "See which way who went?"

"My cat. Little furry thing, about this big." He held his arms out, hands apart. "She came right past here just a second ago."

The bat-creature wrinkled his nose. "I didn't see it. Sorry." The others didn't even stop working.

McCoy walked on past them, looking into nooks and crannies, but the landing bay was *all* nooks and crannies, and open doorways and corridors leading deeper into the station. Nova could be anywhere.

"Dammit," he muttered again, turning once around. A tricorder might find her, but he had left his in the shuttle, and by the time he got it and came back, she could be another hundred yards away.

Scotty came running up to him. "Did ye catch her?"

"No."

"Nova!" Scotty called.

They looked for a few minutes, but there was no sign of her. McCoy went back for his tricorder, but that didn't help. Finally he said, "She's gone. We'll just have to keep the door open and hope she comes back."

"What if somebody catches her?" Scotty said. "They might mistake her for vermin."

He had a point. McCoy thought about it for a moment, frowning. "Then we'll just have to put up posters."

He led the way back to the shuttle. It was the work of a moment to call up an image of a gray tabby cat from the data banks, but it took a bit longer for the computer to translate the message "Lost cat—please return to landing bay 7405, space 93" into the local trade language. The result looked like flyspecks and bird tracks around the photo, but the computer assured them it was the proper translation.

McCoy dithered a moment, then told it to add "reward offered" to the bottom. This was a trading station, after all. He couldn't expect anyone to do anything for free.

They printed out two dozen posters and stuck them all around the cargo bay and in the hallways, then went back to the shuttle and closed the doors until only a hand's width remained for Nova to slip through if she returned. Scotty pulled the power module from the door to make sure nobody could open it any farther, then he turned back toward the station side of the bay and said, "Now we'd best go find us a watering hole and listen for news."

McCoy liked the sound of that. If there was anything like a mint julep to be had around here, he could gladly spend some time sipping one and listening for information.

Chapter Twenty

"WHO EVER HEARD of a tavern that wouldn't serve a paying customer?" Deloric asked. He and Terwolan trudged down the long corridor toward the landing bay where their ship waited. Their footsteps echoed in the metal confines, but they had to compete for volume with the growling of their stomachs. The shuttle hadn't been stocked with food, and the only tavern they could find within walking distance didn't take Kauld military ration chits in trade.

"We'll find a currency exchange booth tomorrow," Terwolan said. "Or a pawnshop. There's plenty of mining equipment we can sell."

"Yes, but I'm hungry *now*," he reminded her.

"Me too, but we'll just have to tough it out. Nothing's open now."

"This is Naresidan! How can all the pawnshops be closed?"

160

She shrugged. "Maybe it's a religious holiday."

They emerged into the landing bay. Deloric shielded his eyes against the glare from the overhead lights until he spotted their shuttle, then led the way down the cargo-choked dock toward it. He considered trying to bum a ration pack from one of the dockhands unloading a ship a few berths down from theirs, and he was still working up his courage when he saw the creature sniffing around the partially melted forward landing leg of their shuttle.

"There!" he said, coming to a stop and holding out an arm to keep Terwolan from getting any closer and scaring it away.

"Where?" she asked. "What do you see?"

"Dinner," he whispered. He pointed toward the gray, furry thing. It looked a bit thin, and that tail would have practically no meat on it, but there had to be enough on its haunches to take the edge off until morning.

Terwolan snorted. "That? I may be hungry, but I'm not desperate. Besides, it looks faster and meaner than either of us. How would you catch it?"

The creature lifted its head and looked at them with wide green eyes, then it stood and rubbed up against the landing strut. It did look like it could move quickly if it had to.

"Maybe if I go around behind it, we could come at it from both sides."

Terwolan pointed at the countless bolt-holes among the unloaded cargo containers that the creature could run into. "We'd have to—hey, wait a minute." She walked over to the wall and pulled down a sheet of paper stuck there. "Look at this. It's somebody's pet."

Deloric looked at the photo. It certainly did look like the creature. Then he noticed the words at the bottom: "Reward offered."

"I wonder what it's worth?" he asked.

"A meal would be good enough for me."

"Me too." He walked slowly closer, then knelt down and held out his hand. "Here, little creature. Come here."

The thing took a step toward him and sniffed, then backed away.

"It can probably sense what you wanted to do to it," Terwolan said. "Let me try." She took a couple more steps toward it, then bent down and held out her hand and the creature trotted right up to her. She rubbed the fur on the back of its head, then stroked its sides. "It's soft," she said. "Let's see if it'll let me pick it up."

It did. Then it climbed up her arm and settled in across her shoulders, holding itself in place on her clothing with tiny hooked claws. "Uh . . . where did that poster say the owners' ship is parked?" she asked nervously.

"Space 93. Only five down from ours."

"Good. Let's go before it eats *me*." Terwolan stood up slowly and set off down the landing bay, walking carefully.

They found the ship easy enough—a modified freighter or tug of some sort that was all engines now— but there was no one home. Both airlock doors were ajar, obviously left that way so the creature could come and go, but nobody answered when Deloric yelled in through the opening.

"Now what?" he asked.

"It's squirming," Terwolan said. "It—ow!" The creature dropped off her shoulder and slipped inside the airlock.

"Oh, great. There goes our reward."

Terwolan looked at the airlock, then at the poster in

Deloric's hand. She tugged it out of his grip and sat down on the ramp with her foot covering the bottommost part of the opening. "Maybe not," she said.

"What do you mean?"

"I mean we brought their—" she looked at the poster again "—their *cat* home. We put it inside where it belongs. Now we're guarding the door."

Deloric looked around at the landing bay, empty except for the team unloading the one cargo ship. "It could be a long wait."

"We can either go back to our shuttle and listen to our stomachs growl, or do it here and hope for a meal. Which would you rather?"

"Well, when you put it like that. . . ." He sat down next to her and stuck his foot in the crack above hers. It felt awkward, and the creature could probably jump right over both of their feet if it wanted to, but they might be able to stop it if they were quick.

They didn't have to try. Only a few minutes after they sat down, they heard footsteps in the corridor and a voice saying, "Who ever heard of a tavern that wouldn't serve a paying customer?"

Two tall, pinkish bipeds entered the cargo bay and headed straight for Deloric and Terwolan. Both wore red leggings; one of them was also dressed in red from the waist up, the other in green.

"Hey now, what are you two doing there?" said the one in red.

Deloric felt the blood drain from his face. He had seen their kind before.

"You're human," he said.

"Aye, an' you're Kauld. What kind of mischief are ye up to with our ship?" The human held his hand near his weapon, but he hadn't drawn it yet.

163

Terwolan held up the poster, moving slowly to keep from startling him. "We found your pet. It ran inside when we set it down, and we were making sure it didn't get out again."

"Did ye, now?" The human didn't relax, but the one behind him unclipped a rectangular sensing device from his belt and held it out toward the ship. It whistled a warbling two-tone note for a few seconds, then the human holding it lowered the gadget and said to the other one, "She's inside the shuttle, all right. And you two," he said to Deloric and Terwolan, "have second- and third-degree radiation burns all over your faces and arms. What happened to you?"

Deloric looked over at Terwolan. Her smooth blue skin was now an angry violet, with blisters beginning to form on her forehead and cheeks. Her forearms were starting to peel. The human could see all that, but could it see the real injury? Deloric could. The haunted look in her eyes no doubt mirrored his own. They had thought they could run away from it, but it had followed them all the way to Naresidan.

His mouth grew dry. To speak would be treason! But to remain silent would be the death of his honor. He heard the rustle of paper as Terwolan crumpled the poster in her fist, and knew she was fighting the same battle.

"What happened?" the human asked again.

He could at least answer that. "We were hit with a laser."

"It sure looks like it. Haven't you done anything for it?"

Nothing can be done, he wanted to say. *It's already been fired.* But he held his tongue.

Terwolan said, "There was an ointment in our medical kit, but we used it up." She flattened the poster again and held it out to him. "You promise a reward. If you will pay us, we can seek medical help."

Deloric's stomach chose that moment to growl. "And food," he said.

The human stuck his sensor back on his belt. "Why don't we cut out the middleman? I'm a doctor, and if you don't mind ration packs, we've got food inside."

The other human said, "But these are Kauld!"

"And they brought our cat back."

"They did that before they knew we were human. We can't trust 'em on board our ship."

Choosing his words carefully, Deloric said, "Not all of us feel the same way about you. We—the two of us—have renounced the war."

The one in red didn't look mollified, but the one in green said, "According to my scan, they're not carrying any weapons. We can feed 'em and heal 'em and send 'em on their way."

"That's fraternizing with the enemy," the other protested.

"The Kauld declared war on us, not the other way around. It's my own choice how I act toward them, and these two are injured. I won't turn them away."

The tension between the humans was palpable. Deloric and Terwolan said nothing, waiting for them to make up their minds.

At last the one in red said, "All right. Be it on your head if there's trouble. If you two would move aside for a moment. . . ."

They stepped off the ramp. Keeping his eye on them, he plugged a power module into the door controls and opened the airlock, disappeared inside for a moment, then came out again, his hand still hovering near his weapon. "Come on in," he said, "but don't touch anything."

That was hard to do. The interior of the ship was cramped even for two. With four people on board it was like a locker room. It was hot enough to be a locker room, too. No wonder their pet had run away; it would be sweltering under all that fur. It was nowhere in evidence now, either, but Deloric assumed it was locked in one of the back rooms to keep it from running away again. All the doors were closed, hiding bunks and engine compartments and who knew what else.

The red-shirted human stood in front of the closed door to the control room. That must have been what he had done before letting Deloric and Terwolan in; sealed off everything but the tiny common area.

There was a tiny table with a padded bench on either side and a set of cabinets covered with food-preparation equipment. Deloric's mouth watered at the sight of it.

The doctor motioned them to sit at the table, then he went into one of the back rooms and returned with a metal case full of medical instruments, one of which he switched on and waved in front of Terwolan's face.

"This will help the burned tissue to heal instead of flake off," he said.

An expression of wonder spread across her face, almost as if the instrument were repainting her features. "It's stopped hurting!"

"Good." The doctor turned his attention to Deloric, and he could feel the effect immediately. The tension in his muscles released, and the constant fiery heat faded back to normal.

"Now your arms," said the doctor, and both Deloric and Terwolan laid their arms out so quickly that everyone—even the human in red—laughed.

The doctor switched to a smaller instrument and went over the same areas again. "This'll cut down on the chance for infection," he explained. He looked at Terwolan's eyes, then nodded, apparently satisfied with what he saw there. "What's your name?" he asked.

"Terwolan," she replied.

"Deloric," Deloric said before the doctor could ask.

"Mine's McCoy. That's Mr. Scott."

Deloric noted the honorific. Anyone holding him at gunpoint could be "Mister" as far as he was concerned.

"Now to take care of your other problem," McCoy said. He unclipped the rectangular scanner from his belt again and examined them both, then nodded. "Looks like anything but shellfish ought to be fine. You like emu?"

Deloric shrugged. "I . . ."

"That was a joke, son." McCoy opened one of the cabinets, selected two ration packs, and set them down in front of his guests. He peeled the top off of one and held it up for them to sniff as the self-heating contents began to steam. It was some kind of brown meat strips on a bed of white grain. Deloric's stomach rumbled again, and Terwolan had to swallow to keep from drooling.

"That will do fine," she said, taking the packet from the human's hands.

McCoy opened the other one and handed it to Deloric, then gave them each a curved, multipointed tool to eat it with.

"So, what brings you to Naresidan Station?" McCoy asked as they set to.

Deloric was swallowing as the human spoke, but the food suddenly stuck in his throat. He coughed, tried to swallow again, but couldn't manage it.

"Easy, man!" Mr. Scott said. "Take your time."

"Wa . . . water!" Deloric gasped as Terwolan pounded him on the back.

McCoy turned back to the galley, filled a mug that was sitting on the counter, and handed it to him. The water tasted of something burned, but he didn't care; he swallowed a big gulp, washing down the lump in his throat.

"You all right?" McCoy asked.

Deloric nodded. He looked at the human, standing there before him so friendly and solicitous, even though the Kauld had caused his people immeasurable harm. He looked over to Terwolan and saw her staring at her food, unable to take another bite either.

"We have to tell them," Deloric said.

She stiffened, but didn't look up.

"Tell us what?" Mr. Scott asked.

Deloric took a deep breath. This was treason. But he had already committed himself. He looked back at McCoy and said, "In four days, a laser beam the width of the planet will strike your colony world, Belle Terre, burning everything in its path down to bedrock."

The humans' expressions were unreadable. McCoy seemed to grow paler, but Mr. Scott merely snorted and said, "A beam the size of a planet? Who are you trying to fool? With that kind of spread, it'd be lucky to melt snow."

"It started out as wide as this station," Deloric told him. "It doesn't have to spread much to cover the planet by the time it gets there. And it'll have more than enough power. The energy source was an olivium chain reaction."

"Was?" Mr. Scott seemed paler now, too.

"Was. We were burned by the flash. The laser has already been fired."

Chapter Twenty-one

KIRK AWOKE to the insistent beeping of a communicator. It took him a moment to place where he was; the room was pitch dark, and it didn't have the familiar acoustics of his shipboard cabin.

Then he smelled the waxy candle smoke and the flowery, feminine aroma that could be found only in a woman's bedroom, and he remembered where he was. He slipped out of bed and felt for his clothing on the chair beneath the window, found the communicator, and stepped into the living room before flipping it open.

"Kirk here," he said softly.

"Captain," said Lieutenant Uhura. "I've got an incoming message from Dr. McCoy."

McCoy? What would Bones be calling him for at this hour? It was even later ship's time than here on the planet. "Put him through," he said, already dreading the news.

"Jim?" came the doctor's voice.

"What is it, Bones?"

"Well, I wish I could tell you I've got good news and bad news, but the fact is, I've got bad news and bad news. Which do you want first?"

Kirk moved deeper into the living room. "I'm not in the mood for jokes," he said.

"Well, that's good, 'cause that's the only humor you're likely to hear for a while. We found that Kauld fleet you were so sure was out here."

Kirk felt the hair at the back of his neck start to stand out. "You did? Are you all right?"

"They didn't spot us. They were doing war games, breaking in three new ships that look like they can beat the pants off the *Enterprise*. But that's not going to be our first problem. According to somebody we met out here, the Kauld built a great big laser about five light-days out from Belle Terre. Olivium-powered, and big enough to fry the whole damn planet when the beam hits."

He felt like he'd been hit already, sucker-punched in the gut. Five light-days out. That was the edge of interstellar space. Nobody had thought to look for problems out there, because nobody *went* there except to pass through under warp power on the way to somewhere else. If the builders were careful with their energy leakage they wouldn't even need Gamma Night to hide their activity until they fired it. That would make a subspace ripple big enough to trigger alarms, but of course if they timed it right, every subspace sensor in the Belle Terre system would be blanked out at the time.

The *Enterprise* had to find it before they fired it, but a spherical shell five light-days out was a big volume to search. "Do you know what direction it's in?"

"I got 'em to draw us a star map of what they could

see from their point of view while they were working on it, so that ought to narrow it down, but it won't do you any good to find it."

"Why not?"

"Because if we can believe the two Kauld soldiers that told us about it, they've already fired it. The beam is on its way."

Kirk looked out the window at the starlight painting the front yard in delicate shades of silver. Some of that light had been millennia in transit from the stars that emitted it. Space was full of crisscrossing light rays sliding along at Einstein's speed limit—and now it apparently contained one enormous laser beam as well.

"How long ago did they fire it?" he asked.

"About a day. Maybe less."

So they still had time. Four days to . . . to what? How could they stop something like that?

"Where are you now?" he asked.

"On our way back," McCoy answered. "Scotty's got us up to warp 12, so we should be there in just a few hours, if we don't blow ourselves up first."

"Good." Kirk had no idea what, if anything, they could do, but he would be glad to have his chief engineer and medical officer back on board when things got ugly. And they would get ugly; he had no doubt of that. At the moment he could think of no way of saving the colonists except evacuation, and he knew what that would be like. Trying to stuff sixty thousand colonists back into the ships that had brought them here would be about as easy as putting a mushroom cloud back into the bomb casing.

"Anything else I should know before you get here?" he asked.

"I think that about covers it," McCoy said.

"I certainly hope so. All right, then, I'll see you when you get back. Kirk out."

He closed the communicator and stood quietly for a moment, still looking out at the starlit yard. Why did peace and beauty always have to be so fragile?

He heard a rustle of motion behind him. When he turned he saw Lilian standing in the bedroom doorway, looking ghostly in a white robe against the darkness behind her. "I heard," she said.

"We'll think of something," he said. "Big mirrors to bounce it right back at them, or . . . I don't know, but we'll think of something."

"And the fleet behind that?"

"We'll take care of them, too."

She shivered. "I don't doubt your ability, but I wonder if it's worth it. Belle Terre, deep-space colonization, quantum olivium—is any of it worth turning this whole sector into a battleground?"

"I don't know," Kirk admitted. "Sometimes I think it's not. Other times I think places like this are the future of the entire Federation. If you're not going forward, you're going backward."

She dabbed at an eye with her sleeve, the motion barely visible in the darkness. "My father told me 'You can tell the pioneers by the arrows in their backs.' Tom and I laughed. We all thought it was funny. Now here we are, and here comes the—what, the third? fourth? fifth arrow? And this one's on fire." She sniffed.

Kirk stepped closer and gathered her into his arms. "It's all right," he said. "We'll find a shield. Then we'll go hunting archers."

He could feel her shivering as she held him. "I have a son," she whispered. "My little boy is one of the targets."

Kirk said, "I will protect his life with my own."

"That's . . . that's what I'm afraid of."

He held her a minute longer, his bare skin cooling in the night air, then he gently let her go and stepped past her into the bedroom. "I have to get back to the ship."

She dabbed her eyes again. "Yes, I know. You've got to save the world."

He didn't know if she meant that to be sarcastic or if she was just stating the obvious. As he began pulling on his clothing he said, "I'm certainly going to try. But just in case I don't manage it, I'm going to need you to help organize the evacuation. If it's done carefully, we can get everyone to safety before the wave front gets here, but if people start to panic we could kill more than the laser will."

"No pressure," she said.

"I've seen you in action. You keep your head during the excitement. You'll do fine."

"I guess I'll have to, won't I?"

"Pardonnet will help, once he realizes the severity of the danger." He pulled on his boots, then went back to the foot of the bed to give her one last squeeze and a long, lingering kiss. "We'll get through this," he said, then he flipped open his communicator and took a couple of steps back. "Kirk to *Enterprise*. One to beam up."

He saw the shimmering colors of the transporter illuminate her for just an instant as the confinement beam locked onto him, then he was squinting in the bright lights of the transporter room. He stepped down from the stage and rushed for the turbolift, nodding to Ensign Vagle at the controls as he swept past.

"Uh . . . sir?" Vagle said.

He stopped himself with one hand on the door frame. "Yes?"

"Your . . . uh . . . jacket?"

He looked down and saw that he had it on inside-out. "Thank you, Ensign."

"Any time, sir."

Another day, Kirk would have told him to wipe that silly grin off his face, but he had no time. He pulled off the jacket as he ran for the lift, ordered the car to the bridge, and donned it correctly on the way.

The bridge was a hive of activity. Uhura was busy coordinating reports from ships spread throughout the system, by the sound of it. Sulu and Thomsen were running deep-space scans of the volume of space five light-days out, no doubt trying to find any energy signatures that would indicate the position of the laser or the beam it had fired. Other officers filled the engineering, weapons, environmental, and security stations, all lending their expertise to the problem. Only Spock, seated at his science station and staring silently into a data screen, seemed immune to the sudden frenetic pace.

"Report," Kirk said as he dropped into his command chair.

Despite his relative calm, Spock was the first to speak. "We are attempting to corroborate Doctor McCoy's story through subspace scans, energy flux readings, gravitational anomalies, and direct optical observation. So far none of our methods have been successful. Lieutenant Uhura is attempting to ascertain if anyone was outside the influence of Gamma Night when the laser was fired. If so, their sensor logs may contain evidence of the energy discharge. Ship's status is operational, all systems on-line and operating at nominal capacity."

"Ready for action, and no idea where to go," Kirk said. "What about that starmap McCoy said he got? Doesn't that help any?"

"Yes, Captain. It narrows the search to a cone only 30 degrees wide. At five light-days' distance, and not knowing the length of the light column, that computes to a target area approximately 1.29×10^{11} kilometers in diameter and 2.6×10^{10} kilometers deep."

"I get the picture," Kirk said. They were looking for a needle in a haystack, but this particular needle couldn't even be seen. Laser beams were practically impossible to detect from the side even in an atmosphere; in space they were invisible unless they hit something and some of their light was scattered toward an observer. Plus this one was coming straight at them, and since everything in normal space traveled at the speed of light, that meant none of that scattered evidence would reach them any sooner than the beam itself. They would have to use warp drive to post observers all through the space where it might be travelling, and hope it hit something natural before it hit an observer.

Or something unmanned.

"How about remote probes?" he asked.

"We are preparing them," Spock said, "but even they will only improve our odds a hundredfold."

"*Only* a hundredfold?" Kirk asked. "That sounds pretty good to me."

"Not when they start out at thirty-seven million to one against us."

"Oh." Kirk leaned back in his chair and rubbed his chin. It was rough; he hadn't shaved since yesterday morning and it was well into the next day now. He ignored it and tried to think of other contingencies. Could they trust this information that McCoy and Scotty had gotten? Or was it a lie designed to send the *Enterprise* off on a wild-goose chase while the Kauld fleet swept in and took Belle Terre right out from under them?

"Keep doing long-range scans for incoming warships, too," he said. "I don't want to get caught with our pants down."

"Indeed," Spock said, his tone of voice absolutely flat. If it had been anyone else but him, Kirk would have sworn that he was being ribbed, but the Vulcan couldn't possibly be kidding. McCoy, yes, but not Spock.

But everyone on the bridge could probably guess where he had been, and his disheveled appearance only lent credence to their speculation. Not that it mattered, but it wouldn't hurt to clean up a bit, he thought. It had been a long day, and who knew when he would next have the chance for a shower. "Let me know the moment you have something," he said, standing up again and heading for the turbolift. "I'll be in my quarters."

Chapter Twenty-two

THE *ENTERPRISE* had never looked so good to Scotty as she did when he pulled the *Beater* up alongside her and prepared to transfer across. The last six hours had been a harrowing roller-coaster ride halfway across the sector, punctuated by two moments of relative calm when the warp coils had fallen out of tune and he'd had to drop back into normal space to readjust them. The heat in the tiny control cabin had been stifling by then. And the shaking. Good God, the shaking! His teeth still ached from it all. At warp 12 even the best gravity generators could barely keep up with the fluctuations as the ship skipped through gravity waves from stellar collisions and supernovas a hundred thousand light-years away.

McCoy had cursed the whole way. So had the cat, when she wasn't hiding under one of the beds. Scotty didn't blame them, but he wasn't about to slow down.

Not after what he had learned from Deloric and Terwolan.

He had wanted to bring them along, but they would have none of that. They had bolted for the door at the first mention of it, and only when he'd promised to let them stay at the outpost had they come back to finish their tale. They really didn't know that much more, anyway. They described how they'd mined the comet and had created the light-minutes-long stream of carbon dioxide, and how the silvered face of the comet and the olivium light source had turned it into a planet-burning laser. It had all seemed incredibly far-fetched to Scotty, but he had to admit it was possible. Practically anything would lase if you hit it with enough light. Carbon dioxide didn't even need that much provocation. It was one of the best light-collimating materials known.

Deloric and Terwolan had given the best description they could of which stars were directly overhead while they worked on the comet, and they had described the firing in hair-raising detail. They had even described the Kauld warship that had supervised the firing. There was nothing left to glean from them that couldn't be discovered on-site.

But now, as he stood in the galley beside Dr. McCoy and waited for the transporter beam, he wondered if he'd made a mistake. Space was vast, even the little bit of it around a solar system. There were millions of comets out there, any one of which could be the source of the death ray. Even if everything the Kauld soldiers said was true—and accurate—it would be nearly impossible to find the one that had been used. If there was anything more that he could have gotten from them, any detail he had misheard or misunderstood, he couldn't go back and ask them now.

McCoy held the cat, who seemed no more eager to face the transporter than he did. Nova squirmed in his grip, meowing pitifully and trying to claw her way up to his shoulders, but he held her close to his chest and gripped her paws so she couldn't scratch him.

At last the *Beater* faded from sight, replaced by the *Enterprise*'s familiar transporter room. McCoy immediately strode across the hall into sickbay, while Scotty headed straight for the turbolift and engineering.

He found it fully staffed, even though it was the middle of ship's night. Technicians were going over every system, running diagnostics and making sure everything was ready for battle. He noted with satisfaction that they were paying special attention to the shields. If the ship found itself in the path of that laser beam, they would need all the shield efficiency they could get.

He had left Lieutenant Hanson, one of his most competent engineers, in charge while he was gone, but now he found her running field tests of the deflector array. By the rumpled look of her uniform and the wild disarray of her short brown hair, it looked like she'd been at it awhile.

"What're you wasting your time here for?" he asked. "You canna stop a laser beam with a deflector."

"Good to see you again, too, sir," Hanson said. "I don't expect to stop laser beams with it, but it would be nice to be able to shove comets out of the way if we have to. We're going to be running back and forth through some pretty dirty space." She pointed to the diagnostic readings, which were way out of spec. "Mr. Spock has been fooling with the system again, trying to boost its gain with olivium-powered sensors. Every time he does that, it knocks the whole works out of whack."

"Out o' whack, eh?" Scotty said. "I suppose that's a technical term."

Hanson reddened. "Yes, sir. With olivium in the circuit, that's about as accurate a description as you can get. Its quantum instability causes some pretty strange macroscopic effects."

"Like what?"

"Like neutrino bursts, for one. Spock blew up his detector the first time he tried it, and he still can't figure out where the neutrinos are coming from."

Scotty looked at the diagnostic readout again. "Neutrinos? They've got to be coming from the olivium itself, don't they?"

"That's what you'd think, but we can get a directional fix on them, and they're definitely not originating on board. Get this: they come from wherever we happen to be pointing the deflector at the time."

"What? That's impossible. It takes a nuclear reaction to produce neutrinos, and they're almost impossible to deflect. They can pass through a dozen light-years of lead without bouncing off a single nucleus. Nothing we can do would just attract a swarm of neutrinos. They'd have to have been on their way toward us long before we pointed our detector at them, and the odds against that happening even once are astronomical."

"That's right." She grinned wickedly. "Now you can start pulling your hair out, too."

He grinned right back at her. "Fortunately, I don't have time for that at the moment. Our first priority is to find that laser beam and figure out how to stop it. And you can bet your life we'll be the ones expected to come up with a miracle when the time comes, so keep your mind on the business at hand."

"Yes, sir."

Satisfied that his department was in good shape, he left Hanson at her job and headed for the bridge, which he found just as busy as engineering, but in a different way. Everyone here was getting ready to take the ship out of orbit and go hunting for photons. Everyone but Spock, at least; the Vulcan was not at his science station. Was he still fooling with the deflector array? Scotty had assumed Lieutenant Hanson was patching things up after the last test, but now he realized she was trying to keep up with Spock in real time. No wonder her hair was frazzled.

Captain Kirk greeted Scotty the moment he stepped out of the lift with, "Good, you're here. Mr. Sulu, set course for the middle of our target area, warp factor three. Thomsen, get ready to release the probes."

Warp three seemed ridiculously slow to someone who had just bored a warp-12 hole across half a sector, but Scotty knew it was plenty fast to get around inside a solar system. Fifteen minutes of flight time would take them anywhere they wanted to go. But where were they going first? Four light-days out to look for the flash of the laser being fired? Four-and-a-half to look for scintillation from the beam hitting dust grains on its way in-system? Five to look for the comet it had come from?

"What's our plan?" he asked the captain.

Kirk said, "From the star map you sent us we know what quadrant the beam is in. We're going to spread a couple of hundred optical sensors through that volume and hope they pick up a reflection. Then we're going to head farther out-system and look for anomalous energy readings. The workers who built the laser had to have left equipment behind. If there's a functioning power source anywhere out there, we should be able to spot it fairly quickly."

"Ah," Scotty said. The sensors were a good idea, but

looking for power sources could be a total waste of time. After the flash that Deloric and Terwolan had described, there might not be anything left but debris. "That's a mighty big 'if,' " he said.

"I'm aware of that, Scotty," Kirk said. "But power readings are the only thing we can search for with subspace sensors, since they warp the curvature of space. Everything else propagates at the speed of light, and catching the wave front of the flash as it passed by would be pure chance. Of course I'd love to have a better option if you can think of one."

Scotty nodded. It wasn't a challenge, not exactly, but as he went to the bridge's engineering station and began catching up on what had happened in his absence, he set himself to work on the problem.

They had a weapon at an unknown point, firing at a moving target. Belle Terre's orbital motion carried it one planetary diameter every . . . what? . . . seven minutes? Eight? Depending on when the laser was fired, it could be pointed at any spot along an arc a few hours long. If they knew exactly when it was fired, and the exact distance to the target, they could calculate the point in its orbit where Belle Terre would intercept the laser beam, but they wouldn't know that until after they found the weapon. In the meantime, the beam itself could be anywhere in a vast region of space, slowly converging on Belle Terre.

So finding its source was the top priority, but the comet's location was also the least constrained variable. Deloric had remembered that Belle Terre's sun was in the constellation of the snake from his perspective, but not exactly where along the serpent's coiled length it had been. "Not in the middle," he had said, which hardly helped at all.

Scotty agreed that looking for the flash was pointless. Oh, they could eventually find it that way by simply planting a string of probes and waiting for the wave front to cross one of them, but that would be a little like dropping a rock in a pond and then scattering leaves over the surface to see which one bobbed up and down first. Except this particular pond was filled with molasses as far as the *Enterprise* was concerned. The speed of light was so *slow* compared to a starship.

What they needed was some way to determine instantly if the wave front had already passed. The *Enterprise* could then simply jump from place to place in the target volume and make a quick sensor sweep. Except the laser had been fired during Gamma Night, which also propagated at the speed of light. He modified his mental picture: the wave front was like the splash from a rock thrown in the ocean, not a pond, with gamma night sweeping through like waves from the infinite distance. One wave held the tiny ripple they were looking for, but they could only work with any efficiency in the troughs between the waves. Even his hypothetical string of buoys watching for the flash wouldn't be able to report until after gamma night had passed.

He groaned as the sudden realization hit him: even after they figured out where the beam had to be, they might never be able actually to find it. Like the flash of light that had created it, the beam itself was in the middle of gamma night! The *Enterprise*'s navigational sensors wouldn't work there. They would be flying blind, trying to pinpoint their position with nothing more than optical measurements of distant planets to go by.

Not that he had any idea what they would do when they found it. How could they stop a laser beam the width of a planet? That was the big question. He wished he had an answer.

Deloric's and Terwolan's burned faces rose to haunt him again. He had been seeing them every time he closed his eyes, imagining every colonist on Belle Terre burned even worse. The Kauld ice miners hadn't even been caught in the direct beam. The flash alone had done that to them.

Scotty wondered again what would be left of the comet when they found it. Would there even be debris, or would everything have been vaporized into an expanding cloud of gas?

An expanding cloud of *hot* gas.

"Stupid!" he said, slapping himself on the forehead. "Stupid, stupid, stupid!"

"Mr. Scott?" Kirk's voice was a blend of alarm and amusement.

Scotty turned around to face him. "What's left of the comet should be glowin' like a beacon in the infrared spectrum. We don't have to look for the flash, or for power sources. We can look for heat."

He saw the realization hit everyone at once. Plain old optical astronomy, practically obsolete since the invention of warp technology and subspace observation techniques, could serve them here. "All we have to do," he said, thinking aloud, "is make a series of jumps around the area we think it's in. If we look for the heat signature, we dinna have to catch the wave front. It'll be visible from anywhere inside the sphere of expanding light."

"Which is one light-day wide now and getting bigger all the time," said Kirk. "That . . . makes a great deal of sense."

"Thank you," Scotty said. He was apparently getting used to thinking in terms of primitive science. He wasn't sure he liked that, but it did have its advantages at the moment. *And for my next trick, I'll use a solder-*

184

ing iron and bailing wire to fix a toaster. The moment he got back to civilization, he swore he would kiss the ground.

Kirk turned to Sulu and Thomsen. "Belay the probe drop. Take us straight for the comet's most likely position. Shields up."

"Yes, sir." The helmsman and navigator got to work, and the *Enterprise* veered onto its new course.

The sensors went dark as they crossed through a zone of gamma night, then came back on-line for a couple of minutes before darkening again. They were plowing through the waves head-on on their way out of the system, a ten-light-hour-wide band of disruption followed by twenty light-hours of clear sailing, all compressed into a few minutes of tension as the ship bore through it at warp speed. If they hit anything during those dark moments they would never know it. The shields might deflect a rock at ultralight velocity, but nothing bigger. And if there was something bigger in their path, Belle Terre would have a brief new star in its night sky for a few minutes . . . and certain death four days later.

They could be flying right through the laser beam at the moment and they would never know it. Not in subspace. The column of photons was crawling toward Belle Terre entirely through normal space.

Sulu was muttering softly, and Scotty realized he was counting the waves. If Thomsen's navigation equipment couldn't handle the recurring blackouts, he would at least know when to stop the ship. Scotty watched his fingers draw closer and closer to the control panel, and he was already reaching out to bring them out of warp when Thomsen said, "We're there."

The *Enterprise* dropped out of warp in a calm spot between waves. They could do optical scans during

Gamma Night, but there was no sense hindering themselves needlessly until they had exhausted the search areas in the clear.

"Start scanning, people," Kirk said, but Scotty was already turning back to his console to do just that.

They had no luck on their first jump, nor on the next five, but on their seventh sweep the omnidirectional infrared detector gave a beep, and a cheer went up around the bridge. Not bad, Scotty thought, considering the odds were about forty-to-one against them. That's how many one-light-day volumes there were inside the search area, but they were spiraling out from the region of most likelihood, so he supposed the true odds were more like fifteen- or twenty-to-one. Spock would be able to tell him exactly, but it didn't matter. They had found it.

Scotty immediately moved to isolate it, and sure enough, there was a single radiation source. It was a bright, hot source, too, which meant they had dropped in close to the edge of the expanding light sphere. They were probably seeing it within an hour after the laser had been fired.

He did some quick distance measurements. Sure enough, the comet was nearly a light-day away. Almost all the way across the clear space between waves of gamma night.

"Uh-oh," he said.

"I don't like the sound of that," Kirk said.

Scotty shook his head. "I dinna like it either. I've found the comet, but we've only got about fifteen minutes to get there and take whatever sensor readings we can before Gamma Night hits it."

Chapter Twenty-three

SPOCK FELT the ship sweeping through the successive layers of Gamma Night. In the science lab the effect was a slight but noticeable difference in the way the deflector array responded to his commands. Much of the signal processing was done on-site, and the onslaught of subspace distortion that accompanied the normal-space effects of the phenomenon played havoc with the exposed computers. Calculations that normally required a single algorithm had to be cross-checked for accuracy using a second method, and sometimes a third when the results didn't match.

He wondered if he was wasting his time here. He might be of more use on the bridge, assisting in the search for the laser beam. That was only the beginning of their problem, however, and he felt sure that the rest of the bridge crew could handle it competently without him. He also felt that someone needed to work on the next and most important question: how could they stop the laser beam from striking Belle Terre once they discovered it?

He didn't know how watching the deflector activity during their successive Gamma Night crossings would help, but there was no sense wasting the opportunity to gather data. He hadn't had the chance to test his olivium-powered sensors since rebuilding them after the neutrino overload; now he could test them four times in a quarter-hour.

They didn't overload on the first transit. That was a good sign, but they didn't report any neutrino bursts, either. On the second transit he set them scanning all the way through the electromagnetic spectrum for the echo frequency, but they were only halfway through when the ship crossed back into clear subspace. On the third transit he finished the scan, finding a peak in the X-ray range that he was able to measure more accurately on the fourth pass.

X-rays in hyperspace. And he had been sending out Berthold rays. It made no more sense than sending out radio and getting back neutrinos.

There were no more Gamma Night crossings to test it in. Spock settled in to analyze the data he had gathered, noting from the flickering of the lights that the ship was now making short hyperspace jumps. They were either dropping probes or searching for the comet from whence the laser beam had come.

Then the intercom whistled, and the captain said, "Bridge to Spock."

He reached out and pressed the reply switch. "Spock here, Captain."

"Get up here on the double. We've found the laser,

but we've only got fifteen minutes to study it before Gamma Night hits."

Fifteen minutes. That wasn't nearly long enough to do a thorough examination, but one didn't argue with the universe. If that was all they had, they would have to make the best use of it they could. "On my way," he said, standing up and heading for the door without even taking the time to switch off his equipment. It could wait until he returned.

When the turbolift doors opened, he saw Dr. McCoy in the car. The doctor nodded to Spock and stood aside; as the door slid closed behind him he said, "I thought I'd come up and see what all the commotion is about."

"All the 'commotion' is about the comet. We've found it."

"Aha. This soon? That's a good sign."

"Take heart in this minor bit of good fortune. It may be the only one we get."

McCoy gave him a critical look, a penetrating, *human* look of the sort that always made Spock feel uncomfortable. He knew just enough about humans—was just human enough himself—to understand what it meant. The doctor was about to make a snap character judgement.

McCoy surprised him, which was almost as annoying as the character judgement would have been. "Want a cat?" he asked.

Spock nearly said, "I beg your pardon?" but then he remembered that McCoy and Mr. Scott had found an abandoned cat on board their exploration ship, which meant he had in fact heard the doctor correctly. He shook his head. "I have no need of a pet."

"You should think about it. She's kind of prickly. Like you."

Spock almost smiled. McCoy hadn't failed him after all.

The door onto the bridge opened, saving him the necessity of a response. He looked immediately to the main viewscreen, where the remains of the comet were displayed. There was no ice left. Chunks of rock, none larger than a shuttlecraft, tumbled slowly among an immense tangle of metal that must have been the olivium-powered exciter for the laser.

Spock gave it only a moment's examination, then went to his science station and immediately got to work with the sensors. He could use his eyes later, during gamma night. For now they needed every electronic measurement they could make before they lost the capability.

He took a molecular scan of the entire debris field, calling out the more interesting details in the data that streamed across the monitors before him. "The heat of the exciter burst was strong enough to vaporize the outer ten centimeters of rock facing it, and melt the rest into slag. My calculations would put it at roughly forty thousand degrees."

"How does that translate into destructive power of the beam itself?" Kirk asked.

That was a very good question, and one which required more information than he had for a precise answer, but he knew enough to speculate. "The amount of energy necessary to reach that kind of temperature is phenomenal, especially when we remember that this was the *leakage* from the exciter, which no doubt directed nearly all its energy down the carbon dioxide column. The evidence here correlates with the data provided to Mr. Scott and Dr. McCoy. I cannot give you a precise energy density for the laser beam, but I agree with the Kauld informants' assessment of its strength. It would indeed be sufficient to destroy Belle Terre."

Nobody responded to that statement. Spock turned back to the sensor displays and called out more observations as they came in. "As expected, I am picking up strong olivium decay signatures. I am unable to determine the amount of olivium the Kauld used, but I suspect it was more than sufficient to ensure the cohesiveness of the laser."

"Cohesiveness?" Kirk asked.

"A laser beam of sufficient power is self-focusing," Spock told him. "It will not spread the way a normal laser would."

Scotty cleared his throat, another human trait that Spock recognized instantly. It meant he was about to contradict what Spock had just said. "Self-focusing works in crystals," he said, "because the light alters the index of refraction inside the beam, but how could that work in space?"

Spock kept the sensors going while he answered. "It's a gravitational effect, not a refractive one. A beam of sufficient energy density actually acts as a solid object, according to the equation $e = mc^2$. The energy's equivalent mass creates gravity, which does affect photons. At a sufficiently high power level, that gravity would be enough to keep the beam from spreading."

Scotty whistled softly. "Aye, I can see how it could, but the amount of power you're talking about would have to be enormous."

"Indeed," Spock said. He looked back to his monitors, studying the data stream from a dozen different scans. Electron, polaron, gravimetric and even temporal disturbances all swept by with dizzying speed. He double-checked that the computer was storing all the data.

This was a treasure-trove of information on the reactivity and characteristics of olivium. The information he gathered from this site would have taken several years of careful development—or an unfortunate accident—to accumulate. Due to olivium's unpredictable nature, he would not have been able to simulate experiments leading to most of this information.

Spock found himself in a surprising moral dilemma. He had great admiration for the people who designed and engineered this feat. The efficient use of existing resources would please any logical being. Likewise, the decision to build a self-consuming device for a one-time need reflected in their favor. The Kauld had built something extraordinary; yet even the fact that they had done it in an elegant manner was of no consequence. What they'd produced was a weapon powerful enough to destroy a planet and all who lived on it. Worse yet, they had fired it at Belle Terre and the people the *Enterprise* was there to protect. It was not his job to admire the craftsmanship but to determine how to stop it before it reached its target.

"Can you pinpoint the time when the laser was actually fired?" Kirk asked.

Spock looked at the radiation decay figures from the rocky debris. "I can only narrow it down to a time between twenty-five and twenty-seven hours ago."

McCoy, who had taken up his customary position behind the captain's left shoulder, said, "What the heck kind of answer is that? Where's your 'approximately 25.48762 hours' accuracy?"

Spock tore his attention from the incoming numbers scrolling across his data charts long enough to say to McCoy, "I assure you, doctor, if there had been more precision to be gleaned from these readings, I would have given it. Perhaps if you could provide me with a chronometer conveniently stopped by the blast, or a reflection from an object at a calibrated distance, my work would be more accurate."

McCoy didn't answer back, but the look on his face told Spock that his explanation had had the desired effect. With any luck, it would be some time before the good doctor felt compelled to interrupt his work with any more frivolous comments.

He turned back to his monitors and noticed that the data streams were slowing down. Sensors were double-checking their readings and rejecting some outright as unreliable. "Gamma Night is nearly upon us," he said.

"Hmph." said Kirk. He sat in the command chair, rubbing his chin with his right fist, his eyes glued to the viewscreen, searching every piece of debris. Spock had seen that look on his face before. The captain was pondering his options, weighing his possible moves, just as he did when the two of them played a game of three-dimensional chess. He was also waiting for more information from Spock.

Spock turned back to his consoles. There was still plenty to be observed in the visual spectrum. He peered into the debris field with the ship's main telescope, noting how the separate pieces drifted away at varying speeds according to their density. From that he could probably calculate the strength of the final explosion that wrecked the olivium-powered exciter beam, but the fact that there was any debris left at all proved that the explosion was only a tiny fraction of the total energy delivered into the laser. He looked for more revealing objects, and eventually found them nearly twenty kilometers distant. "It appears that at least two other vessels were caught in the flash of the laser and destroyed. They appear to be Kauld ships."

"On screen," Kirk ordered.

Spock complied. The charred and broken remains of two ships hung like shadowy ghosts amid an expanding sea of small—those weren't rocks. They were all the same size, and they had arms and legs. Those ships hadn't merely been staffed; they had been jammed full of people.

Spock closed his eyes against the sight, then forced himself to look. There could be valuable information here. The ship closest to the comet was little more than cinders and pieces of broken frame, but the hull of the second one showed an interesting burn pattern as it tumbled slowly end over end.

Kirk saw it too. "It looks like they were caught completely off-guard when the laser was fired."

"How do you figure?" McCoy asked.

"Well, aside from the fact that they were here at all with that many people on board, the farthest one sustained all its damage on its starboard side. That means it was stationed side-on to the comet. It wasn't even trying to escape, or it would have been burned on the backside. If they'd known what was coming, they would have at least tried to get out of here."

"Are you saying that the Kauld ambushed their own people?" McCoy asked.

"It's possible. It could be Vellyngaith's way of ensuring that nobody compromised the mission. Leave no witnesses."

Mr. Scott nodded. "It would fit with the information we got from Deloric and Terwolan. They weren't told the purpose of the work they were doing, and they weren't warned that the laser was about to be fired. If they hadn't figured it out themselves and jumped ship, they'd have been out there."

"Maybe it went off prematurely," Sulu said. Everyone on the bridge looked over at him as he continued. "We could be worrying about nothing. If they pushed the button too soon, the beam will pass right by Belle Terre."

McCoy nodded. "Which could be why they're drilling their ships for a big battle. They know this isn't going to do us any harm!" He grew more excited as he spoke. "Yeah, they blew it, but they're hoping we waste all our time out here trying to stop it while they get into position to take us out with their fleet. Deloric and Terwolan were probably sent to us straight from the high command!"

Spock looked at him with narrowed eyes. "How easily you cling to false hope. According to your report, you saw the Kauld fleet conducting war games at nearly the same time the laser was fired. That fleet included three new ships and dozens of refitted ones—not an impromptu attack force. And unless the Kauld knew of your presence there and followed you—at warp 11—to Naresidan Station, how would they have known to plant their agents there?" He looked back at the two wrecked ships and the debris field surrounding them. "No, it is far more likely that they fired it just when they intended to, but they simply didn't expect the flash to be as strong as it was."

Kirk rubbed his chin again. "Intentional or not, we need to find the beam itself and find out exactly where it's aimed before we dismiss it as a threat."

"Indeed, Captain. To that end, I believe we should plant our remote probes along the wave front in the laser's most likely path."

Kirk nodded. "Give us your best estimate of where that would be, and let's do it."

Spock turned back to his monitors. They were now exactly 5.23 light-days out from Belle Terre. If he assumed the middle of the window of possibility for firing time, that would put the planet . . . there when the laser beam arrived. And if he drew a direct line from here to there, and stopped twenty-six light-hours out, that would be it.

He transferred the coordinates to the navigation console.

"Course locked in," Thomsen said.

"Shields up," Kirk said.

"Shields at maximum."

"Engage."

The *Enterprise* leaped into subspace. For just a second, they were flying blind, then they shook free of Gamma Night and locked on course.

Chapter Twenty-four

THE *ENTERPRISE* crossed the gap between waves of Gamma Night in only a few minutes. Kirk kept his eyes on the viewscreen as they swept on into the next area of sensor blackout. The chances of him seeing something before they hit it were infinitesimally small, but they were better going into this with his eyes open than completely blind.

Gamma Night had seemed like a personal affront to him from the very first time he had encountered it. Things were tough enough out here on the edge of nowhere; the universe really didn't need to throw this periodic torment at him as well. But it did, and he was slowly learning how to deal with it.

So were his helmsman and navigator. Sulu and Thomsen had certainly earned their pay in the months since they had come to Belle Terre. With only a few nearby planets to provide reference points, and light-speed lag to mask their true position at that, they were still able to take readings and calculate the ship's position whenever they dropped back into normal space. Under warp they weren't so lucky, but they knew the design parameters of the ship and could calculate its position, with a cumulative error of only ten or twenty thousand kilometers per minute.

No wonder Chekov had taken that position on board the *Reliant*.

"Coming up on the first drop point," Thomsen said.

"Release the probe," Kirk replied.

The *Enterprise* dropped out of warp. On the viewscreen a tiny spark of light shot away from the ship. When it was far enough away to escape the warp field, Sulu took them back into warp for the next drop point.

It took less than a second of flight to cover the distance, even at warp one. They weren't talking about a lot of volume here, not on the cosmic scale of things. The beam could be as little as twelve thousand kilometers wide and still cover the entire planet. But that meant they had to drop a probe every twelve thousand kilometers if they wanted to detect it.

It would almost make sense to do it on impulse power alone. Almost, but not quite. They were planting the probes in a spiral, weaving a web ever outward from the beam's most likely path. The total distance they had to travel was six times the target zone just for the first layer, and six times that for every extra layer they put on. It could take hours to cover that distance under impulse power. The beam could slip past before they got all their probes in place, and they would never know it.

Besides, without a gravity well to bend the ship's path, flying in a spiral was incredibly wasteful of fuel. It also put Kirk on edge. He already felt like he was going in circles with this whole Belle Terre situation; he wasn't about to start doing it literally.

They settled into a routine. Jump, drop, wait. Jump, drop, wait. Jump, drop—

Wham!

The viewscreen flashed brilliant white. The ship lurched sideways, throwing Kirk against the arm of his chair. McCoy flew up against the handrail around the command chair and did a spectacular gymnast's flip, turning completely over before landing flat on his back on the other side of the rail. Thomsen wound up on the floor beside him, and Sulu wound up in Thomsen's chair.

"Take us out of here!" Kirk shouted, his voice only a heartbeat ahead of half a dozen alarms.

In the intense glare from the viewscreen he saw Sulu slap at the controls, and a moment later they leaped into darkness.

He looked to see if McCoy had broken his back, but the doctor scrambled to his feet and moved like a man twenty years his junior, helping other crew members back to their seats and making sure that nobody was badly hurt.

Alarms screamed for attention from every control console. The entire bridge crew rushed back to their stations and began working frantically to correct the problems, but no sooner did they silence one alarm than two more took its place. The telltale smell of burnt electronics filled the air, and within a few seconds Kirk began to feel the heat seeping through the bulkhead and radiating from the walls. The outer hull had to be glowing like the surface of a star for that to happen.

Through the noise of the alarms, he heard McCoy say to Thomsen, "Lady, you're bleeding."

"I am?" The navigator raised a hand to her forehead,

above her right eye. When she dropped her hand, her fingers were covered in blood. "It doesn't hurt. I'll be fine," she said as she wiped her fingers on her black trousers.

"Let me at least put a topical coagulant on that, or you'll be dripping into your controls and sending us off to who knows where," McCoy said.

Thomsen didn't argue with that. Kirk felt a trickle on his own brow, but when he wiped it away it was just sweat. It was growing uncomfortably warm in the bridge.

"Environmental controls?" he asked.

"Off-line," Scotty said. "I'm working on 'em."

"Shields?"

Sulu said, "They're down. It was just an overload though, not a failure, so they'll be okay as soon as the generators can radiate their excess heat."

Maybe easier said than done. Kirk turned to Uhura. "How's the rest of the ship?"

"Damage to the outer hull on all decks. Breaches on decks 14 through 21, and the portside warp nacelle." She listened to the intercom for a moment, then said, "Injuries reported in engineering."

Scotty looked up from his console, but another alarm drew his attention back to the job at hand. Without prompting, McCoy ran for the turbolift.

"Spock?" Kirk asked.

"Forward and portside sensor arrays damaged. No response from the navigational deflector."

Kirk remembered the ships they had seen near the comet—melted, twisted wrecks. The *Enterprise* hadn't been exposed for as long, but she'd taken the laser full-on. All this time he'd been thinking of the search for the beam as looking for a needle in a haystack. Well, what better way to find that needle than to take a walk barefoot through the hay? Without trying, they'd flown the ship right into the path of the beam.

"Launch a probe," he said.

"Sir?" Thomsen asked.

"I want to see what the hull looks like."

"Oh! Yes, sir."

The image on the viewscreen looked dim, but whether that was from damage to the display or simply from his eyes having not yet recovered from the flash Kirk didn't know. He could see well enough to spot the probe moving away, but instead of rushing on into space, this one braked to a halt just off the bow, and the screen shifted to a view from its perspective.

The *Enterprise*'s light gray paint had flashed to vapor in the first few milliseconds; every surface that had faced the laser now showed the silvery luster of bare hullmetal. That was by design, but even 99.9% reflective alloy couldn't withstand a laser of that intensity. The hull had been partially melted across the saucer section and the port warp nacelle. Any antenna arrays or equipment housings that had stuck out on that side had simply ceased to exist. Atmosphere was venting from the breaches in the secondary hull. And while the hull wasn't white-hot, it was glowing a deep red; the color of perfect barbecue coals.

They had been in the beam for maybe two seconds. It had been strong enough to do all this in that brief moment, and strong enough to shove the *Enterprise* sideways as well. *Light pressure* had done that.

Kirk looked over at the science station. "Spock, did we get any useful information out of our . . . encounter?"

Spock looked up from his station. "Yes, Captain. We now have readings of our relative position at the time of impact with the leading edge of the laser. We also know the wavelength and the energy density. Unfortunately, many of our instruments failed before we could gather more data. Most importantly, we do not know the width nor the length of the beam."

Those were the crucial details. Especially the length. Had the olivium laser expended its charge in one instantaneous burst, or had the carbon dioxide column continued to lase for a while? That would make a big difference in how they fought it.

They had actually been inside the laser beam for a moment, but they still didn't know its extent. "Then our work out here is only half finished," Kirk said.

"Less than that," Spock replied.

He was right, of course. They were still at a loss as to how one goes about stopping a laser of *any* length from frying a planet. There were only so many ways to prevent a laser strike. Reflecting the beam away from the target, blocking it with something massive, or just not being in the path in the first place were the three standard defense tactics.

However, there was no mirror of sufficient dimension—or durability—available. Simply blocking the beam would take an ablative shield as wide as the planet, and who knew how thick? Maybe just a few meters if the beam was short, but it could take a few kilometers if the beam was more than a few minutes long. In either case it would have to have the mass of a good sized asteroid to cover the entire planet.

On the other hand, Belle Terre had eight moons. There had been nine to begin with, but shortly after the colonists had arrived here, Kirk had sacrificed one of them in the collision that released the internal pressure of the olivium moon before it could explode. The relatively minor release of energy from the collision had caused the Burn, but it had at least saved the planet from total destruction. Was there some way to sacrifice another moon to prevent destruction a second time?

It might be possible. Tow it into the right position and blow it into fragments that would absorb the worst of the light. . . . But even if they could do that, that wouldn't prevent the beam from shoving the fragments into the planet at a high fraction of the speed of light. Even a vapor cloud hitting at that speed would flatten continents.

That left dodging it. If they could harness the total power of the olivium moon itself, that would probably be enough energy to hold back Belle Terre in its orbit long enough for the laser to slide harmlessly by. But even if that were possible, Kirk knew that the already fragile planet would suffer as much damage from that kind of manipulation as from the laser. Tides, winds, volcanos, landslides; they might as well let it burn.

He hoped Lilian and the governor were working toward an orderly evacuation. In light of the other options, it might be the only way to save the colonists' lives. But it still wouldn't save Belle Terre, and with the Kauld fleet waiting in the wings, the Federation would probably lose the olivium moon, too.

That left only option four: think of something else.

Chapter Twenty-five

SPOCK CHECKED his science station one final time. All but one of his optical sensors were operational. The data storage buffers were ready for input. The library computer was on-line and ready for heuristic analysis of the data.

The rest of the ship wasn't in quite as good shape. It was capable of flight, but it would be days before many subsystems would be repaired. The environmental system was only now bringing the bridge back down to its normal, uncomfortably cool (for a Vulcan, at least) temperature, and the viewscreen was still much dimmer than usual. However, it would do for the task at hand.

Spock kept his eyes on the monitors as the *Enterprise* prepared for another look at the laser beam. They had found the leading edge of it easily enough, but the trailing edge would not be so simple. They couldn't just wait for it to pass over them the way they had done with the front. For one thing, that would put them inside the beam while they waited, and they had already seen how well the ship could handle that.

They could park a probe ahead of the beam and wait for it to pop out the back, but there was no known material or force field strong enough to protect even the smallest probe from the onslaught of photons. Besides, anything less dense than neutronium would be shoved down the beam path by the light pressure, rendering any measurements it could make meaningless. For the same reason, they couldn't just scatter dust in its path and watch the dust delineate its edges the way it might a less powerful beam. All they would see would be a scintillating disk receding at the speed of light as the wave front pushed the dust ahead of it.

They couldn't sneak up on it from behind, either. They could approach under warp drive, but the moment they popped back into normal space they would either be inside the beam again or behind it. Neither possibility would be much help.

It had taken him a moment to convince himself that they couldn't catch up with it using any combination of warp drive and impulse power, either. The beam was traveling ridiculously slow by warp drive standards, but by the rules of normal space it was traveling at the ultimate speed. Relativistic effects came into play at light-speed, and they were as counterintuitive as any produced by quantum olivium.

For instance, no matter how fast the *Enterprise* travelled through normal space, they could never even keep pace with the light beam, much less catch it. The laser would always be receding at the speed of light, completely independent of the *Enterprise*'s velocity. If they launched a probe at 99 percent of light-speed and left another one at rest, the laser would outrun them both at the same velocity: light-speed. It was difficult to accept, but that was the way the universe worked. Such seeming paradoxes were the foundation of relativity, and every one of them had been proven true by experiment.

So they were going to try a different method, starting at the end they could reach first and working their way back.

"Ready, Spock?" Kirk asked.

"Ready here."

"Thomsen? Sulu?"

"Ready," they both replied.

"All right, then. Take us in."

Everyone seemed to be holding their breath as Sulu and Thomsen sent the ship into warp. They knew where one point along the leading edge was, but they didn't know where along the beam's considerable width that point was. It could have been dead center, or all the way to one side for all they knew, so they were planning to stop well outside the farthest likely distance, and well ahead of the beam.

Of course, with Gamma Night compromising their navigation, their safety margin could easily disappear in their margin of error.

When the ship popped out of subspace, everyone gripped the edges of their consoles for support, but space was as clear and serene as ever. "Let's not waste time, gentlemen," Kirk said, and Sulu immediately executed stage two of the plan.

Full impulse power barely shook the ship. Its gravity generators were designed to compensate for accelerations a thousand times greater. But Spock's monitors showed what was happening outside, as the starship's immense fusion engines poured their high-velocity exhaust out the back. Long streams of plasma shot out behind the ship, directly into the path of the oncoming laser beam.

Or so they hoped. It would be minutes before they knew for sure. By then the *Enterprise* would be moving away from the laser at a significant fraction of light-speed itself, and the evidence of the encounter would take even longer to reach them.

Uhura had put the aft view on the main screen. Nobody spoke as they waited to see what would happen. Waited to see if they had miscalculated and the laser was bearing down on *them* and not the exhaust stream.

In the far distance the plasma trail grew less and less distinct as it expanded and cooled. *Any time,* Spock thought, then he chided himself for allowing the humans' anxiety to affect his impartial reason. The time to impact was a datum, like any other. There was no reason to have an emotional stake in it. It would happen when it happened, and then they would know the cross-sectional area of the beam.

Captain Kirk shifted in his command chair. "Any time," he said.

As if responding to his order, an oblong patch of light blossomed in the distance, then immediately streaked away to the right, toward the inner solar system. It was bright as a strobe light, and left an afterimage in Spock's eyes.

No, that was a true image. It stayed put when he moved. Somehow, he was seeing the length of the laser beam itself, not just the leading edge, as it reheated the exhaust plume to incandescence and swept it out of the way. But how could that be? The exhaust stream couldn't be moving fast enough for more than a few molecules to hit any given kilometer of the beam's flank as it flashed past. He had expected that much—had counted on it, and had planned on reviewing his recordings at high amplification to determine the structure of the beam later—but this was far more illumination than he had expected.

And the beam was far wider than he'd imagined it, too. Not just a line in the distance; it was a scintillating wall blocking out a quarter of the starfield. Of course if it was the width of a planet, that should not have been surprising, but his mental picture had not accounted for the scale of it, seen from only a few thousand kilometers away.

Scotty said, "Kind o' pretty, isn't it? In a deadly sort of way."

"It's very puzzling," Spock replied. "We should not be seeing the side of the beam that clearly. It's almost as if—" He stopped, his mental picture of the situation shifting yet again.

"Spock?" asked Kirk.

"The beam is angled."

There was a moment of silence, then Kirk said, "Explain."

Visualizing it even as he spoke, he said, "We have been thinking of the laser beam as a straight line drawn between the emitter and its target. That is usually a close approximation to reality when the travel time is measured in milliseconds, but in this case we have a beam of apparently some seconds' duration, aimed at a moving target. The Kauld would have been tracking that target, pivoting the exciter beam inside the carbon dioxide column as it lased. The result is a laser beam that moves sideways as it moves forward."

Scotty nodded. "Like sprayin' water from a hose and swingin' it around at the same time."

"A crude analogy, but yes. The actual angle is less than—" he did a quick calculation "—three minutes of arc, but it is a significant deviation from true. Significant enough that the side of the beam is colliding with our exhaust stream, rather than the other way around."

"I notice it's still doing it," Kirk said. "How long has it been?"

Spock consulted his readouts. "Thirty-two seconds," he said.

The beam continued to roar past.

"Forty seconds."

"Are we in any danger here?" Kirk asked.

"No," Spock said. "We are moving away faster than it is moving toward us." Of course they were, he realized as soon as he said that. The beam was tracking the planet, and even a few seconds of impulse power would get the ship moving much faster than a planet's orbital velocity around its sun.

Spock watched the chronometer. "Sixty seconds."

The beam grew smaller as they raced away from it, but it was still quite visible as a bright blue, almost ultraviolet streak against the black backdrop of space.

"Do we need to keep thrustin' away, or should we turn back and get a closer look?" Scotty asked.

"We do not yet know the duration of the beam," Spock said. "We must keep a continuous exhaust stream pouring into it until it passes."

"It canna be more than a couple o' minutes long, can it?"

Spock looked back to his chronometer. "Two minutes and twelve seconds and counting."

Uhura upped the magnification on the viewscreen. The beam looked like a searchlight shining through fog.

"There is structure to the flank," Spock reported.

"The significance of that?" Kirk asked.

"Unknown. No, wait. It must mean that the carbon dioxide column was growing turbulent from the thermal effects."

Kirk shook his head. "No, I meant what's the significance for *us?* How's that going to affect our ability to deal with it?"

The question brought Spock up short. How would it? He thought about it for a moment, but came up blank. "Since we have no idea what our strategy will be, I cannot speculate."

"Great," said Kirk. His tone of voice made it clear it was anything but.

They watched the beam slide past. Three minutes. Five. Ten. Uhura kept raising the magnification on the main screen to keep the beam about the same width as a person's forearm held out in front of them, but on his own monitor Spock periodically checked the direct, unmagnified view. From the *Enterprise*'s distance of nearly a million kilometers, the beam was a bright gash in space, extending in-system as far as the eye could follow. It was tens of millions of kilometers long, and still coming.

How *could* they stop such a thing? With each passing minute, the immensity of the task grew more apparent. It was ten minutes—now fifteen—of pure destruction, any *second* of which could wipe out all life on the planet.

And yet, despite its magnitude, it was still just a streak in the distance. If he thought of it in the right terms, it almost seemed manageable. After all, it was only the width of a planet. A small, terrestrial planet at that. Its length might seem vast even on that scale, but compared to the solar system itself, it was no more than one or two percent of the total diameter. And if it missed Belle Terre and swept on through the system, it would be quickly lost in the vastness of interstellar space. It wasn't even aimed along the plane of the galaxy, but outward, into intergalactic space. The odds of it encountering anything ever again were infinitesimally small.

If it would just miss the planet.

He double- and triple-checked its position. No such luck. The Kauld had taken very careful aim. Not only would it hit Belle Terre; it would do so when the main city, Buena Vista, was facing directly into the beam. It would be just a few minutes past midnight there.

And the olivium moon? Spock displayed the visual ephemeris for that moment. It would be on the other side of Belle Terre, of course. Safely protected from harm by the bulk of the planet. The Kauld, it seemed, had thought of everything.

Twenty minutes. Spock struggled against a growing sense of annoyance. Surely this was overkill. What little admiration he had for the elegance of their construction faded under the continual barrage of its product. They had failed to understand the fundamental principle behind artistic beauty: enough is enough.

At last the fluorescing exhaust stream began to lose its sharp-edged definition, and a moment later it winked out as the last of the laser beam receded into the distance. Spock checked the chronometer.

He read the number aloud for all to hear. "Twenty-one minutes, fourteen seconds."

Mr. Scott was standing beside his engineering station with his fists planted on his hips. "Good God," he said. "Do ye realize that's more firepower than all o'

211

the weapons in all o' the fleets in all o' the Federation put together? What could we possibly do to stop that?"

Spock had no answer for him. Neither did the captain. Kirk rubbed his chin thoughtfully, then said softly to Sulu, "Take us home."

Chapter Twenty-six

THE GLITTERING vision of the laser lingered as an after-image whenever Kirk closed his eyes. He didn't need Spock's assessment to know that the beam was powerful. Powerful and unstoppable. He clenched his hand into a fist, pushing all his frustrations into the spaces between his fingers.

Once again the *Enterprise* rode the waves of Gamma Night back to the beleaguered fort that was Belle Terre. Spock immersed himself in the data that scrolled in a constant stream across his instruments. The rest of the bridge crew waited in unnatural silence while Sulu flew them home. Kirk suspected that they had more on their minds besides the wild ride. He certainly did.

The moment they dropped out of warp, however, the bridge resumed a more normal level of activity. Uhura's fingers danced across her communications panel, imposing order on the confusion of the dozens of incoming hails they were receiving all at once. Scotty, apparently satisfied with the state of the bridge's repairs, set off for engineering.

The viewscreen now displayed an image of Belle Terre, three of its eight remaining moons visible from their position. From here, the Burn wasn't apparent. Kirk could see clouds forming over the ocean, building up at the coastline. It seemed like such a peaceful place. The thought of it being burned to a crisp made his stomach roil.

"Captain, I have Governor Pardonnet for you," Uhura said.

"Onscreen."

Pardonnet's handsome face replaced the blue-and-white planet. "Captain, what the hell's going on! I got a message from you telling me to start evacuation procedures, but when I try to contact you, poof! You're gone! Out of communication and it isn't even Gamma Night!"

Maybe not where you were, Kirk thought. "Sorry, Governor, but it couldn't be helped. You couldn't be reached at the time, and we couldn't wait for you. I hope you've already started on that evacuation, because we don't have time to waste."

"No, we haven't started! I'm not about to abandon everything on your say-so. My office is working with Dr. Neville, Mrs. Coates, and the mayors of our various settlements to form a plan, but they're waiting on my go-ahead before they implement anything. I've got to tell you Captain, this had better be damned good. I'm not about to crush what's left of the colonists' spirit with this kind of defeat, being chased from our homes like vermin." The muscles along Pardonnet's jaw clenched.

Kirk wished the governor's sheer determination could actually help this time, but after what he had just seen he knew it couldn't. "Trust me," he said, "evacuation is the only option available. We've got to get these people loaded up and headed back to Federation space."

"I thought we were *in* Federation space."

"We're trying to make it that way, but the Kauld are trying just as hard to prevent it. Unfortunately, I think they just outgunned us. Uhura, play the video of the laser. Give me audio."

"Yes, sir."

Kirk heard the electronic bleep from her console, noted Pardonnet's eyes shifting slightly to account for the change in his view, and said, "What you are seeing here is a laser that's over twenty light-minutes long aimed directly at Belle Terre. We sustained substantial damage during an exposure of only a second or two."

The governor was silent a long minute while he watched the screen. At last he spoke. "*Twenty* light-minutes long, you say."

"Yes. And if you can think of a way to stop it, I'm all ears."

"I . . . see," he said, all of his bluster evaporating like the paint from the *Enterprise*'s hull. "How much time before it hits?"

Kirk softened his own tone. "Approximately three days. We've got to move on this *now*."

"So that's it. This is how we lose Belle Terre, by turning our tails and running." Pardonnet shook his head sadly. "There are people down here who won't run, you know. They've paid for Belle Terre over and over again with their sweat, their tears and blood, and the blood of their loved ones. They would rather die than evacuate."

"I'm well aware of people's attitudes, but I can guarantee that anybody who chooses to stay *will* die. They can burrow into the deepest cave on the planet and they'll still be cooked. Even if they somehow manage to survive the twenty minutes of inferno, there won't be a breathable atmosphere left. We've seen the result of the Burn, how devastated that left the planet. Well, that'll be a walk through paradise compared to *this* burn." He shook his head. "I have orders. I've been charged with protecting the planet of Belle Terre, but when I can no longer do so, I will protect the colonists' lives any way I can. I believe those were your orders as well, were they not?"

Pardonnet looked down and nodded.

Kirk took the quiet moment as an opportunity to drive forward. "We'll need to get all the *Conestoga*-class vessels loaded as soon as possible, even those without drive capability. We can tow them far enough away to escape the laser and get them travel-worthy once the dust clears. Everything that can be salvaged from the planet will have to be packed up, too. There won't be anything worth coming back for."

The look that crossed Pardonnet's face was his "are you crazy?" look. But to the man's credit, he didn't say it. Instead he said, "This is going to take a full-blown mobilization effort. Getting people moving without panicking them is going to be nearly impossible. We'll need to find ways to store fresh food for the duration of the trip. We'll need refrigeration equipment, medical equipment—the whole infrastructure. We can't wedge it all into the remaining Conestogas in three days."

He was right. It had taken months to off-load everything. There was no way they could put it all back in the time they had left. "You'll just have to beam it into space, then," Kirk said.

"What?" Pardonnet's eyebrows tried to disappear

216

over the top of his head. "Did I hear you correctly? Beam it into space?"

"That's right. Put it in the Lagrangian point between Belle Terre and the olivium moon. It'll be in the planet's shadow when the laser hits, so it should be safe there. We can come back and pick it up afterward."

"But . . . but . . . do you know what exposure to vacuum and extremes of heat and cold can do to things?"

"Oh, I have some idea," Kirk replied, and he heard Uhura stifle a snicker. "Believe me, it's better than what they'll face on the ground. Imagine what it would be like if the sun went supernova. That's what it's going to be like under that laser beam. Get anything you want saved in the shadow of the planet."

Pardonnet swallowed hard, then nodded. "Very well." He reached forward to switch off, but stopped with his hand halfway to the button. "What about the moon?" he asked.

"It should be safe," Kirk said. "The Kauld timed their shot so it would be in the planet's shadow, too."

"That's what I mean. We aren't going to just leave it for them, are we? The most concentrated energy source in the universe in the hands of hostiles?"

"It's either that or blow it up on our way out," Kirk said. "It's tempting, but that's not the way the Federation does things."

"And why not?"

Kirk suppressed a sigh. Starfleet spent years drilling the ethics of engagement into their cadets, and here he was trying to explain it to Pardonnet in a few seconds. "Because that olivium could offer a wealth of opportunity to every civilization in the galaxy, that's why not. The Kauld may not be the best stewards of it, but we would be no better if we destroyed it just to keep them from getting their hands on it. Besides, if we leave it intact, there's always the possibility that we could take it back at a later date."

Pardonnet nodded his grudging acceptance. "Maybe so, but do the Kauld know we think that way?"

"Probably not. What's your point?"

"My point is, they'll expect us to blow it up. They're going to try to stop us."

Kirk stared at the governor for a moment, his opinion of the man rising another notch. Kirk would have thought of that eventually, but Pardonnet had beat him to it. "You're right," he said. "And now the last piece of the puzzle has clicked into place. Lieutenant?" He turned toward Uhura. "The fleet video."

"Yes, sir." Another bleep from her console.

"Mr. Scott and Dr. McCoy discovered this while doing some reconnaissance in neighboring star systems. I was wondering why they were still building up their fleet when they had just fired their ultimate weapon, but now I know. They expect they'll have to prevent us from destroying the moon before we go."

Pardonnet seemed to go a little paler as he watched the enemy warships in action. "That does seem likely," he agreed.

"Which means we'll be fighting a battle while we evacuate unless we're already gone when they get here. We need to be ready in two days, not three."

Chapter Twenty-seven

SPOCK STACKED his olivium-powered sensor experiment on the far end of the science lab's counter. He could work on that later, during the long flight home. He suppressed a shudder at the thought of escorting twenty Conestogas full of angry, defeated colonists back to civilization, but there truly seemed no other option. Everyone expected the *Enterprise* to work some miracle to save them, and Spock would work right up to the final hour to give them that miracle, but the final hour was now less than three days away.

Even if it had been three weeks away, the odds of success would not be good. How could they stop the Kauld superweapon? How could any number of ships stop such a thing?

Mirrors, mass, and motion. Those were the traditional methods for defending against laser attacks, and none of them would work here.

That left more exotic methods. Spock rested his hands on the bare tabletop before him, facing the grav board covered with tools at the back of the workspace, then closed his eyes and considered the possibilities. Despite the laser beam's size, it was still made up of photons, and the individual photons were still subject to quantum effects. They behaved like both particles and waves, depending upon the circumstances. They would, for instance, create interference patterns if they passed through two side-by-side slits. Their own wave-forms would cancel one another out in narrow bands of interference, and amplify one another in alternate bands.

He didn't bother calculating the size of the slits required to create an interference pattern big enough to neutralize a light beam this size. If they could make a diffraction grating that big, they could make a mirror that big.

What else? He let his mind go blank, allowing the synapses to seek new connections on their own, letting the quantum uncertainty of raw creativity work for him where logic was little help.

The laboratory door slid open behind him. Footsteps, then: "I should have known I'd find you here. Looks like *you're* working hard." The Southern drawl and the derision it carried were unmistakable.

Spock didn't open his eyes. "It may be difficult for you to fathom, Doctor, but yes, I am indeed working hard."

"Yeah, I can practically smell the smoke." Another three footsteps. McCoy stood just behind his left shoulder now. "What are you working *on?* Looks like all your equipment is at the other end of the bench."

"That is another experiment, irrelevant to the matter at hand."

"Oh? What's it do?"

Spock took a deep breath. "It was an attempt to increase our ship's long-range sensing capabilities utilizing the quantum instability and extreme energy density of an olivium power supply. Unfortunately, it does not function as designed."

"Why not?"

Spock opened his eyes and turned his head toward the doctor. "Did you have a purpose in coming here other than to disrupt my thought processes?"

"Not really." Instead of taking the hint, McCoy came around and sat on the countertop beside him. "I've got everybody patched up as best I can after our little encounter with the laser beam out there, so I thought I'd check out the wounds that aren't so obvious on the surface."

T'plana-Hath save me, thought Spock. *He's talking about human psychology.*

Sure enough, McCoy said, "We're lookin' defeat in the eye and we haven't got so much as a pop-gun to even the odds. The depression around here is thick enough to cut with a knife. And you and the captain are under the most pressure of all. I wanted to see how you were holding up."

"Thank you for your concern," Spock said. "I am fine."

"I'm the doctor. Let me be the judge of that. Are you eating okay? Sleeping at all? Sleeping *too* much?"

Spock thought of the antiphase wave cancellation headphones resting against the grav board just a half-meter away. He could put them on, adjust them to the pitch of a human voice, and Dr. McCoy could ask all the questions he wanted. The headphones would generate an exact duplicate of the sound waves that made up

221

his voice, only out of phase with the original, effectively cancelling it out. McCoy could natter on at length, and Spock could get on with the business of figuring out how to neutralize the laser.

Unfortunately, decorum and basic civility required that he endure the doctor's personal inquisition instead.

"My caloric intake is adequate. I have not slept in seventy-nine hours, but this is not unusual for a Vulcan."

"You're half human. We need eight hours a day; you should get at least four."

Antiphase wave cancellation, Spock thought. Then he suddenly said it aloud. "Antiphase wave cancellation." He nearly inflected his voice with excitement, but McCoy would never let him hear the end of it if he did.

"What?"

Spock stood up. "Thank you, doctor. You have provided the solution to our dilemma."

"I have? How?"

"Lasers are collimated light beams, with all the waveforms aligned peak-to-peak. We merely need to fire another laser beam of exactly the same frequency, but out of phase with the first, along the same path as the original. The two beams will cancel one another out."

McCoy squinted at him as if he had confessed to an emotional fondness for Klingons. "You, uh, want to fire *another* laser at Belle Terre?" His right hand edged nervously toward his communicator.

"It would work," Spock said. He moved down to the end of the bench and carried his sensor experiment back to the center. It hadn't behaved as he had designed it, but with a little more modification it might suffice to detect the wavefront of the approaching laser beam. "When light waves cancel out, they leave no trace. Both beams would simply cease to exist."

"*If* they cancelled out. I don't know a whole lot about optics, but isn't it true that two light waves can reinforce each other just as easily?"

Spock nodded. "That is true, but only if they are in phase. We will be sure not to allow that to happen."

McCoy slid off the bench to give him room to set his breadboarded circuitry. "How are you going to do that? A wavelength of light is, what, a couple of microns across? How are you going to position your second laser that accurately? It'd be impossible under the best of conditions, but yours would have to be fired during Gamma Night! We'd be lucky if we got within a country mile of where we needed to be."

"That is what this equipment is for," Spock said. "I believe I can modify it to provide a subspace echo off the laser beam. Its efficiency is less than two percent, which makes it useless for general scanning because of the poor signal-to-noise ratio, but since we already know roughly where the beam is, we should be able to filter out extraneous signals and eventually locate it with the necessary precision."

"You *think*. You're going to trust people's lives to an untested gadget?"

Spock started plugging in his equipment. "No, Doctor, I plan to trust their lives to a tested one, which will be much easier to do if you allow me to get to work."

"You're nuts! You've cracked under the pressure. You—"

"Is that your professional evaluation?"

"It is."

Spock counted slowly to ten. As the ship's chief surgeon, McCoy could order him to sickbay for mental evaluation. It could be hours before his monitors proved that there was no pathological illness, if indeed the doctor believed his monitors. By the time Spock was free of his clutches, the point could be moot.

Choosing his words with care, he said, "I propose to fire a second laser beam at a planet that is already doomed if we do nothing. If we fail, we do no harm. If we succeed, we save the planet, the colony, and with it the Federation's control of perhaps the most valuable resource in the galaxy. I believe the idea has enough merit to at least do a feasibility study."

McCoy cocked his head to the side. Listening to inner voices, perhaps. But whatever they told him, they were apparently on Spock's side. "All right," McCoy said. "I agree that the *concept* has merit. But even if you could fire a second beam with enough precision to do the job, we can't build the laser in the time we've got left. We'd have to drag a comet down here ahead of it, cut it in half, silver it, build the light source . . . it can't be done. Not in three days."

"You are correct," Spock said, powering up the sensor array.

"Look, I'm telling you—what?"

"Your logic is impeccable. We will do it another way."

"I . . . how?"

"I do not yet know, but the sooner you allow me to begin experimentation, the sooner I will."

"Oh. Right." McCoy shook his head as if he were trying to coax a different answer out of it, but at last he took a few steps toward the door. He turned around halfway there. "Do sleep on it before you do anything drastic, okay?"

"I will," Spock promised. As he watched the doctor leave the science lab, he vowed to keep that promise, too. But he had made no promise regarding how long he would sleep.

Chapter Twenty-eight

SCOTTY LOOKED sadly at the immense starship before him. He was in one of the shuttles, coasting backwards nearly five kilometers ahead of her in orbit, but even from that distance the damage was obvious. Half the ship was still its normal light gray, but the other half was the pearlescent silver of bare hull. Tiny specks of light on the silver side showed where work crews were busy repairing the damage, but Scotty knew they were only patching holes. There was more damage inside that couldn't be fixed, not this far from a starbase. They were at the far end of a tenuous supply chain, and they could only stockpile so much equipment.

He cursed Vellyngaith, cursed the laser the Kauld had built, cursed the damage it had done to Scotty's beautiful ship. So the very notion of sitting here in space and waiting for the signal to fire *another* laser at her felt like betrayal of the worst sort.

Still, Spock had the only plan going. It had about as much chance of working as an arrow had of stopping a cannonball, but if the cannonball was on its way, he supposed the archer might as well shoot. A last act of defiance if nothing else.

Besides, Scotty had set the shuttlecraft's laser to a tiny fraction of its maximum-rated power. At this setting, it would barely warm the *Enterprise*'s hull even if it missed the target: a light sensor mounted dead square in the middle of the deflector array. Scotty wondered how valid a test this would be of their ability to cancel out a beam of the strength that was bearing down on them, but he supposed they had to start somewhere.

The Vulcan's voice came over the comm. "Ready here, Mr. Scott."

"Aye," Scotty replied, reaching for the firing stud. "Here goes nothin'."

The laser fired, and in the same instant the interior of the shuttle lit up with grainy red light. Scotty had scattered a couple kilograms of atomic iron dust on his way out here so the ship's sensors could track the light beams, but the scatter shouldn't have been anything like this.

"Hey!" he yelled. "You hit *me!*"

"That shouldn't have happened," Spock said.

"You're darn tootin' it shouldn't!" Scotty said, blinking rapidly and watching the afterimages flash in his field of vision. That had been *bright*.

"What was your energy setting?" Spock asked.

Scotty read the digital meter. "One watt, just like we agreed."

"My beam was one watt as well. Wavelength?"

"Six hundred nanometers."

"Mine also. They should have cancelled—wait a moment."

"What?"

"Mine apparently *did* cancel yours. Unless you missed the target."

"I can shoot a laser, laddiebuck."

Spock took a moment before he replied. "Let's run the test again."

"Just a sec." Scotty polarized the window to cut down on the glare if he was hit again, then made doubly sure he was aimed at the target. "Ready."

"Fire at will."

He pressed the stud again. Brilliant light flooded the cabin for just an instant; not as bad as before, but only because of the polarizing filter. The *Enterprise*'s beam had hit him again.

"Interesting," Spock said.

"I still got zapped over here. Did my beam get cancelled out again?"

"I don't believe it did either time. Yours seems to have disappeared before mine reached it."

Scotty rubbed his eyes. "Not to contradict you, but that's flat-out impossible, isn't it?"

"Apparently not," Spock said.

Scotty thought through the stages of the test. When he fired his laser, Spock's souped-up subspace scanner would detect the energy pulse as the leading edge of the beam plowed through the dust. It would return a very faint but detectable subspace echo that would pinpoint the advancing beam long before it reached the ship. That would trigger the *Enterprise*'s return beam, which should have met Scotty's beam head-on. Normally that would do no good, since light beams have to be travelling in the same direction to interfere with one another, but they had used an old trick known as temporal waveform inversion to make the outgoing wave look like an incoming wave. And since the two were out of phase and had the same power level, they should have cancelled each other out.

Okay, so where in that process could Scotty's beam have been cancelled out prematurely?

"It's got to be your scanner pulse," he said. "That's the only other thing that's hitting my incoming beam."

"There is also the dust," Spock reminded him.

"Aye, but we've been firing lasers through dust for centuries and nobody's ever had one disappear on 'em before. Not at this thin a density."

"It does seem unlikely that the dust is the cause," Spock admitted. "That would leave the questing beam, as you say."

There were a few seconds of silence as both men tried to puzzle out what was going on. Scotty watched the *Enterprise* floating before him in space while his mind soared farther and farther away . . . but his thoughts swooped back to the present when Spock said, "Neutrinos?"

"What about neutrinos?"

"When I first tried an olivium-enhanced scanner, I detected a large pulse of neutrinos every time I sent out a signal. I was unable to determine where the neutrinos were coming from. What if they were ordinary photons, quantum-shifted by the olivium?"

Scotty tried to imagine how that would work. "That's not just a quantum shift; that's a shift from one kind o' fundamental particle to another."

"Not an uncommon occurrence," Spock reminded him.

"Not in a nuclear reaction, maybe, but in free space it certainly is." Scotty chewed his lower lip in thought, then said, "We ought to be able to test that theory easily enough. Set up your receiver to look for neutrinos, and

I'll fire another laser at you. If the neutrino count spikes when I shoot, we'll know that's it."

He could hear Spock tinkering with the circuitry, then, "Ready."

"Here we—wait a second." Scotty stopped with his finger poised over the button. "Have you shut off *your* laser? There's no need o' me getting blinded for this one."

"Good point. The laser is now off-line."

"Here goes." Scotty fired the laser. This time he could see the beam lance out toward the *Enterprise*, but it never connected. About a third of the way between the shuttle and the starship, the bright red thread of light simply faded out.

"Neutrino burst detected," Spock said.

"Let's try a patterned pulse," Scotty said, "just to make sure it's not coincidence." He tapped the fire button once, then twice in quick succession, then three times, then five, then seven, then eleven.

"I am receiving a sequence of prime numbers," Spock said.

"That's what I sent." A sudden thought made Scotty laugh.

"What do you find amusing about prime numbers?" Spock asked.

"I'm thinking about where these neutrinos might wind up. They can travel right through a planet without being absorbed. That sequence of prime numbers could make it halfway across the universe before they finally hit something. Can you imagine what could happen if somebody in another galaxy detects them?"

"They would think they were being hailed by an intelligent entity. Yes, I see the irony."

Scotty frowned. "Spock, you have an uncanny way with words, do you know that?"

"My apologies, Mr. Scott. It was not my intention to insult you. I was merely pointing out the—"

"Aye, never mind." He didn't really care. They had just discovered an unexplained new phenomenon that might just save their collective bacon from the fire. He said, "It looks like we've got a magic transmutation ray that'll turn photons into neutrinos. Are you thinkin' what I'm thinkin'?"

"Unfortunately, the distance between us is too great to allow a mind-meld, but if you are proposing to aim our olivium-enhanced sensor array at the oncoming Kauld laser beam, then the answer is yes. But before we do that, we should test its ability to transmute photon streams at the energy density required."

"Which means shootin' a bigger laser beam at the *Enterprise*."

"That is correct. Also, we should determine whether or not the neutrinos *stay* neutrinos outside of the influence of the modified sensor array."

"You could send a probe out in the opposite direction from me."

"I will do so." Scotty heard Spock tapping at the science lab's control station, then he saw a bright spark shoot away from the back of the *Enterprise* and disappear into warp drive.

"I am steering the probe into position one light-second away," Spock reported. "Checking alignment . . . on station. You may fire when ready."

"I'm setting it at one kilowatt," Scotty said. If a beam of that strength hit the *Enterprise*, it would do some damage to the target, but not to the hull behind it. "Firing." He pressed the fire button.

The streak of red light was much brighter this time,

but it disappeared in the same place as far as he could tell.

"Neutrino burst detected here," said Spock. "Probe data coming in. This is . . . fascinating."

"What?"

"Your laser beam destroyed the probe."

"It turned back into photons?"

"That would seem to be the case."

Scotty slumped back in his chair. So close. For a moment there he had allowed himself to believe that they had found a way to beat the Kauld's superweapon, but it wouldn't work if the beam reappeared the moment it left the influence of the olivium-powered scanners. It would just reappear a few meters underground, and would cook the planet just as well as if it hit from space.

Spock said, "That is not encouraging, but the neutrinos did make it all the way through the *Enterprise*'s primary hull before they reverted to their original state. That implies a definite duration beyond the influence of my sensors. We should experiment with probes closer to the ship and see if we can determine the point at which the transition occurs."

"Aye, that we should," Scotty said. They'd had their moment of serendipity; now it was time to do the science to see if it would amount to anything. It was going to be a long afternoon.

Chapter Twenty-nine

"WAIT A MINUTE," Kirk said. "You want us to do *what?*" He had been at his desk in his briefing room, going over progress reports on the repair and refitting of the colony's starships, when Spock and Scotty had come up from the science lab with the most bizarre cock-and-bull story he'd ever heard.

"Use the deflector array to turn the laser beam into neutrinos," Spock repeated. "Mr. Scott and I have determined the parameters of the effect, and we believe that a sufficient number of olivium-enhanced deflector units can effect a temporary transmutation of the beam long enough to allow it to pass harmlessly through the planet."

Kirk couldn't read the Vulcan's poker face at all. He looked over at Scotty, who was grinning like a rube with four aces. "You actually think this could work?" he asked.

"Yes, sir. I know it sounds a wee bit daft, but we've tested it every which way and it's a real phenomenon."

" 'Wee bit daft' doesn't begin to describe it," Kirk said. "You're asking us to risk every—"

The intercom whistled for attention. Kirk reached out and snapped it on, and Uhura's voice said, "Captain, incoming message from Shucorion."

Oh damn. In all the excitement, he had completely forgotten the Blood leader. "Put him on."

Shucorion's blue face filled the desktop monitor. "Captain! I'm proud to report that we are on our way with your emergency building materials. We've managed to fill your school administrator's request for desks and chairs as well."

"That's, um, that's wonderful," Kirk said. He couldn't tell Shucorion to stay home and save himself the trouble, not on an open channel. He couldn't tell him even on a secure channel, because there were bound to be Kauld spies on board his ships, and he couldn't afford to tip off the Kauld that they had learned about the laser. "When will you arrive?" he asked.

"Two days," Shucorion said.

Just in time for the fireworks. "Wonderful," he said. "Watch out for Kauld ships on the way. We believe they're building up their presence again." That was for any Kauld who might be listening. It didn't give away anything, but if the enemy thought Kirk was expecting them, they might wait until after the laser strike to attack, in the hopes that some of the Federation ships would be taken out by the beam.

"It is the Blood way, to watch out for the Kauld. My thanks for the thought." Shucorion signed off.

Kirk turned his attention back to his senior officers. "As I was saying, 'daft' is too mild a word. You're actually suggesting that we place ourselves in the path of the laser in order to convert it to neutrinos with modified deflectors?"

"Aye," Scotty said, still grinning.

"How many ships do you think you'd need to make it work?"

Scotty lost his smile and held a hand to his lips while he cleared his throat. Kirk stared at him impatiently, waiting for an answer, but it was Spock who said, "All of them."

Those three words hung like a soap bubble between them. Kirk spoke first. "You mean all of the fighters."

Scotty found his voice. "No, sir. He means every ship we have left. Even the Conestogas and tugs. We need them all to cover the area of the beam."

"Couldn't the *Enterprise* and a few other ships make multiple passes through it?"

Scotty and Spock exchanged glances.

Kirk recognized that look. This wasn't going to be good news. "What? Out with it."

"The effect is temporary," Spock said. "It lasts for less than a tenth of a second before the neutrinos turn back into photons."

"A tenth of a second!" Kirk's jaw dropped.

Scotty said, "It doesn't sound like much, but light— and neutrinos—travel thirty thousand kilometers in a tenth of a second. More than far enough to pass through the planet."

"But we'd have to wait until just before the beam hit," Kirk protested.

"That is correct," said Spock.

Kirk digested this new information. It would mean the end of the evacuation. There would be no point in putting everyone on the ships, then putting the ships right back in the path of destruction. He was faced with an either/or situation. He looked back at Spock and asked, "What are the odds that we'll succeed?"

"Approximately two point three to one."

"For or against?"

"Against. A great deal of the uncertainty depends upon the timing of the Kauld invasion. If left to our own devices, our odds of success become nearly even."

Even those weren't the odds he was hoping for, but they were frankly better than the odds of successfully getting everyone off the planet and all the way back to Federation space. And it certainly beat running away with their tails between their legs.

"Get ready to move on this, but find a way to do it with fewer ships. The Kauld aren't likely to leave us alone once they see that their laser beam isn't hitting the planet, so we're going to need some defense capability."

"Aye," said Scotty. "There's truth in that. We'll see what we can do."

"Good. Now if you will excuse me, I have to do a little adjusting of the governor's vision of events here. I'll get back to you."

As Scotty and Spock left the briefing room, Kirk took a deep breath to steel himself for the call he would make to Pardonnet. Once the man got moving on a plan, it was nearly impossible to get him to switch horses in midstream. That was generally considered a virtue, but sometimes Pardonnet's determination bordered on the hidebound.

Well, Kirk would just have to ruffle his hide.

He toggled the intercom. "Lieutenant Uhura, get me Governor Pardonnet."

"Yes, sir."

The screen blanked out while she made the connection, then Pardonnet's harried visage appeared. "What now, Captain?" he demanded. He rustled the sheets of paper on his desk, pointedly letting him know how busy he was.

"Good news for a change," said Kirk. "You wanted an alternative to evacuation; my science officer and chief engineer have come up with one."

That got his attention. "What kind of alternative?"

"They've discovered how to turn the laser into neutrinos, which will pass harmlessly through the planet before turning back into photons on the far side."

"They . . . have?" Pardonnet didn't look any more credulous than Kirk had been at first.

"They have. Problem is, it's going to take every ship we've got, including the Conestogas, and it requires putting them right in the path of the beam. We won't have a Plan B if anything goes wrong."

"That's unacceptable," Pardonnet said. "I won't risk my people to a mad scientist's experiment."

"That's what I told Mr. Spock. Good enough, then; we'll continue the evacuation. That will be a lot easier for us, anyway. I just didn't want to make your decision for you without at least giving you the chance to think it over."

"Chance to think it over?" Pardonnet said indignantly. "You just told me about it!"

"And you've already made your customary snap judgement," Kirk replied. "As I expected, and quite frankly, as I was counting on. Sorry, but I've got it recorded in case you start complaining later when the going gets tough."

Pardonnet's face turned red. "Now just one damned minute! I refuse to be railroaded here. I demand to hear the details of this plan before you so blithely assume what my response will be."

"It's a moot point," Kirk said. "You've already decided."

"I have not! Give me enough information to make an informed decision, *then* I'll decide."

Kirk gave a theatrical sigh, then described what Spock and Scotty had found. "Trouble is," he concluded, "we have to wait until literally the last second before we start the conversion process, and even then we can't protect the moon. The neutrinos will turn back into photons well before they reach it. It won't set the olivium off, but we'll lose our mining facilities there for sure."

That was the icing on the cake for Pardonnet. He had never wanted the mining operation to begin with; his interest was in the colony. Still, he made a great show of thinking it over before he finally said, "I understand that sacrifices may have to be made, but this plan does at least preserve the colony."

"Provided it works," Kirk said.

"Yes, yes, provided. But whatever I may think of your priorities, I have learned that you do at least take your job seriously. Protecting the lives of the colonists is your job, and if you thought this was more dangerous than evacuation, then you wouldn't have suggested it." He looked straight at Kirk, trying for the image of a stern conscience. "If you think this will work, then it's your duty to do it, no matter how difficult it may be."

"I see," said Kirk. "And that's your final word."

"Yes."

Another theatrical sigh. Then he nodded and said, "All right. I'll put Spock and Scotty to work on the modifications to the Conestogas. You'll have to offload whatever supplies you've stowed already. We'll need those ships light and maneuverable. And you'd better beam back anything you've parked in space."

"That, ah, won't be a problem," Pardonnet said.

Kirk bet it wouldn't. He hadn't beamed anything up yet. He'd been too busy "organizing" things. Kirk didn't say anything about that; he had gotten what he wanted from the governor. "All right, then. We'll do it your way. Kirk out."

He looked out the viewport at the planet below. Two days. Sighing for real this time, he picked up the status reports and began sifting through the ship rosters, trying to decide which ships to put on the firing line and which to reserve for battling the Kauld; but he had hardly begun the process before the intercom whistled and Lieutenant Uhura said, "Incoming transmission from Lilian Coates."

He felt a lump rise in his throat. He hadn't called her since he'd returned. He swallowed, then said, "Put her through."

She looked even worse than Pardonnet. She had evidently been spending her time actually working as well as organizing the evacuation.

"I assume you've heard the word?" he asked her.

A puzzled expression crossed her face. "What word? I just called to talk to you about logistics. I need to know what to pack into which ships."

"We're . . . not evacuating after all."

She blinked a couple of times. "Oh. I see. How long have you known this?"

"About two minutes. I just talked with Pardonnet."

"Oh. How did he convince you to let him stay? Isn't there a death ray headed right for us?"

Kirk nodded. "There is, but we think we know how to stop it."

"You think."

"We're pretty sure. It worked when we tested it." He described to her what they were planning to do.

She listened quietly, then when he was done she said, "And we're supposed to just wait down here at ground zero to see if it works?"

"It wouldn't make any sense to put the colonists into the Conestogas," he told her, "because the Conestogas are going to be right in front of the laser, too. So is the *Enterprise*. I'm stationing it right over Buena Vista." He hadn't realized he was going to do that until he heard the words coming out of his own mouth, but he instantly knew it was the right choice. The only way anything would happen to the colony's largest town would be if the *Enterprise* went up in smoke first.

She didn't say anything, just looked at him, biting her lower lip.

"If you'd like, you can ride it out up here with us. It won't be any safer, but I'd be glad to have you aboard."

She shook her head. "It wouldn't look good. Whether it's any safer or not, people would think I was trying to save my own skin at their expense. And they'd jump to conclusions about us."

Kirk almost said, "Let them," but he realized it wasn't that simple. Not for her. This was a frontier society, and she ran the schools; if there was even a hint of impropriety, she could find herself in serious trouble. He suddenly realized the risk she had taken in simply spending a day with him, much less most of a night. Thank heavens he had beamed out of her living room rather than simply walking out her front door in the morning.

"That would make things difficult for you," he acknowledged. "I'm ... sorry if I've complicated your life."

240

That brought a faint smile to her face. "Don't apologize. Some complications are worth the trouble."

"And others aren't," he said. "I do apologize about the wild-goose chase, but I really did think we were going to have to evacuate until just a few minutes ago."

She nodded. "I hope this is the right decision."

"Me too," he told her. "Me too."

That brought a faint smile to her face. "It'll work
nice. So and nice," she murmured with joy, thanks.
"And so so well," he said. "I do not figure out
he will work close. She literary did pack so well
along to luckless environmental just a few minutes ago,
she added. "I hope this is the right motion."
"As for this and not," He told ...

Chapter Thirty

"YOU MEAN this is it?" Scotty asked Kirk, as the captain delivered the specs of all the ships that were available for modification. "Not to be ungrateful, sir, but I dinna know how we're going to cover the entire area with only twenty-four ships. At the power levels we can sustain, the transmutation effect is only good for about a thousand kilometers on a side."

Scotty leaned back in his chair and felt the vertebrae between his shoulders pop. He'd been bent over his workstation in engineering for hours now, coordinating the efforts of his crew.

With a shrug, Kirk said, "We have to make do with what we have." He pointed to the top left corner of the data pad and added, "These ships have essential systems missing. Pardonnet started dismantling them for ground shelter before I could stop him. And I have to hold some ships back for defense. The ones on the front line are going to be sitting ducks for twenty minutes."

Scotty pulled up the schematics and studied the revisions. "Aye, you're right about that, but except for the *Greeley,* none of the others are missing their deflector arrays. There's no need for engines; we can tow 'em into place and they'll be usable as they are."

"Good. That gives you thirty-two ships. Will that be enough?"

Scotty didn't know. There would be practically no overlap in coverage that way. If even one ship failed, a section of the laser beam a couple thousand kilometers across could reach the planet's surface. That was only three percent of the total area, but could Belle Terre survive even that much damage to its ecosystem? "I guess it'll have to," he said.

"How are the modifications going?"

Scotty stretched his arms out in front of him and said, "I have sixteen teams out on as many ships installing Mr. Spock's modified sensors. We've had crews working constantly on producing and testing the new units—"

"How are you *testing* these units?" Kirk asked, his brows knotted over the bridge of his nose.

"Carefully," Scott answered, deadpan.

Kirk looked at him in silence a moment longer and finally said, "Good."

Scotty couldn't remain straightfaced. He cracked a smile and said, "Not to worry, Captain. We've taken every precaution. Just because we're short on time doesn't mean we've taken leave of our senses."

Kirk smiled back, then said as he headed toward the door, "I'm glad to see you can still maintain a sense of humor. Keep me posted on your progress."

"Aye, sir."

Scotty's smile faded as he turned back to the roster of ships. It was going to be a long shift getting everything installed and tested.

He returned to his schematics. There were so many kinds of ships and just as many different sensor arrays that he and his crew had to be able to manipulate in order to get everything to work properly. Fortunately Lieutenant Hanson was in charge of tuning the units after the installation crew finished. She seemed the likely candidate for the job, since she had had so much experience recalibrating the sensors on the *Enterprise* while Mr. Spock had them tied up in his experiments. Besides, she did a good job of keeping focused on the problems at hand.

There were plenty of those to go around. Scotty had originally planned to adapt the most defendable, maneuverable ships, leaving the slow Conestogas and tugs to take as many evacuees as possible and get them out of the line of fire. But when Spock finished his calculations, it had become obvious that there could be no evacuation—every ship was needed in the front line to face the laser. That meant that *every* ship needed modifying. Some of these buckets of bolts barely had the sophistication of a handcart, and he was supposed to turn them into antilaser defense platforms.

His communicator beeped. "Lieutenant Hanson to Mr. Scott."

"Scott here. What is it, Lieutenant?"

"I'm on the *Hudson,* trying to finish the calibration on the new sensors."

"Trying?"

"We're getting background interference. Nothing I've tried takes care of it."

Background interference? "Did you check the phase rotation?"

"First thing."

"The inverter angle?"

"It checks out."

"It's not Gamma Night, or I wouldn't be hearing from you."

"Obviously."

"Have ye checked the leads? It's not installed backwards, is it?"

She let a note of exasperation creep into her voice. "I can tell red wires from black. It's installed correctly."

"Check the sensor itself. Are there any physical anomalies in the antenna array?"

"Negative."

"How about—"

"Excuse me, sir, but I've run down the entire troubleshooting list. I'm at the point where I have to call tech support. Tag. You're it."

He sighed heavily and said, "I'll be right there, Lieutenant. Scott out."

The change would do him some good, he supposed. Get out, stretch his legs a bit. He left orders with Ensign Young to start replacing the missing deflector on the *Greeley,* and headed for the transporter room.

By now, Scotty's face had become well known to most of the other ships' engineers over the duration of the mission. They had to work together, and though some at first had felt insulted that Scotty had authority to go in and tell them what to do, most of them were becoming good friends. This wasn't the case with the *Hudson*'s crew, the most sullen-faced group to pilot a supply ship this side of the Alpha Quadrant. The head engineer, a big burly man from the Martian Settlements by the name of Jonder, had never accepted Scotty as his superior.

The *Enterprise*'s transporter room faded away to be replaced with the *Hudson*'s unkempt, cramped equivalent. As soon as the confinement beam released him, Scotty's nose was assaulted with a sour odor.

"My God, what's wrong with your environmental controls?" he asked the transport tech.

"Sorry sir," the young man replied. "The ventilation has been off-line for a couple of days now. Jonder's been too busy realigning the warp coils to get to it."

"He could ha' asked for help. I could have sent somebody from the *Enterprise* to work on it for you."

The technician snickered. "No offense, sir, but I doubt that the idea ever crossed his mind."

Scotty rolled his eyes and shook his head. "I suppose you're right. Well, if my crew has to work on board, ye'll have breathable air." He flipped open his communicator. "Scott to Ensign Young."

"Young here."

"Ensign, the *Hudson* is in need of environmental repair. Send over someone who can fix it quickly."

"Aye, sir."

Scotty hung his communicator back on his belt. "That ought to do it," he said to the technician, then he left the transporter room for the ship's engineering level.

He found Hanson sitting cross-legged on the floor by the main deflector electronics housing. Her short hair was once again in disarray from her habit of running her fingers through it while she thought. She'd apparently been doing a lot of thinking.

"Any luck, Lieutenant?"

"No sir. I've uninstalled it, reinstalled it, run every known diagnostic on it, reinstalled it backwards on purpose, and just now I installed a whole new unit. All to no avail."

Over his shoulder, Scotty heard Jonder's nasty laugh. "What's the matter, Mr. Scott? Can't getcher toy to run?"

Scotty's already tight shoulder muscles tensed further. He didn't have time to get into an argument today. "I canna take credit for this one," Scotty said. He certainly couldn't. The device was wholly the work of Mr. Spock. He'd be hard pressed to explain its basic premise, let alone the intricate details of how it worked. What he did know was how to install and debug them. He hoped.

"Oh, don't be modest. And don't be shy. If you need help I'll be over here with the warp engines." Jonder walked away, laughing. The man obviously hadn't been told what the modifications to his ship were for, or he wouldn't have that cocky grin on his face.

Scotty watched him leave, the tension in his neck leaving with him. He turned back to the problem at hand. "Let's see what's going on here," he said as he waved his tricorder over the recalcitrant sensor, flipping from scale to scale to check its various subsystems in operation.

Lieutenant Hanson's assessment was correct. The unit appeared to be functioning properly, but the signal-to-noise ratio was atrocious. No amount of adjusting could clean up the dirty background.

Scotty had been leaning over the whole time; now he sat down on the deck with his back against a support beam and wiped his brow with his forearm. Either someone from the *Enterprise* had already fixed the ventilation, or he had grown used to the smell, but that didn't take care of the heat down here in engineering. He looked over at Lieutenant Hanson, who looked just as uncomfortable as he felt. "As Mr. Spock would say, there's got to be a logical explanation for this," he said.

Hanson smiled weakly. "Great. Maybe *he* should come on over and join the party."

"Let's give it a minute before we call him. It's time to think about what the diagnostics are tellin' us." He stood up with a groan. "I'm not as young as I was last week. I've got to get up and stretch my legs a wee bit." He headed out the engineering room door and down the corridor, meaning to walk its length a time or two and study his tricorder readings, but the instrument's display flickered like a bad light fixture. He'd hate to think that *it* was on the blink.

He ran a self-diagnostic check, then a background check. Then he ran it again. The energy readings were astronomical. He rushed back to engineering and down to the warp controls. "Mr. Jonder, what has the *Hudson* been doing lately?"

Jonder turned from his console to face Scotty with a scowl. "What do you mean, what have we been doing? Working hard, I'll tell you."

"I don't doubt that, man. I merely want to know what it is that ye've been working hard *at.*"

"We've been loading up ore, that's what."

"Olivium . . . ore?"

"None other. We were almost full, too. Woulda been on our way back home by now if your captain hadn't stopped us." He turned away from Scotty.

Well, *that* would explain the interference. "Ye gods, man. We canna have you full of olivium on the front line. Tell your captain he'll have to unload."

"Tell him yourself."

The insolence of this man was unbelievable. "I'll do you one better." Scotty grabbed his communicator. "Scott to *Enterprise.*"

Uhura answered, *"Enterprise* here, go ahead."

"Tell the captain that we've got a bombship in our midst."

The briefest of pauses passed before Kirk said, "Scotty, what's going on?"

"I just found out that the *Hudson*'s cargo hold is full of olivium ore. It's playing havoc with the new sensors and it'll play more havoc if it gets hit during battle."

"Understood. I'll have a word with her captain. Kirk out."

Scotty closed his communicator and hung it back on his belt. A glance in Hanson's direction confirmed his suspicion. She shook from the effort of suppressing laughter.

Jonder wasn't laughing. "Front lines? Hit during battle? I thought we were preparing for an evacuation."

"And you figured a few tons of olivium ore wouldn't take up that much extra room, eh?" Scotty shook his head. "Be glad we caught it, or you'd have gone up in a flash o' light to rival the Big Bang, and probably taken the rest of us with you."

He helped Hanson pick up her tools. When she appeared to be in control of herself again, he said, "Lieutenant, why don't we move on to the next ship and leave these kind gentlemen to their unloading. You can come back when they're finished."

She smiled and said, "I'd be delighted."

Well, he thought as they walked to the transporter room, *on to the next problem.*

Chapter Thirty-one

DR. MCCOY took a deep breath of the fresh evening air as he walked down the main street of Buena Vista. It had rained earlier that day; nothing much, but enough to knock down the dust and the afternoon heat. Now a couple of dozen people walked along the sidewalks, coming and going from shops and public buildings. No one hurried. There was no sign of trouble, no sign that anything was wrong unless a person looked closely.

Up close he could see the chinks in the façade. Nobody was smiling. Their purchases tended to be luxury items: bottles of genuine Earth vintage wine, caviar, cultured roses. McCoy would have liked to think that people were planning to celebrate the great victory over the Kauld's sneak attack, but he suspected most of that wine and food would be gone before midnight.

Five hours and counting. In five hours and a couple of minutes, everyone would either be celebrating for real or vaporized. Including McCoy. He had decided he would be more use on the planet's surface than in orbit. If through some miracle Spock's crazy notion worked, there was a great potential for injury from the very revelry that would erupt in the wake of the threat. And if it didn't work—well, McCoy would have preferred to end his days with his friends on board the *Enterprise,* but he could take what little comfort there was in knowing that he would only outlive them by one four-thousandth of a second before the laser beam got him, too.

A few colonists were hiding in a cave a few kilometers up the valley. Others had roofed their houses in bright metallic foil. The universe had no shortage of fools, he thought, but he had to admit that the glittering foil provided interesting punctuation to the sunset that slowly stretched out from the western sky.

There was one other sign of the recent trouble. Everyone's garden looked abandoned. Apparently nobody had thought it worthwhile to water them if they were just going to leave them behind anyway. McCoy wouldn't have guessed that the plants would be so fragile that they would show the neglect so quickly, but he wasn't a gardener.

He looked at the school as he passed it. The windows were dark. Everyone was home with their families, waiting to see what would happen.

The hospital, in contrast, was brightly lit and busy. Fortunately, most of the people were coming and going from the cafeteria wing, not the medical wing. It would be hours before the traffic shifted over, if it ever did. But if that happened, McCoy and Dr. Neville and the rest of the staff were ready.

He entered the cafeteria himself, joining the line of people waiting for food. Might as well stoke up for the long night. It looked like everyone else had the same idea, too. The hospital cafeteria was one of the biggest meeting halls in town, and it had the added advantage of hot food. Reynold Coates waved to him from a table in the corner, and he waved back. When he had filled his tray with steak and vegetables and a slice of chocolate cake for dessert, he went on over and sat down beside the boy. Lilian was sitting across from him with her back to the room; he hadn't realized it was her until he sat down.

"May I?" he asked.

"Of course," she replied.

"How're you feeling?" he asked Reynold.

"Fine, sir," Reynold replied. "I think I must have just swallowed some muddy water or something."

"Or something," McCoy agreed. "Well, I'm glad nothing came of it."

"Me too."

McCoy turned to his food for a moment, asking between bites, "So, Lilian, how're *you* feeling?"

She smiled faintly. "You mean aside from being scared to death?"

He looked into her eyes. If she was scared, she sure didn't show it. "I mean how are you coping with all this back-and-forth business? Gearing up to go back home, then being told you have to stay put." That was as much as he could say in front of her son, but she had to know what he was really talking about.

"It's been difficult," she said. "I thought I would be happy to go, after all we've been through, but when it came time to pack I started to realize just how much of myself I've planted here. And your advice to get out and do something fun helped me put things in perspective a little bit, too."

"She went flying with Captain Kirk!" Reynold said loudly. Lilian blushed, and Reynold lowered his voice conspiratorially to whisper to McCoy, "I think she's sweet on him."

"Reynold!" she said. "I don't go around telling everyone you're sweet on Kelly Taylor."

"Mom!"

"Oh, I'm sorry, was that a secret?"

McCoy laughed. She certainly had mothering down to a science.

He also noticed that she hadn't denied her affection for the captain. What was it with him, anyway? McCoy had watched him woo his way across half the Alpha Quadrant, and he still didn't understand how Kirk did it. He'd gone so far as to check him for pheremones during a routine medical evaluation, but there had been no sign of anything unusual about him. The man simply attracted women the way a light attracts moths.

If it had been anyone else, McCoy might have felt jealous. Hell, maybe just this once he did feel a little bit jealous. He had grown fond of Lilian himself during their months of contact. He'd come to care about her welfare. Yet when he had encouraged her to go out and live a little, who was the first person she had turned to?

It was a mystery. If he and Kirk were together another twenty years, he would probably never figure it out.

He hoped he would have the chance to try. While he sliced another piece of steak, the lights flickered, and the voices in the cafeteria all stilled for a moment. He knew what everyone was thinking.

Gamma Night. Four hours and thirty minutes before impact.

253

Chapter Thirty-two

IT'S AMAZING *what lasers can do,* Kirk thought as he watched the fleet of colony ships assemble in space between Belle Terre and its olivium moon. They were in the thick of Gamma Night now. Radio was useless, both the normal and the subspace variety, but the ships stayed linked through message lasers beamed directly from ship to ship. It was a cumbersome system that required constant adjusting for position, but it worked like a charm when it worked, and it had one big advantage: the Kauld couldn't listen in on their transmissions.

He knew they were out there, hovering at the edge of the system and watching to see how their plan was progressing. Every few minutes a lookout would report a ship warping in close to Belle Terre for an instant before disappearing again, physically entering the gamma-blocked section of the solar system to gather information and then warping back out to report to the rest of the Kauld fleet.

Hopefully, what they saw would both puzzle and trouble them. Kirk had assembled his ships on the wrong side of the planet! The fact that he was hiding in the planet's shadow gave away the fact that he knew about the oncoming laser beam, but it must look damned strange for him to be hiding there without even attempting to evacuate or even shield the colonists on the exposed side. It could only mean that he had been caught by surprise, and was desperately saving his own skin.

Would they make the next logical conclusion, as Governor Pardonnet had?

Kirk looked at the time. Only ten minutes left. The Kauld weren't taking the bait.

Time for Plan B. "Mr. Sulu, the moment the next Kauld observer warps into range, fire a low-yield photon torpedo at the moon."

"At the moon, not the Kauld ship, sir?" Sulu asked.

"That's right."

The miners had been evacuated hours ago. Most of their equipment was on the farside, where the impact that caused the Burn had exposed raw olivium veins. A photon torpedo fired from this angle would hardly damage a thing, but the Kauld wouldn't know that. They would just see a big flash, and would think that Kirk was destroying the moon so they couldn't have it.

Uhura, listening to the field reports, announced, "Kauld ship." Sulu hit the fire button, and a bright ball of light shot out from the *Enterprise,* illuminating the moon's dark night side with its approach and impacting on the rough gray surface in a bright explosion.

"Kauld ship just warped out," Uhura said.

Kirk felt his heartbeat start to rise. This was it. "All

ships, battle stations," he said. "Shields to maximum. Engage the enemy until T minus one minute, then take your positions on the laser side of the planet. Nonmodified defenders, continue engaging the enemy until T minus five seconds, then get to safety." That was cutting it close, but it was the only way to play this one. They couldn't give the Kauld time to react.

He barely had time to give the orders. Space was suddenly filled with battleships. The computer immediately began identifying targets, and it quickly became clear that the entire fleet had warped in at once. Even Vellyngaith's command ship had joined the party.

The Federation ships leaped into action, firing and dodging, firing and dodging, sometimes warping out for mere milliseconds, then reappearing behind the enemy and firing again. Phaser fire splayed across enemy shields, pinpointing weaknesses and overloading them one after another, leaving the ships wide open for the next shot to rupture the hull.

The Kauld weren't having nearly as much luck hitting the Federation ships. Of course they didn't have the advantage the Federation had, either: nearly half an hour of sensor readings of their enemy's fleet in action during their most recent war games. Kirk had distributed Scotty and McCoy's surveillance information to all his ships, and the captains and gunners had all pored over it to learn the Kauld strategy, capability, and soft spots.

Space filled with debris as ship after ship erupted in fiery balls of destruction. There was no communication now; not even Uhura could keep track of targets that kept warping in and out of normal space every few seconds.

Not surprisingly, the *Enterprise* was the Kauld's biggest target. Sulu and Thomsen flew the immense starship like an atmospheric fighter, swooping, banking, and corkscrewing around the attackers while simultaneously pounding them with phaser fire and the occasional photon torpedo. The viewscreen filled with images of Belle Terre's day side, blue oceans and white sky shining brightly, then the dark of space, then the planet again, as the starship took evasive action. The shields flared every few seconds, their power ratings steadily dropping, but the Kauld paid dearly for every shot.

Vellyngaith's flagship dogged them through every maneuver, but the three new olivium-powered ships were a worse threat. If Kirk hadn't watched them in action, he would have been hard pressed to fight even one of them. As it was, they more than made up for his strategic advantage with sheer speed and power. The Enterprise shuddered under blow after blow from their disruptors, and warning alarms began sounding at the engineering and life-support stations. Kirk ordered return fire with everything he had, but when their captains realized that the *Enterprise* wasn't giving up easily, all three of the new ships focused their attack on it at once.

"Phasers, wide spread," Kirk ordered as the ships swooped in from three different directions. "Blind them." Everyone was limited to optical maneuvering here; not even the new ships could see to navigate through a flaring shield. Even as the phasers were reaching out, he said, "Keep firing, and fire photon torpedoes on the one dead ahead. Full salvo. Hit 'em while they're blind."

A string of bright stars shot out toward the enemy ship, each one impacting on the shields in the same spot. Not even olivium-enhanced generators could withstand that many hits; the third shot flared through, and the fourth one buried itself deep in the ship itself before exploding and ripping it into two ragged halves.

The fifth and sixth torpedoes raced right through the debris and onward toward the *Hudson* until Sulu detonated them remotely.

"Two minutes to laser impact," Spock said from his science station.

Had it been eight minutes already since the start of battle? It felt more like eight seconds, but Kirk knew how time could telescope in a fight. "Rush the moon," he said. "Let's look like we mean to destroy it."

Sulu turned the *Enterprise* toward the pocked gray surface and accelerated at one-quarter impulse power. The other ships, taking their cue, all turned toward it as well. The Kauld ships in front of them pulled together into what looked like a solid wall of defense, while the ones behind poured fire into the Federation ships' aft shields. The Federation returned fire in both directions, giving it everything they had for another sixty seconds and blasting at least a dozen more Kauld out of space, then Spock said, "One minute," and Kirk said, "Hard around to the far side! Go, go, go!"

The *Enterprise* swooped into warp drive. Sulu guided the ship around the planet in a precalculated arc, bringing them out just a thousand kilometers above the surface and directly in the path of the oncoming laser. There was nothing to be seen yet, of course, not in visual wavelengths, but Spock was ready with his modified sensors and he instantly took a reading. "Forty-five seconds to impact," he said.

Forty-five light-seconds ahead of them, a patch of the laser beam quantum-shifted into neutrinos, then a tenth of a second later shifted back to photons. At least Kirk hoped it had. If it hadn't, everyone was in deep trouble.

Thomsen quickly checked the *Enterprise*'s location

with respect to optical beacons on the ground, and Sulu flew them the few hundred kilometers it took to put them directly over Buena Vista.

"Other ships are taking up position," Uhura said. Kirk wished he could see what was going on on the other side of the planet, but without subspace sensors, he was blind. That worked both ways, though; so were the Kauld. From their point of view, the *Enterprise* and most of her support ships had just fled the battle; even if Vellyngaith had stationed observers on this side of Belle Terre—a suicidal proposition—they would never spot the Federation ships against the night side of the planet. And the remaining ships were still fighting, leading the Kauld into a tight knot between Belle Terre and the moon while their captains counted down the last few seconds.

"Ten." Spock said. "Deflectors on line. Five. Four. Three. Two. Now." He hit the manual override button in the same instant that the computer triggered the enhanced sensor beam.

Kirk held his breath. Enough energy to vaporize him was pouring right through his body, but neutrinos reacted so poorly with normal matter that all but the tiniest fraction of them passed right through—and right through the planet as well. There would have been no sign that anything at all was happening if the *Enterprise* hadn't salted the beam front with its impulse drive exhaust four days earlier; but those ions were still being pushed along by the front of the beam, and they hadn't turned into neutrinos. They had been accelerated almost to light speed, but not quite; they lagged behind by a couple of seconds, just long enough to let the crew begin exhaling before a sudden wall of gas slammed into the *Enterprise,* rocking it backward.

Involuntary screams echoed around the bridge.

"Keep station!" Kirk ordered, and Sulu brought them back into position again.

The night side of Belle Terre momentarily lit up as the gas layer struck the atmosphere, and the ground sparked in places as sections of the laser beam slipped past the suddenly jostled ships, but the light show only lasted a moment. A few thousand square kilometers had just gotten cooked, but it had been nothing like what the full force of the beam would have done.

Kirk imagined what was happening on the other side of the planet. The neutrinos, about a third of the way between planet and moon, would turn back into photons, which would slam at full intensity into the remains of the Kauld fleet, who would have stayed put, thinking they would be safe in the shadow of the planet.

That mental picture burst like a balloon when Uhura said, "Shipboard spotters report Kauld vessels appearing ten to fifteen thousand kilometers to the side of the beam."

"They jumped away," Kirk growled.

"Some of them did," Uhura said. "We're only spotting about half of the ones we left behind, and most of those are badly burned."

"Good." They were well outside the path of the laser beam, he noted, but they must be curious as hell about why it was cooking the moon on the other side of the planet and not even in evidence on this side. Let 'em wonder.

Kirk realized that Spock was tapping furiously at his controls and speaking softly on a private channel to engineering. He turned toward the science station. "Spock, is there a problem?"

"I am detecting a 12 percent variation in output

power," the Vulcan replied. "I believe the emitter might have been damaged in the battle."

Before Kirk could say anything about that, Sulu yelled, "Incoming ships!"

"On screen!" Kirk ordered.

The main viewscreen lit up with the view from Sulu's console. On it, three Kauld warships, including one of the new ones, were rushing toward the Federation fleet.

"All ships hold your positions!" Kirk warned. If anyone turned to fight, they would be instantly cooked by the laser beam. They could, on the other hand, narrow the beam they were emitting. . . .

Just as the lead Kauld ship approached within firing range of the Federation ship closest to it, that ship, the privateer *Zavada,* shifted its deflector a few degrees inward. In an instant, the Kauld ship flared brilliant white, then exploded in a shower of melting fragments. It had been just outside the diameter of the planet; the *Zavada*'s maneuver hadn't even exposed the surface to the laser.

The other two Kauld ships veered away, but another one from farther out rushed toward the planet, ducking in low and flying beneath the Federation shield before anyone could maneuver to burn him.

"Aft phasers," Kirk ordered. "All ships concentrate fire on that intruder!"

Two dozen phasers lanced out toward the ship, but without active sensor guidance to lock them on target, only a few hit. The enemy ship snapped off a shot at the *Enterprise* that rocked them sideways, but the shields held.

"Spock, can you angle our deflector to burn that guy?"

"Not at the moment," Spock replied. "Mr. Scott and I are currently having difficulty maintaining emissions at all. If we try to alter the beam, we could destabilize the tuning to the point where the entire system goes down."

Yeow. Kirk felt his heart skip a beat at that news. The deflector had to work for over twenty-one minutes. If it was starting to flake out on them now, they were in big trouble.

The Kauld ship fired again at the *Enterprise,* but three more phaser beams caught it in a crossfire and it veered away before it could do more damage. The phasers didn't destroy it, though, and its success encouraged others to follow it. Soon there were five Kauld ships darting around beneath them, including the new olivium-powered one that had attempted to cross into the beam's path moments before.

Things were getting dicey fast. The Federation ships were sitting ducks; they couldn't budge without letting major sections of the planet burn, and without mobility their fighting capability was severely limited.

"Where are those damned reserve ships?" Kirk demanded. Had they been caught in the beam?

"Unknown," Uhura replied, "but our spotters report twenty more Kauld vessels coming out of warp."

"What? Where did they come from?" The entire Kauld fleet had been committed to the battle. Unless Vellyngaith had held some ships in reserve even from the war games, the ones they had been fighting were the only ones the Kauld had.

Disruptor beams lanced into the fray, but they were aimed at the Kauld ships, not the Federation defenders.

"Disruptor patterns indicate Blood vessels, not Kauld," Spock said. A moment later the viewscreen image swirled around to show twenty ships accelerating hard toward them, and twenty immense cargo containers tumbling free in space behind them.

"Shucorion," Kirk whispered. "That son of a bitch used warships to haul the cargo hulls." He had never been so glad to see an order disobeyed in his life.

Two of the Kauld ships flared and died under the assault. The others blinked out under warp drive, then Uhura said, "We're being hailed."

"Put him on."

Shucorion's smiling face filled a quarter of the viewscreen, while the tactical display remained in place around him. "Greetings, captain," the Blood leader said. "My apologies for shooting first and asking questions later, but it looked as if you were in trouble there. May I ask why your ships are all facing away from the obvious danger?"

"Because we're stopping an even worse one from overhead," Kirk replied. "Whatever you do, don't send any of your ships out beyond our cordon."

"Why not? I see no danger there."

Just then, the Kauld supership warped back into position and fired a full disruptor barrage at the *Zavada*. The ship's shields went down almost instantly, and a moment later the ship itself exploded. There was barely time to blink at the flash before the scene grew brighter still: the section of laser it had been converting blasted through its space unchanged, vaporizing the fragments of starship and slamming into the planet below.

The *Zavada* had been over ocean. Instantly, huge gouts of steam rose up off the water as the surface boiled. The white vapor scattered the beam in all directions, but the lion's share of its energy punched right through. In a few seconds, it would spawn major hurricanes; a few more seconds would change the global climate for years to come.

"All ships, increase power and close up that gap!" Kirk ordered. They had planned for this contingency. There was a little bit of overlap in deflector coverage; now the defenders shifted sideways until that overlap was all but gone, but the combined extension of range was enough to cover the area that had been the *Zavada*'s. The laser light blinked out again, and the ocean below ceased boiling.

"You've convinced me," Shucorion said. "We'll stay well clear of that!"

"Take a look on the other side of the planet," Kirk said. "Something has happened to our support ships over there."

"We'll check into it," Shucorion said. His fleet peeled away, and another video image sprang into place on the main screen as he relayed what his scouts saw: the olivium moon glowing like a magnesium torch under the brunt of the laser, and dozens of tiny specks of light milling around in its starkly defined shadow. Aggressors and defenders had both taken refuge there when the laser hit, and like bugs in a jar, they were fighting one another to the death.

The Blood ships moved closer, cautiously testing the space ahead of them with probes until they found the edge of the laser beam, then they parked just beyond it and opened fire on the Kauld.

Hit from two sides, the Kauld ships were immediately overpowered. Four of them flared and died, and the rest turned and ran. About half of them—including Vellyngaith's flagship—warped away, but the rest used impulse power to flee down the long column of shadow. Their warp nacelles had evidently been damaged in battle or by the beam.

"Let them go," Kirk said. If they couldn't warp out,

they would be easy to catch later. It might even be possible to capture them intact.

But Shucorion wasn't interested in that. His ships kept pounding the Kauld, blasting one after another as they attempted to flee. One veered sideways out of the shadow and instantly flashed into vapor in the laser beam.

"That's enough!" Kirk ordered. "Let them go!"

Shucorion shook his head. "This is my fight," he said. "I will do it my way."

"Damn it, that's not—" Kirk began, but Spock's voice stopped him cold.

"Captain, we have a problem."

Chapter Thirty-three

SPOCK WAS keenly aware of the battle raging around him, and he knew he could probably be of considerable use in a tactical capacity, but he was already fighting a battle with equally serious consequences entirely on board the ship. Something was wrong with the modified sensor array. Power levels were fluctuating, and worse, the signal from the various antenna elements was drifting in and out of phase. Twice the condition had reached the critical point where the photon/neutrino transmutation effect became unstable, and twice he—and Mr. Scott down in engineering—had pulled it back into operational parameters with only moments to spare. Their fixes were only temporary; the oscillations were starting up again, and this time they were building faster than before.

"We are treating the symptoms," he said on his private link to engineering, speaking softly so he wouldn't interfere with the bridge activity around him. "We must find the source of the problem and fix it if we expect the deflector to last another fifteen minutes."

"We're tryin' to!" Scott answered. "I've got people checkin' every circuit between here and the deflector dish, but we're not finding anything wrong. The problem's outside."

"Then you must go outside to fix it."

"Do you have any idea how much energy is pouring through that dish?" Scott asked.

Spock consulted his data displays. "At the moment, 14.6 megawatts, but that is diminishing at an alarming rate. In another 2.5 minutes, the power level will drop below the critical threshold, and we will begin receiving a thousand times that much energy in the form of laser radiation."

"Aye, I can see that," Mr. Scott said. "We'll have to go outside, all right, but we can't do that with the antenna active. We'll have to close up the gap and drop out of formation while we shut 'er down and replace the Klystrons."

Spock tried to think of another way, but after a full ten seconds he came up blank. "You are correct. Prepare for EVA." He looked up at the captain, who was busy arguing with Shucorion. There was no time to spare; he interrupted Kirk in midsentence and said, "Captain, we have a problem."

The captain gave him his full attention. "What is it, Spock?"

"We must stand down and make repairs to the deflector array."

"Stand down? We can't just duck out for repairs. We're shielding Buena Vista!"

"The other ships will have to cover for us. I estimate our down time at no more than three minutes, but if we don't make the repair, we will suffer systems failure before half the beam is past."

Kirk didn't waste time arguing. "All ships," he ordered, "Increase power again and shift to cover the *Enterprise*'s position."

In the exterior view, Spock could see the other ships moving into new positions. He calculated their deflector paths based on their design parameters, and the moment they overlapped, he shut down the *Enterprise*'s array and said to Mr. Scott, "We are covered. Commence your repairs."

"Aye, here goes."

Spock noted transporter activity on the ship's status monitor. Good; Mr. Scott was wasting no time. It was risky during Gamma Night, but it would probably work over such a short distance. Radio wouldn't, though. From outside the ship there would be no progress reports. Spock directed an outer hull camera down at the deflector and zoomed in until he could see four spacesuited figures around the central emitter housing. They didn't bother with the bolts. One of them merely phasered the housing loose and flung it out into space, then all four people leaped upon the Klystrons and began ripping them loose, replacing them with new units that continuously beamed into easy reach beside them.

Then the figures backed away, and a second later they vanished in a sparkle of the transporter beam.

Spock immediately powered the array back up, noting with satisfaction that the phase instability was much less prominent. "That seems to have done it," he said.

"Good," replied Mr. Scott. "Now let's get back into place and finish the job."

"Agreed." Spock relayed the message to the captain, and within seconds they were back on the front line.

"Time?" Kirk asked.

Spock directed the computer to answer. "Ten minutes twenty-four seconds to laser terminus."

They were just under halfway into the beam. Even to Spock, whose time sense was exquisitely accurate, this ordeal had already felt like forever.

He checked his monitors again. "I read a 15.21 percent increase in power. However the focus is not optimal."

"I'm on it," Scotty said.

Suddenly the *Enterprise* lurched, throwing everyone on the bridge from their chairs. Spock grabbed the edge of the console before him and managed to keep upright. He helped Uhura back to her chair, then returned to his station.

"Report!" Kirk ordered as he got up from the floor.

Uhura listened for a moment to her intraship monitor, then said, "We took a hit portside from a Kauld disruptor. It looks like Shucorion must have missed one."

"Shields down twenty-five percent," Sulu said.

"Compensating," Spock said, trading precious energy from the deflector array. They could spare what Mr. Scott had just gained.

Uhura said, "Minor damage restricted to decks seven through nine. No injuries reported."

"Find that Kauld ship," Kirk ordered. "Knock him out before he hits us again."

Shucorion's face vanished off the screen as the tactical display expanded to fill the entire space. It was hard to spot the Kauld against the dark planet below, but the moment they fired again, a streak of red light pointed straight at them. Sulu was ready for them; he swiveled the *Enterprise*'s phasers to the source of the beam and fired at full power. Two other ships did the same, and the night lit up momentarily as the Kauld ship detonated in a bright flash.

"Eight minutes to laser terminus," the computer said.

Spock checked his monitors again. "Deflector efficiency has dropped to ninety-two percent."

"I'll have to recalibrate it, but it'll continue to drop until I'm finished," Scotty warned.

"Understood. I'll boost the power input for the duration."

"Shields down thirty percent," Sulu reported as he did so.

Kirk said, "Thomsen, start routing power from auxiliary sources. We've got to keep both our shields and our deflector going on max."

"Yes, sir."

Spock could feel the humans' anxiety as everyone watched the tactical display for enemy ships. Without their usual sensors, they were clearly distressed, worried about sneak attacks. He wondered if that was an instinctive response to the unknown, learned when their kind huddled in caves at night to avoid nocturnal predators, or if, like him, theirs was an intellectual fear based on a logical assessment of their danger.

The captain said, "Uhura, tell Shucorion to get back over here where he'll do the most good."

"Yes, sir."

"Seven minutes to laser terminus," the computer said.

Spock kept his eyes glued to the internal monitors, watching the power fluctuate to the deflector array. "Mr. Scott, we are still losing stability."

"Hold onto your britches. We're about done here."

The signal degradation continued for two more minutes before it bottomed out at seventy-six percent, then it just as slowly began to improve. "That seems to have done it," Spock said.

Suddenly the viewscreen filled with streaks of light. The Kauld were rallying for one final attack before their master weapon was neutralized completely. But this time the remains of the Federation's mobile defenders were hot on their tails, and Shucorion's fleet swooped in from all sides to join the battle directly beneath the antilaser shield.

It must have been a spectacular sight from the ground. Space battles were usually distant sparks and glints of light for all but the participants, but this time it raged across the night sky of the whole planet. Antimatter explosions actually lit up the ground like day for seconds at a time, and debris from disintegrating ships rained down in showers of multicolored meteors.

"Four minutes to laser terminus," the computer reported.

Vellyngaith's ship suddenly winked into view, plowing through the defenders as it built up ramming speed straight for the *Enterprise.* The Kauld leader had put all his ship's energy into shields and engines, but at the last moment he couldn't resist firing a disruptor at his nemesis as it hung there unmoving before him. In that moment of vulnerability, Kirk ordered full phasers from every ship in the fleet concentrated on the battleship, and its shields flared out. One of Shucorion's ships fired at it at close range, blasting a huge section out of its flank, and a moment later the Kauld warship vanished back into warp drive.

"Three minutes to laser terminus."

Vellyngaith's flight broke the resolve of the Kauld attack force, and the rest of his ships fled the battle right behind him. Shucorion's ships patrolled back and forth across the dark face of the planet, reminding Spock of a pack of sehlats strutting their stuff during mating season. Or a pack of humans, for that matter.

The power readings continued to fluctuate, but with Mr. Scott's assistance they were able to keep the deflector array well within operating parameters. The computer counted down the final few minutes, then the final few seconds. At last it said, "Laser terminus has passed," and a cheer erupted around the bridge. Spock was mortified to realize that he had nearly joined in, but he stopped the impulse at the last moment and stoically accepted the backslapping and the hugging that humans felt obliged to perform when things worked out as planned.

Chapter Thirty-four

ENGINEERING looked like a cyclone had hit it. Scotty and his crew had removed several access panels under the various workstations in his need to keep the deflector array running. He left them where they lay as markers for repairs that would have to be completed. Bluish smoke rose in thin columns from the master engineering console as well as from the environmental controls. It could all be fixed, and would be soon, but just now it didn't matter. They were alive, and they'd managed to beat the laser.

Cheering filled the room as the reality of their success dawned on everyone, and Kirk's voice echoed through the shipwide network: "We made it."

Scotty wiped his brow with the back of his hand and felt the muscles in his neck truly relax for the first time since he and Dr. McCoy had found the

Kauld fleet practicing their war games. He glanced over at the master engineering station again. All the major components it took to keep the *Enterprise* intact and operational were up and running, if not pretty. Around him, other engineering crew members were starting to poke around their stations too, reconnecting the obviously disconnected. They could take care of themselves for the moment.

The flashing red lights in the corners of the room shut off, indicating that the captain had taken them off alert status. Lieutenant Hanson nearly ran him over as she came around from behind with an armful of helical tensors. "Sorry, sir," she said, dropping a tensor from her cache.

He bent over to retrieve it for her. "Watch where you're going, lass, or you'll be spending all o' your time fixing what you crash into."

"And thank you for your help too, sir," she said, a smile tugging at her lips.

Scotty smiled back. "Aye. Good work out there on the EVA. Spock's right. We'd never have made it with the array in the shape it was in."

"Tensors?" a voice called out from deeper into the room.

"Gotta go," Hanson said.

Scotty peered through the thinning smoke and watched as his crew stepped over debris and pushed aside ruined displays to make room for replacements. He proudly listened to them discuss their options, debate the merits of each, and come to the same conclusions *he* would have. They were indeed a fine crew.

His communicator whistled for his attention. "Scott here."

"How long before the warp drive is up again?" Kirk asked.

He looked at the status monitor. "Captain, I canna possibly have it fixed before Gamma Night is over. Another five or six hours, anyway." *That* ought to give the laddies working on it time enough.

"That'll do. Keep me posted. Kirk out."

Scotty returned his communicator to his belt and turned once around, looking for the job that needed him most, but he realized everything that needed doing was already being done. He might actually have a moment to breathe before the next crisis came along. A moment, even, to relax.

He turned to the wall where the storage lockers held sets of specialized tools, the rare personal item for the crew members on duty, or even—in this case—an heirloom. He cleared a space on the nearest workbench, then cautiously opened the locker that held the Brandons' toaster. It had survived the hubbub of the fight with the Kauld and the defending of Belle Terre without so much as a scratch. It had already survived the trip out here and the blacksmith's shop. It would probably outlast the *Enterprise* herself. Kaylene Brandon had placed her faith wisely after all. If her family was anything like her toaster, they were a tough lot.

Carefully placing it on the bench, Scotty grabbed a stool and sat down to admire the toaster's antiquity.

Lieutenant Hanson came up beside him, her arms free of their load. "Are you okay, sir?"

He angled his head slightly to look at her. "I'm fine, Lieutenant. I'm just taking a little time to relax, and I happen to have this unfinished project that's been bothering me."

She looked at the silvery object, recognition absent from her face. She finally said, "Okay. Call me if I can help," and disappeared into the melee.

"Now then," he said to himself, turning back to the toaster. "I need a Phillips screwdriver, and a soldering gun, and . . ."

Chapter Thirty-five

GOVERNOR PARDONNET'S office looked like a blizzard had hit it. Kirk had never seen so much paper in one room outside of a library, and never so much of it lying loose on desktops, chairs, and filing cabinets. There was no place to sit for anyone but Pardonnet, but the governor made no apology for it.

"This is the way I do things," he said when he saw Kirk's expression. "I know it would all fit into one datapad, but if I can't see it nagging me for attention, I'll never get to it."

Kirk looked at a few sheets. Inventories, status reports, schedules—the detritus of a bureaucratic job. Kirk wondered how big a pile the contents of *his* datapad would make if he printed it all out.

That pile would be a bit smaller today than yesterday, at least. He could cross saving the world off his list. And patching it up, too. He smiled at the governor, then turned to Shucorion and Lilian, who stood by his side.

"Shucorion has brought all the building supplies he could fit into his ships," he said. "Plus the furnishings for new schools, medical centers, and community halls." He looked askance at the Blood leader and said, "Quite a packing job, considering the cargo containers were form-fit around the hulls of his warships."

"You're complaining?" Shucorion asked.

"No. I make it a point not to complain when somebody pulls my bacon out of the fire. But I do wonder what made you think you could get away with it before you knew what the Kauld had planned."

Shucorion shrugged. "I have my sources. I didn't know exactly what they had planned, but I knew they were about to spring it on either you or us. Travelling armed seemed a prudent precaution."

"Well, it certainly was," Kirk admitted. "And I thank you."

"The colony thanks you as well," Pardonnet said.

"Helping defeat the Kauld was my pleasure," Shucorion said. "But the building supplies were a business deal, and there is now the matter of payment. Your olivium mine is temporarily shut down. How long before you can resume production?"

Pardonnet narrowed his brows, then began searching among the papers on his desk. "I have that report here somewhere. Just a moment."

Kirk took that as his cue to make a graceful exit. He turned to Lilian and said, "Why don't we leave them to their business."

"Certainly," she said. "Would you care to walk me home?"

"I'd be delighted."

Pardonnet glanced up at them, his eyes full of questions, but he said nothing. Kirk held the door for Lilian, and they walked out of the building and into the street.

He was a bit surprised when she reached for his hand, but he accepted the familiarity. If she wanted to be seen this way in public, that was fine with him.

"That was quite a light show in the night sky," she said as they walked toward her house.

"It was pretty exciting from overhead, too," Kirk replied.

She nodded. "I imagine it was."

They walked a couple blocks in silence, just enjoying each other's company. They were about to turn off the main street when Kirk spotted the familiar figure of Dr. McCoy walking toward them from the other direction. He was carrying something gray in his arms, and when he drew closer Kirk could see that it was a cat.

"Hello, Lilian," McCoy said when he came closer. "Jim. Fancy meetin' you here."

"Likewise," Kirk said. "Looks like you've found a friend."

"I'm looking for a good home for her," McCoy said. "Sickbay is no place for a cat. She's getting into everything. And I refuse to let Scotty keep her in engineering, either. She'd get herself electrocuted, first thing." He held her up so Lilian could see her. "So I thought I'd see if you could use a mouser."

Lilian started to shake her head, but then she looked at McCoy again and stopped in midmotion. "I don't know," she said. "Maybe. Why don't you bring her up to the house and we'll see how she takes to it." She took his arm in her free hand and started walking again between the two men. "Why don't you both stay for dinner? My garden is looking kind of shabby at the moment, but I'm sure we can rustle up something worth eating."

McCoy scratched the cat between the ears and said, "I'll never turn down a home-cooked meal."

"Sounds wonderful," said Kirk. As they walked on up the street, he couldn't help thinking how close they had come to losing all this. Pardonnet and Lilian and the others were building a real community here, and for the first time since he'd taken this mission he understood why they had gone to all the trouble to do it. Life wasn't all duty and honor and glory; someone had to live the life that people like him fought to protect, or the whole thing would be meaningless.

He wasn't about to give up the glory, but just this once, for a little while, he was happy to stop and smell the roses.

Chapter Thirty-six

THE OUTPOST TAVERN thumped and gyrated to the sound of squealing yeerids in heat—or perhaps it was alien music. Deloric couldn't tell. He and Terwolan had finally managed to exchange their pay chits for local currency, and were now busy trying to learn enough about their new home to find a niche they could fill while they planned their new lives, but it was proving more complicated than they had hoped.

Deloric was still a bit stunned to think that he was no longer a soldier, and equally stunned to think that a woman like Terwolan would cast her lot with him. In all the time they had worked together, he had never guessed the depth of her thoughts, nor their similarity to his own. Now he could hardly imagine life without her, no matter where that life might lead.

He was just about to ask her to dance with him when two Kauld soldiers entered the bar.

He turned away and whispered to her, "Don't look, but trouble just walked in."

Neither he nor she were wearing their uniforms anymore. Those had been the first things they had gotten rid of. Still, they were the only other blue-skinned bipeds in the bar. He tried to look nonchalant as the soldiers stomped through the bar right past him and pulled up chairs at the empty table behind his back.

A large-eared, peg-toothed trader at the next table over said, "I hear the Kauld got their butts kicked a couple of days ago in the Beltar system. Any truth to that?"

The soldiers looked at one another, then in one fluid motion they rose up and grabbed the trader.

"Hey!" he squealed as they carried him to the door. "I was just making conversation!"

"Make it outside," one of the soldiers said, and they heaved him out the door.

"Damn ear-flapper," the other one said as they came back to their table and sat down again. "The news must be all over the sector by now."

"It doesn't matter," said the first. "It's a setback, nothing more."

"Oh? Does Vellyngaith have another bright idea up his sleeve?" The one who spoke punched his companion on the shoulder. "Get it? Bright? Huh, huh, huh."

The optimistic one ignored him. "I don't know about Vellyngaith, but I know Yanorada's got one, and the clock's already ticking. Those humans may be laughing now, but they just traded a fast death for a slow one, that's all."

Deloric looked at Terwolan. She raised her glass and drained it, then stood up. "Time to go," she said softly.

"Right." He dropped a half-credit on the table and

followed her out into the corridor toward their apartment.

"Those poor sons of bitches," she said when they were out of earshot of the bar.

"Who, the soldiers?" asked Deloric.

"No, the humans. They've stepped into the middle of another mess."

"They do seem to have a talent for that," Deloric said. "Do you think we should try to warn them?"

She snorted. "What are we, their guardian angels? We paid off our debt to them already. They're not our problem anymore."

"I suppose not." He followed her toward their apartment, but his eyes weren't seeing the space station any more. He was remembering the view from the comet, how Belle Terre's sun was just a bright star in the sky, and how the planet had been a barely visible speck of light beside it. Just one planet among millions, circling a nondescript star in an average sector of the galaxy. By all rights, a person should be able to go through his entire life without encountering another of its inhabitants ever again, but he got the feeling he hadn't heard the last of these humans. They might be the newcomers here, but they were by no means helpless. No matter what this Yanorada's plan was, Deloric was glad he was on their good side.

Pocket Books
Proudly Presents

STAR TREK®
NEW EARTH #5
THIN AIR

Kristine Kathryn Rusch
and Dean Wesley Smith

Coming Soon from Pocket Books

Turn the page for a preview of
Thin Air . . .

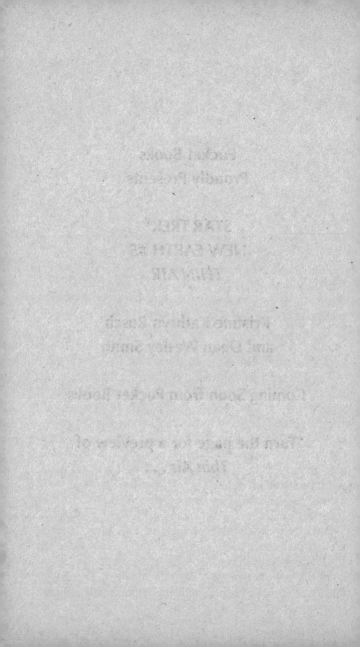

The clear canister sitting on the *Enterprise* science lab bench held no more than a few handfuls of brown dirt taken directly from a field just outside Belle Terre's main colony on the island side of the planet. It was farm soil, nothing more. Recently tilled, the dirt smelled of rich possibilities, seasons full of fresh, crisp vegetables, and the very future of Belle Terre.

Only there was something very wrong with this soil. And Spock was trying to figure out exactly what that was.

On the counter beside the canister were almost two dozen other canisters, all containing dirt from different areas of Belle Terre. The soil from the explosion-blasted side of the planet seemed darker, almost black with the radiation damage from what the colonists were calling the "Burn." Two canisters seemed to be full of light sand.

But, from what Spock had been told, areas of soil around the planet were "going bad," as the colonists put it. Plants were dying, and in places the soil even smelled foul and rotten. Lilian Coates had asked Captain Kirk to look into it, and the captain had assigned

Spock to help the colonist scientists discover what was wrong.

All the soil canisters in the lab were carefully labeled and sorted by region and continent. It had taken three *Enterprise* crew members most of a day to collect all the soil samples for Spock. And he had spent the last two hours analyzing the data from scans of each sample. His findings had not been what he had expected. The soil contained polymers that logically just didn't belong on Belle Terre, let alone in every sample from every region of the planet.

Spock held his tricorder over the sample of rich dirt from the largest island on the undamaged side of Belle Terre, then inserted a small silver probe into the soil. He again checked the readings of the soil, then stepped back and flipped a switch on a nearby panel, sending a slight jolt of electricity into the soil through the probe. What he had expected from his readings was a small puff of smoke as the electrical jolt broke down unknown gel molecules he had discovered in the soil.

That wasn't what he got.

The soil sample exploded with the force of a large bomb.

The impact smashed Spock back against the wall, knocking the wind from him. The room swirled with smoke and Spock's ears rang. He could feel a dozen cuts and gashes on his body from flying glass and debris.

He ignored the wounds, the shortness of breath, and his damaged ears and forced his attention completely on the explosion. He had not expected it, and did not know why it had happened. Simple farming soil did not normally explode when touched with electricity. Clearly the soil problem developing on Belle Terre was far worse than he had first thought.

Alarm bells were sounding throughout the ship as he slowly stood.

"Spock! Spock! Come in." Captain Kirk's voice carried over the alarms.

Spock stumbled a few steps through the glass and debris, and tapped the comm link on the wall. "Spock here, Captain." His own voice sounded hollow and distant in his ears, and he had to lean against the wall for support.

The captain's voice came back instantly. "Spock, what happened? Are you all right?"

Spock looked through the smoke at the completely destroyed science lab, then said, "I fared better than the science lab. And I made a discovery."

"What?" Kirk demanded as two emergency personnel shoved the jammed door aside and rushed into the lab. They stopped, clearly stunned at the destruction, then one moved toward Spock as the other moved to stop the small fire in a panel.

Spock understood the men's reaction. He was surprised as well by the force of the explosion. He had grossly miscalculated and it had cost them a lot of important scientific equipment. It was equipment that would not be easily replaced this far from Federation space. It was also lucky that he had been the only person in the lab at the time. A human would have had little chance of surviving such an explosion.

At that moment Dr. McCoy shoved in through the half-open door and glanced around. "For the love of—" He instantly moved toward Spock, his medical tricorder in his hand. "What in green-blooded blazes have you done?"

"Spock?" Kirk demanded over the comm as McCoy scanned him. "What discovery?"

"Belle Terre is in trouble, Captain," Spock said.

"Explain," Kirk said.

"Jim," McCoy said to the comm unit on the wall before Spock could say a word, "if you want to talk to your first officer, it's going to have to be in sickbay."

McCoy waved for the two emergency crewmen to help him with Spock.

"I can walk, Doctor," Spock said, pushing himself away from the wall.

"I doubt that," McCoy said, his voice not hiding his disgust. "But you are more than welcome to try."

Three stumbling, painful steps later Spock realized the logical choice was to have help getting to sickbay. In fact, it was the only choice.

Spock was thankful that McCoy had the good sense to not say "I told you so."

Lilian Coates awoke with a start, gasping for air, sweat dripping from her forehead, her hair stuck to her cheeks. What an awful nightmare.

She looked around her bedroom, trying to get back something familiar while forcing herself to take a few deep breaths. That was the worst dream she had had since right after the Burn. For weeks after that she had dreamed she was back in the cave with the children, trying to save them, but always failing. Luckily, in real life she had been successful. She, her son, Reynold, and five other children had ridden through the explosion of the planet's olivium-filled moon inside a cave. After a month or so the nightmares of Reynold dying, just as her husband had done, ended. But the memory of them always seemed just below the surface of every minute of every day.

She took another long, deep breath and blew outward, letting the fresh air clear her mind. Then she swung out of bed and in the faint light she padded to Reynold's room and glanced in at him. Their cat, Nova, a gift from Dr. McCoy, lay curled around Reynold's feet. Both seemed to be sleeping fine, so she moved on into the kitchen area, trying not to think about the nightmare until she calmed down some.

A large glass of cold water helped, and she sat at the

kitchen table, still cluttered with a few dishes left from last night's dinner with Reynold and Captain Kirk. Jim had returned to his ship shortly after dinner and she just hadn't felt like cleaning up. Right now she wished he was here. Someone to talk to, someone to tell her that staying on Belle Terre, not going back to Earth, was the right thing to do for her and Reynold.

Slowly she let the nightmare back into her thoughts.

She is outside, standing in her garden, under clear, sunny skies. Around her all her plants are dead and wilted. Suddenly her feet become rooted to the soil, as if she is a plant as well.

She can't move.

Then she feels pressure around her face, as if someone is putting a hand over her nose and mouth, choking off her air. But there is no one there.

She can't run.

She can't breathe.

She is dying, just as her garden is dying.

Reynold is beside her, also planted, also unable to breathe.

She can't save him, either.

She knew they were about to suffocate when she awoke.

Awful nightmare.

Another long drink of water pushed the images back again. It seemed she was more worried about her garden, and other plants around the area, than she had even told Jim. No doubt the plants' dying had something to do with the Burn and the extreme changes in climate and weather. She knew there was a logical explanation for it.

But it seemed her subconscious didn't.

She glanced at the time. Two hours until she and Reynold had to be up. There wasn't going to be any getting back to sleep now. Not after that nightmare. She stood and picked up the last of the dishes from last night's dinner and moved to the sink, where she could wash them.

She was the school administrator and librarian for the colony. She had more than enough work to keep her busy.

Two hours later, as she fixed breakfast for herself and Reynold, the nightmare still haunted her, like a shadow she didn't want.

As they headed off to school, she looked at the slowly wilting plants in her garden. She knew that part of the nightmare was truth. The question that worried her was, *Which part?*

Governor Pardonnet smiled at Tegan Welch as if she were a child, giving her his best false smile. She desperately wanted to smash it into his face. It was that smile that had at first convinced her to trust the man, to follow him for light-years to this planet. And it was that smile that was condemning her son, Charles, to death.

She was a short woman, at best five-foot-one, but she knew how to fight and defend herself and her son. She stepped right up close to him, staring up into his face, forcing him to step backward in the tight space of the medical lab. "Take a look in that room again, Governor." She pointed to a closed door. "My son and four others are going to die unless you get us back to Federation space."

"I understand that, Ms. Welch," Pardonnet said, trying to ease sideways from where she had him pinned against a medical stand. The small medical supply room was no bigger than a closet. It was where she had asked for a word privately with him the minute they learned the cause of the illness affecting her son and the others.

"So what ship are you planning to send and when?"

"We're going to get them to the hospital ship first," Pardonnet said, "now that we know the cause of their illness."

She shook her head. "Not enough and you know it."

All the doctors, including Dr. McCoy from the *Enterprise,* had been clear that the only way to save these people was to get them a long distance away from olivium and the subspace radiation it was emitting. After the explosion of the Quake Moon, olivium had pelted the planet and spread like a wave through the system. Her son and the four others were allergic to the standard radiation treatments—and all the others McCoy had been able to whip up. Deathly allergic.

Her son would die unless he was away from the olivium, and she was going to make sure he got away from it, one way or another.

"We don't know that getting them to the medical ship won't be enough," Pardonnet said, anger in his voice as he pushed past her, trying to get to the door. She moved to block his way.

Pardonnet stopped and stared at her. "Ms. Welch, getting your son out of the atmosphere might stop the spread of the reaction. On the medical ship we can get him and the others into a sterile, protected ward."

"And what exactly did Dr. McCoy say about that idea?" she asked.

Pardonnet stared and said nothing.

"It seems I remember him saying along the lines of 'That would work when pigs fly.' Am I correct?"

"Dr. McCoy can be wrong," Pardonnet said. "We're going to try it first, then face the next step."

"The lives of my son and the others are not worth a ship to you, are they?"

Pardonnet actually looked stunned at the accusation; then his eyes hardened and he said, "I have thirty thousand lives to worry about every minute of every day. Now excuse me." He shoved past her and out into the ward.

She had been right. Five lives were not worth a ship to the governor.

She stood staring at the medical supplies for a moment. Somehow there had to be a way to get her son away from the olivium—ideally, back to Federation space. But at least away from the olivium first.

And if there was a way, she was going to find it. The first step was getting Charles off the planet and to the hospital ship. From there she'd figure out what to do. If it meant stealing a ship and flying it herself, she'd do it. She just hoped it wouldn't come to that.

But if it did, she wouldn't hesitate.

Look for
Thin Air
Coming Soon
Wherever Books Are Sold

OUR FIRST SERIAL NOVEL!

The Final Chapter . . .

**The very beginning of the
Starfleet Adventure . . .**

**STAR TREK®
STARFLEET: YEAR ONE**

A Novel in Twelve Parts®

**by
Michael Jan Friedman**

Chapter Twelve

As soon as Hiro Matsura reached the *Yellowjacket*'s bridge, he took stock of its viewscreen.

He could see what his first officer had described to him via communicator minutes earlier—a formation of fourteen alien ships, each one a deadly dark triangle. And without a doubt, they were bearing down on the colony world from which Matsura's pod had just returned.

The last time he had seen the aggressors, they had all but crippled his ship—a setback from which the crew of the *Yellowjacket* was still trying desperately to recover. The ship's shields, lasers, and atomic weapon launchers had yet to be brought back online, and her impulse engines were too sluggish to be effective.

In short, the *Yellowjacket* wasn't fit to engage the enemy. If she entered the field of battle, she would be nothing more than a target—and therefore a liability to her sister ships.

The odds against Matsura's comrades were considerable. It galled the captain to have to hang back at a safe distance and watch the aliens tear chunks out of their Christophers.

But it didn't seem like he had much of a choice.

Aaron Stiles glared at his viewscreen, which showed him so many enemy ships that they seemed to blot out the stars.

It would have been a daunting sight even if three of his fellow captains weren't butterfly catchers. As it was, only he and Hagedorn could point to any real combat experience—a deficit which prevented the five of them from executing maneuvers as a group.

Stiles would have much preferred to fly alongside his old wingmates—veteran space fighters like Andre Beschta and Amanda McTigue and his brother Jake. Then they would have *had* something.

Of course, Shumar, Dane, and Cobaryn had plenty of former Earth Command officers on their bridges. If they paid them some mind, they might have a chance to come through this.

Yeah, right, Stiles thought. *And I'm the King of Tennessee.* If he and Hagedorn couldn't beat *four* of the triangle ships, how was their little fleet supposed to beat *fourteen?*

He scowled and began barking out orders. "Raise shields. Power to all batteries. Mr. Bagdasarian, target atomics."

Weeks, the better weapons officer, was still in sickbay. But with the aliens packed into such a tight formation, Bagdasarian wouldn't need a marksman's eye to hit something.

"Atomics targeted," came Bagdasarian's reply. And a moment later, he added, "Range, sir."

"Fire!" bellowed Stiles.

A black-and-gold missile erupted from the *Gibraltar* and shot through the void in the enemy's direction. For a fraction of a second, it was on its own. Then four other missiles came hurtling after it.

Apparently, the captain's colleagues were all thinking along the same lines he was. It was more than he had expected.

As his missile found a target, it vanished in a burst of blinding white light. The other missiles struck the enemy in quick succession, each one swallowed up in a light show of its own.

But when the alien armada became visible again, it wasn't clear if the atomics had done any damage. The enemy vessels looked every bit as dangerous as they had before.

A voice came through the comm grate in Stiles's armrest. "Stay outside them," Hagedorn advised the group. "The longer they remain bunched that way, the better our chances."

The man was right, of course. Stiles regarded his weapons officer. "Fire again!" he snapped.

The *Gibraltar* sent a second black-and-gold missile hurtling toward the alien formation. Over the next couple of heartbeats, the other captains followed Stiles's example.

Unfortunately, their second barrage wasn't any more productive than the first. It lit up the void for a moment, but the enemy shook off its impact and kept coming.

And by then it was too late to launch a third barrage anyway. They were too close to the aliens to risk atomics.

"Target lasers!" Stiles roared.

As if the enemy had read his mind, the triangle ships abandoned their formation and went twisting off in pairs. Suddenly, they weren't such easy targets anymore.

"Fire at will!" the captain told Bagdasarian.

The weapons officer unleashed the fury of their laser batteries on the nearest pair of enemy vessels. At the last possible moment, the triangles peeled off and eluded the beams.

Then they came after the *Gibraltar*.

Stiles glowered at them. "Evade!" he urged his helm officer.

Urbina did her best to slip the aliens' knot, but it tightened altogether too quickly. The *Gibraltar* was wracked by one blinding-white assault after another, each barrage like a giant fist punishing the vessel to the limits of her endurance.

A console exploded directly behind the captain, singeing the hairs on the back of his neck. As sparks hissed and smoke billowed darkly, the deck lurched one way and then the other like a skiff on a stormy sea.

But Stiles held on. They all did.

By the time the enemy shot past them, the *Gibraltar* was in a bad way. The captain knew that even before he was told that their shields were down eighty-five percent, or that they had lost power to the starboard nacelle.

"They're coming about for another shot at us!" Rosten called out abruptly, her voice hoarse and thin with smoke.

Stiles swore beneath his breath. "Shake them!" he told Urbina.

The helm officer sent them twisting through space, even without any help from their damaged nacelle. And somehow, she did what the captain had demanded of her. She shook the triangles from their tail.

It looked as if they were safe, at least for a moment. Then Stiles saw the two alien vessels sliding into view from another quarter, setting their sights on the poorly shielded *Gibraltar*.

"Enemy to port!" Rosten called out.

The captain felt his throat constrict. This must have been how his brother Jake felt before the Romulans blew him to pieces.

"Target and fire!" he thundered.

If they were going to go down, it wouldn't be without a fight. Stiles promised himself that.

But before the aliens could get a barrage off, a metallic shadow swept between the *Gibraltar* and her antagonists. It took Stiles a second to realize that it was one of the other Christophers, trying to shield him and his crew from the enemy.

He couldn't see the triangles' weapons ports as they fired, but he saw the ruddy flare of light beyond the curve of the other Christopher's hull and the way the Starfleet vessel shuddered under the impact.

The captain didn't know for certain which of his colleagues was risking his life to save the *Gibraltar*. However, he guessed that it was Hagedorn. It was the kind of chance only a soldier would take.

The aliens pounded the interceding ship a second time and a third, but Stiles wouldn't let his comrade protect him any longer. Glancing at Urbina, he said, "Get us a clear shot, Lieutenant."

"Aye, sir," came the reply.

"Ready lasers," the captain told Bagdasarian.

"Ready, sir."

"Fire as soon as you've got a target," Stiles told him.

As Urbina dropped them below the level of the other Christopher, Bagdasarian didn't hesitate for even a fraction of second. He unleashed a couple of devastating blue laser volleys that struck the enemy vessels from below, forcing them to give ground—at least for the time being.

Stiles turned to Rosten, taking advantage of the respite. "Raise Captain Hagedorn," he said. "See how badly he's damaged."

But when the navigator bent to her task, she seemed to find something that surprised her. "It's not the *Horatio*," she reported crisply. "It's the *Maverick*, sir."

Stiles looked at her. *Dane?*

A moment later, the Cochrane jockey's voice came crackling over the *Gibraltar*'s comm system. He sounded as if he were talking about a barroom brawl instead of a dogfight.

"Looks like I bit off more than I could chew," said Dane. "Everything's down . . . shields, weapons, you name it. I'm not going to be much help from here on in."

"I'll do what I can to protect you," Stiles assured him.

There was a pause, as Dane seemed to realize to whom he was speaking. "You just want to make sure nothing happens to that pistol I won."

"Damned right," said Stiles.

But, of course, the pistol was the farthest thing from his mind. He was trying to figure out how he was going to repay Dane's favor without getting his ship carved up in the process.

* * *

Hiro Matsura had never felt so helpless in his life.

The other captains were fighting valiantly, dodging energy volley after energy volley, but it wasn't getting them anywhere. With one of their ships disabled—perhaps as badly as the *Yellowjacket*—the tide of battle was slowly but inexorably turning against them. In time, the aliens would blow them out of space.

But Matsura couldn't do anything about it—not with his ship in its current state of disrepair. With his weapons down and his shield generators mangled, he would only be offering himself up as cannon fodder.

He wished he could speak to the aliens. Then he would let them know that he understood the reason for their hostility. He would make them see that it was all a misunderstanding.

But he *couldn't* speak to them—not without programming their language into his ship's computer. And if he knew their language, he wouldn't require the computer's help in the first place.

As Matsura looked on, Hagedorn's ship absorbed another blinding, bludgeoning barrage. Then the same thing happened to Shumar's ship, and Cobaryn's. Their deflector grids had to be failing. Pretty soon, they would all be as helpless as the *Yellowjacket*.

The captain's fists clenched. *Dammit,* he thought bitterly, *there's got to be* something *I can do.*

His excavation of the mound on Oreias Eight had put the key to the problem in his hands. He just had to figure out what to unlock with it.

Unlock? he repeated inwardly.

And then it came to him.

There might be a way to help the other ships after all. It was a long shot, but he had taken long shots before.

Swinging himself out of his center seat, Matsura said, "Jezzelis, you're with me." Then he grabbed the Vobilite's arm and pulled him in the direction of the lift.

"Sir?" said Jezzelis, doing his best to keep up.

The captain punched the bulkhead pad, summoning the lift. "I need help with something," he told his exec.

"With what?" asked Jezzelis.

Just then, the lift doors hissed open. Moving inside, Matsura tapped in their destination. By the time he was finished, his first officer had entered the compartment too.

"Captain," said Jezzelis, "I would—"

Matsura held up a hand for silence. Then he pressed the stud that activated the ship's intercom. "Spencer, Naulty, Brosius, Jimenez . . . this is the captain. Meet me on deck six."

A string of affirmative responses followed his command. All four of the security officers would be there, Matsura assured himself.

His exec looked at him askance, no doubt trying to figure out what could be so pressing about deck six. After all, there was nothing there except cargo space and equipment lockers.

"Mr. McDonald," the captain went on, "report to the transporter room and stand by."

"The transporter . . . ?" Jezzelis wondered out loud.

Then they reached deck six and the doors opened. Spencer, Naulty, Brosius, and Jimenez were just arriving.

"Follow me," said Matsura, swinging out of the lift compartment and darting down the corridor.

He could hear the others pelting along after him, matching him stride for stride. No doubt, the four security officers were every bit as curious as Jezzelis. Unfortunately, there was no time for an explanation.

If his plan was going to stand a chance, he had to move quickly.

The captain negotiated a couple of turns in the passage. Then he came to a door and pounded on the bulkhead controls beside it. A moment later, the titanium panel slid aside, revealing two facing rows of gold lockers in a long, narrow cabin.

Matsura knew exactly what each locker contained—a fully charged palm-sized flashlight, a small black packet of barely edible rations, and an Earth Command emergency containment suit.

There were two dozen of the gold-and-black suits in all, each one boasting a hood with an airtight visor. As bulky as they were, a normal man wouldn't be able to carry more than four of them at once—which was why Matsura had brought help along.

As Jezzelis and the others caught up with him, the captain tapped a three-digit security code into a pad on one of the lockers. When the door swung open, he grabbed the suit inside the locker and gestured for his assistants to do the same.

"Take them to the transporter room," he barked.

Invading one locker after the other, Matsura dragged out three more suits. They weighed his arms down as if they were full of lead. Satisfied that he couldn't carry any more, he made his way back to the lift.

Jezzelis was right behind him. With his powerful Vobilite musculature, the first officer didn't seem half as encumbered as his captain did. As Matsura struck the bulkhead panel and got the doors to open for them, Jezzelis helped the human with his ungainly burden.

"Thanks," Matsura breathed, making his way to a wall of the compartment and leaning against it for support.

The Vobilite took advantage of the respite to pin the captain down. "If I may ask, sir . . . exactly what are we doing?"

Matsura told him.

Then the others piled into the turbolift with them, and the captain programmed in a destination—the transporter room. As luck would have it, it was only a deck below them.

The ride down took only a few seconds. Jimenez was the first one to bolt into the corridor with his armful of containment suits. Matsura was last—but not by much.

As they spilled into the room, McDonald was waiting for them at the control console. He looked confused when he saw what the captain and his helpers were bringing in.

"Sir . . . ?" said the transporter operator, staring at Matsura as if he was afraid the man had lost his mind.

"Don't ask," the captain told him, dumping his suits on the raised transporter platform. "Just drop what's left of our shields and beam these out into space—say, a hundred meters from the ship."

McDonald hesitated for a fraction of a second, as if he thought he might have been the butt of a very bizarre joke. Then he activated the transporter system, overrode shield control, and did as Matsura had ordered.

The captain pointed to Jezzelis. "Yours next."

His first officer deposited his load on the platform. At a nod from Matsura, McDonald beamed that into space as well.

It seemed to take forever, but the captain saw every one of their two dozen Earth Command–issue containment garments dispatched to the void. Only then did he take a deep breath, wipe the sweat from his forehead with the back of his hand, and start back in the direction of the turbolift.

He had to get back to the bridge. It was there that he would find out if his idea had been as crazy as it seemed.

Connor Dane didn't like the idea of being protected by Aaron Stiles. For that matter, he didn't like the idea of being protected by *anybody*.

Unfortunately, he wasn't in much of a position to complain about it. It wasn't just *his* life on the line—it was his crew's lives as well. And he had no one to blame but himself.

If he hadn't risked the *Maverick* to keep the aliens from destroying the *Gibraltar*, his ship wouldn't be a useless piece of junk now. He would still be trading punches with the enemy instead of cringing every time a dark triangle veered his way.

Of course, the enemy had all but ignored him since the moment his ship was disabled. Obviously, they had more viable fish to fry. But eventually, they would finish frying them—and then Dane's ship would be slagged with a few good energy bursts.

Not a pleasant thought, he mused. He looked around his bridge at his officers, whose expressions told him they were thinking the same thing.

They deserved a lot better than the fate he had obtained for them. But then, so did everyone else in the fleet. There were brave, dedicated people serving under every one of Dane's colleagues.

And it looked like their only legacy would be a few odd scraps of charred space debris.

"Sir," said his navigator, "something seems to be happening in the vicinity of the *Yellowjacket.*"

Dane turned to her. "Are they being attacked?"

Ideko shook her black-and-white-striped head from side to side. "No, sir. It's something else. I—"

"Yes?" said the captain.

Ideko frowned and called up additional information. Then she frowned even more. "Sensors say they're containment suits, sir."

Dane looked at her. Then he turned to his screen, daring it to show him what his navigator had described. "Give me a view of the *Yellowjacket,* Lieutenant. I'd like to see this for myself."

A moment later, an image of Matsura's ship filled the screen. And just as Ideko had reported, there was a swarm of black-and-gold containment suits floating outside the vessel.

"I'll be deep fried," the captain muttered. He leaned forward in his chair and studied the *Yellowjacket* more closely. "There's no sign of a hull breach," he concluded.

"None," agreed Nasir, who had taken up a position on Dane's flank.

"So what are they doing out there?" Dane wondered.

No one answered him.

The captain was still trying to figure it out when one of the triangles separated itself from the thick of the battle and headed in the direction of the *Yellowjacket*.

Like the *Maverick*, the *Yellowjacket* was defenseless. It had no weapons, no shields . . . no threat to keep the enemy at bay.

Damn, thought Dane, feeling a pang of sympathy for his colleague. *This is it for Matsura*.

Of course, he expected Matsura to give the aliens a run for their money—to buy as much time as possible for his crew, or maybe even try to maneuver the enemy into the sights of another Christopher.

But the captain of the *Yellowjacket* didn't do a thing. He just sat there, as if resigned to the fact of his doom.

Dane was surprised. Matsura had seemed like the type to fight to the end, no matter how small the chances of his succeeding. *Apparently*, he thought, *I was wrong about him*.

As the alien ship bore down on the *Yellowjacket*, Dane grimaced in anticipation. But the deadly energy burst never came. Instead, the triangle slowed down, came to a stop in front of the toothless Christopher . . .

And just sat there.

Nasir muttered a curse.

"You can say that again," Dane told him.

The triangle reminded him of a dog sniffing something new in the neighborhood. But what was new about the *Yellowjacket*? Hadn't the aliens run into Starfleet vessels twice before?

Then it came to him. But before the captain could make mention of it, his comm grate came alive with Matsura's voice.

"Don't ask questions," said the captain of the *Yellowjacket*. "Just transport all your containment suits into space. I'll explain later."

Dane looked at his first officer. "You heard the man, Mr. Nasir. We've got work to do."

Before Nasir could utter a protest, Dane swung out of his chair and headed for the turbolift.

Alonis Cobaryn was stunned.

A scant few minutes earlier, he had been entangled in the fight of his life, battered by an implacable enemy at every turn. Now he was watching that same enemy withdraw peacefully from the field of battle, its weapons obligingly powered down.

Except for one triangle-shaped ship . . . and that one was hanging nose to nose with the *Yellowjacket* in the midst of nearly a hundred and fifty black-and-gold containment suits, looking as patient and deliberate as a Vulcan.

Clearly, it wanted something. Cobaryn just wished he knew *what*.

Tapping the stud on his intercom, he opened a channel to the *Yellowjacket*. "Captain Matsura," he said, "you offered to provide an explanation. This might be a propitious time."

"Damned right," said Dane, joining their conversation. "Exactly what did we just do?"

"And," added Cobaryn, "how did you know it would work?"

"Believe me," said Matsura. "I didn't. I was wishing I could speak to the aliens, tell them somehow that we weren't trying to dishonor their burial mounds . . . and it occurred to me that what we needed was some kind of peace offering. But it had to be an offering they understood—something they would immediately recognize as precious."

"Something like . . . a year's supply of containment suits?" Dane asked, clearly still in the dark.

"Remember," said Matsura, "the aliens had never seen a human being—or, for that matter, a member of any other Federation species. I was hoping they would identify the suits as our *shells*—or at least what passes for shells in our society."

Cobaryn was beginning to understand. "And if we were anything like them, these so-called shells would have great spiritual value."

"Exactly," said Matsura. "And anyone who's generous enough to present offerings of great spiritual value can't be all bad."

Dane grunted in appreciation. "Nice one."

"Indeed," remarked Cobaryn. "However, now that we have achieved a stalemate, we must capitalize on it. We must build a basis for mutual understanding with the aliens."

"As I understand it," said Matsura, "a couple of our colleagues are gearing up to do just that."

"Hagedorn here," said a voice, as if on cue. "Stand by. Captain Shumar and I are going to attempt to make first contact."

"Who died and left *him* boss?" asked Dane.

But Cobaryn could tell from the Cochrane jockey's tone that he didn't really have any objection. It was simply impossible for Dane to cope with authority without making a fuss.

As the Rigelian watched, a pod escaped from the belly of the *Horatio* and made its way toward the waiting triangle ship. No doubt, both Shumar and Hagedorn were aboard.

"Good luck," Cobaryn told them.

A hundred meters shy of the alien vessel, Daniel Hagedorn grazed the last of the Christophers' seemingly ubiquitous containment suits.

The protective garment seemed to want to latch onto the escape pod, desiring rescue, but Hagedorn urged his vehicle past it. Then there was nothing but empty space between him and the triangle ship.

Twenty meters from it, Hagedorn applied the pod's braking thrusters. Then he sat back and waited.

"What do you think they're going to do?" wondered Shumar, who was ensconced next to him in the copilot's seat.

Hagedorn shook his head. "You're the scientist. You tell me."

"I'm not an ambassador," said Shumar. "I'm a surveyor. I've never made contact with anything smarter than a snail."

"And the only contact I've made has been with a laser cannon. Apparently, we're at something of a disadvantage."

For a moment, silence reigned in the pod's tiny cabin. Hagedorn took advantage of it to study the alien ship. For all its speed and power, it didn't appear to be based on a very efficient design.

"It must be gratifying," he said, using the part of his mind that wasn't focused on the triangle.

Shumar looked at him. "What do you mean?"

"Your work on Oreias Eight . . . it gave us this opportunity. You can be proud of that."

"You mean . . . if we don't make it?"

Even Hagedorn had to smile at that. "Yes."

Shumar looked at him. "Either way, Captain, it's been a pleasure working with you."

"You don't have to say that," Hagedorn told him.

His colleague nodded. "I know."

Suddenly, something began to move underneath the triangle ship. Hagedorn could feel his pulse begin to race. He willed it to slow down, knowing they would need to be sharp to pull this off.

"Is that a door opening?" asked Shumar, craning his neck to get a view of the alien's underside.

It certainly looked like a door. Hagedorn said so.

"Then let's accept their invitation," Shumar suggested.

It was why they had come, after all—in the hope that they might obtain face-to-face contact with the aliens. Carefully, Hagedorn eased the pod down and under the triangle, all the while gaining a better view of what awaited them within.

The first thing Hagedorn saw was a smaller version of the alien vessel, sitting alongside the open bay door. Then he spotted some of the aliens themselves, standing back from the opening behind what must have been a transparent force field.

They were tall, angular, and dark-skinned, with minimal, vividly colored clothing, and white hair drawn back into thick, elaborate braids. Their pale, wideset eyes followed the pod as it came up through the open doorway into an unexpectedly large chamber.

Hagedorn landed his vehicle and the door closed behind him. He took a moment to scan the aliens more closely. He noticed that all four of them had hand weapons hanging at their hips.

"They're armed," he observed.

"Wouldn't you be?" asked Shumar.

It was a good point.

Of course, neither of them had figured out yet how they were going to communicate with their hosts. But then, it wouldn't be the first time Hagedorn had been forced to improvise.

He flipped the visor of his containment suit down over his

face, grateful that he had had the foresight to hold a couple of the garments back when he received Matsura's instructions.

Then, his fingers crawling across his control console, he cracked the pod's hatch and went out to meet the aliens.

Lydia Littlejohn paced the carpeted floor of her office, remembering with crystal clarity the last time she had felt compelled to do so.

It was during the last push of the war, when Dan Hagedorn led the assault on the Romulan supply depot at Cheron. The president of Earth had paced well into the night, unable to lie down, unable even to sit . . . until she finally received a message from her communications specialist that the enemy's depot had been destroyed.

And even then, she had been incapable of sleep. She had remained awake thinking about the brave men and women who had given their lives to see the Romulans defeated.

At the time, some people had predicted that Earth had seen the last of war. Littlejohn hadn't been one of them. However, she had hoped for a respite, at least—a couple of years without an armed conflict.

Surely, her people had earned it.

But mere months after the creation of the Romulan Neutral Zone, Earth colonies were again being attacked by an unknown aggressor, and the Federation had been forced to send its fleet out to address the situation.

Officially, it wasn't Earth's problem. But the endangered colonies were Earth colonies, and the ships they sent out were Earth ships, and the largest part of their crews were Earth men and women . . . and Littlejohn couldn't help feeling as if her world were at war all over again.

"President Littlejohn?" came a voice.

She looked up. "Yes, Mr. Stuckey?"

"We've received a communication from Starfleet Headquarters. Apparently, the mission to the Oreias system was a success. The fleet has made contact with the raiders and achieved a peaceful resolution."

Littlejohn felt a wave of relief wash over her. Thank God, she thought. "Were there many casualties?" she asked.

"None, ma'am."

She couldn't believe it. "None at all?"

"I made sure of it, ma'am. I knew you would want to know."

Littlejohn smiled. "Thank you, Mr. Stuckey."

"Have a pleasant evening, ma'am."

She glanced out her window, where she could see the first stars emerging in a darkening and more serene-looking sky. *I'll do that,* she answered silently. *I most definitely will do that.*

Aaron Stiles was feeling pretty good about himself as he felt his ship go to warp speed and saw the stars on his viewscreen go from points of light to long streaks.

After all, Hagedorn and Shumar had patched things up with the aliens—a species who called themselves the Nisaaren— and engineered an agreement under which Earth's colonists could remain in the system without fear of attack. It was a far better outcome than any Stiles would have predicted.

And he and his colleagues had secured it by working together—as a unified fleet, instead of two irreconcilable factions. Sure, they'd had their differences. No doubt, they always would. But they had made compromises on both sides, and found a way to construct a whole that was a little more than the sum of its parts.

Dane had surprised Stiles most of all. The Cochrane jockey had struck him as a misfit, a waste of time. But when push came to shove, he had shoved as hard as any of them. And though Stiles would never have admitted it in public, Dane had risked his life to save the *Gibraltar.*

That was the kind of action he would have expected from a wingmate in Earth Command, not a man whom he had shown nothing but hostility and disdain. Clearly, he had misjudged Connor Dane.

In fact, he conceded, he had misjudged all *three* of the butterfly catchers. It was a mistake he wouldn't make again.

"Captain Stiles?" said his navigator, interrupting his thoughts.

He turned to Rosten. "Yes, Lieutenant?"

"There's a message coming in from Earth, sir. Eyes only."

The captain smiled, believing he knew what the message was about. It was high time Abute had called to offer congratulations. But why had the man declined to address the crew as a whole?

"I'll take it in my quarters," said Stiles, and pushed himself up out of his center seat.

It wasn't until he reached his anteroom and activated his terminal that he realized why Abute had chosen to be secretive. According to the director, the board of review had made its decision . . . and selected the captain of the spanking-new *Daedalus*.

Abute had spent a lot of time overseeing, discussing, and inspecting the construction of the Federation starship *Daedalus*. In fact, he probably knew the vessel as well as the men and women who had assembled her.

So it was a special thrill for the fleet director to be the first to beam aboard the new ship, bypassing her transporter room and appearing instead on her handsome, well-appointed bridge.

He took a look around, enjoying every last detail—down to the subtle hum of the *Daedalus*'s impulse engines and the smell of her newly installed blue carpeting. He even ran his hand over the silver rail that enclosed her spacious command center.

However, Abute wasn't alone there for very long. He was soon joined by a host of dignitaries, human and otherwise, including Admiral Walker of Earth Command, Clarisse Dumont, and the highly regarded Sammak of Vulcan.

Both Walker and Dumont looked a little fidgety. But then, they had been campaigning for a long time to secure the *Daedalus* for their respective political factions—and to that very moment, neither of them knew who had been given command of the ship.

Of course, Abute knew. And for that matter, so did the fleet's six captains. But they had been ordered not to tell anyone else, so as to minimize the potential for injunctive protests and debates.

Even so, the director had expected at least a little feedback . . . if only from the captains themselves. After all, at least half of them couldn't have been thrilled with the board's decision, and Abute had expected them to tell him so.

But they hadn't. They hadn't uttered a word. In fact, in view of what had gone before, their silence had begun to seem a little eerie to him.

The director wished all six of them could have been given command of the *Daedalus*. Certainly, they deserved it. The job they did in the Oreias system, both collectively and as individuals, had exceeded everyone's expectations—including his own.

It was unfortunate that only one of them could win the prize.

Just then, he heard the beep of his communicator. Withdrawing the device from its place inside his uniform, he said, "Abute here."

"Director," said the transporter technician on a nearby Christopher, "we're ready to begin transport."

"Do so," the administrator told him. "Abute out."

He turned to the bridge's sleek silver captain's chair and waited. A moment later, Abute saw a vertical gleam of light grace the air in front of the center seat. As the gleam lengthened, the outline of a man in a blue Starfleet uniform began to form around it.

After a few seconds, the director mused, many people there would have a good idea of who the officer was. Nonetheless, they would have to wait until the fellow had completely solidified before any of them could be certain. Finally, the materialization process was complete. . . .

And Hiro Matsura took a step forward.

The man cut a gallant figure in his freshly laundered uniform, his bearing confident, his gaze steady and alert. If appearance meant anything, he was precisely what Starfleet had been looking for.

But it wasn't just Matsura's appearance that had won him the *Daedalus*. It was the uncanny resourcefulness he had displayed in the encounter with the Nisaaren, which had saved the Oreias colonies from destruction and invited the possibility of peace.

Of all the qualities the review board had considered, ingenuity was the one they had valued most—the one they believed would prove most critical to the fleet's success as the Federation moved into the future.

And Hiro Matsura had demonstrated that he had this quality in spades.

The assembled officials exchanged glances and even a few muffled remarks—some of them tinged with disapproval. But then, the director mused, it was an understandable reaction. The research faction had been made to swallow a rather bitter pill.

The military, on the other hand, had won a great victory. If anyone doubted that, he had but to observe the ear-to-ear grin of Admiral Walker, who was gazing at Matsura with unabashed pride.

Of course, neither the admiral nor anyone else had any inkling how narrow Matsura's victory had been. Right to the end, Abute had learned, the board had been vacillating between two and even three of the candidates—though no one had revealed to him the identity of the other choices.

But that was all water under the bridge, the director told himself. Captain Matsura would sit in the *Daedalus*'s center seat. The decision had been made and no one could change it.

"Ladies and gentlemen," said Abute, "I give you the commanding officer of the *U.S.S. Daedalus* . . . Captain Hiro Matsura."

The announcement was met with applause from all present—with varying degrees of enthusiasm, naturally. In the director's estimate, it was to the credit of the research people that they applauded at all.

"Congratulations," Walker told his protégé, stepping forward to offer the younger man his hand.

Matsura shook it, a bit of a smile on his face. "Thank you, sir," he responded in crisp military fashion.

Clarisse Dumont came forward as well, albeit with a good deal more reluctance. She too extended her hand to the captain of the *Daedalus*.

"I wish you all the luck in the world," she told Matsura. "And despite the disdain *some* have displayed toward the advancement of science, I hope you will see fit to—"

Unfortunately, Dumont never got to finish her statement. Before she could accomplish that, another gleam of light appeared in front of the center seat. Abute looked wonderingly at the admiral and then at Dumont, but neither of them seemed to know what was going on.

As the newcomer gained definition, the director could see that it was Captain Hagedorn. When he had finished coming together, the fellow moved forward to stand alongside Matsura.

Abute shook his head. "I don't understand," he said.

Neither Matsura nor Hagedorn provided an answer. However, another glint of light appeared in front of the captain's chair.

This time, it was Aaron Stiles who appeared there. Without

looking at Admiral Walker or anyone else, he came forward and joined his colleagues.

Walker's eyes narrowed warily beneath his thick gray brows. "What's the meaning of this?" he demanded of his former officers.

They didn't respond. But the director noticed that there was yet another gleam of light in front of the center seat, and someone else taking shape around it.

To his surprise, that someone turned out to be Bryce Shumar. And to his further surprise, Shumar took his place beside the others.

Now Abute *really* didn't get it. What did Shumar have to do with the military contingent? Hadn't he been at odds with Matsura and the others right from the start?

But Shumar wasn't the last surprise. Thirty seconds later, Cobaryn appeared as well. And after him came Dane, completing the set.

Starfleet's captains stood shoulder to shoulder, enduring the stares of everyone present. And for the first time, the director mused, the six of them looked as if they might be able to stand one another's company.

The admiral glowered at them. "Blast it," he said, "exactly what are you men trying to pull?"

"I'd like to know myself," Dumont chimed in.

Matsura turned to her. "It's simple, really. You tried to make us your pawns. You tried to pit us against one another."

"But we had a little talk after Oreias," Shumar continued, "and we realized this isn't about individual agendas. It's too important."

"Damned right," said Stiles. "My fellow captains and I have come too far to let bureaucrats of *any* stripe tell us what to do."

Dane glanced at Walker. "Or whom we should respect. After all, we're not just a bunch of space jockeys anymore."

"We're a fleet," Hagedorn noted. "A *Star*fleet."

"And in spirit, at least," Cobaryn told them, "we are here to assume command of the *Daedalus together.*"

The admiral went red in the face. "The *hell* you are! I'll see the lot of you stripped of your ranks!"

"Perhaps you would," Abute told him, "if you were in charge of this fleet. But at the risk of being rude, I must remind you that *I* am the one in charge." He glanced at the six captains. "And frankly, I am quite impressed by what I see in front of me."

Walker's eyes looked as if they were going to pop out of their sockets. "Are you out of your mind?" he growled. "This is rank insubordination!"

The director shrugged. "One might call it that, I suppose. But I prefer to think of it as courage, Admiral—and even you must admit that courage is a trait greatly to be admired."

Dumont sighed. "This *is* unexpected. But if that's the way these men feel, I certainly won't stand in their way."

Abute chuckled. "Spoken like someone who has nothing to lose and everything to gain, Ms. Dumont. I wonder . . . had it been Captain Shumar or Captain Cobaryn who was granted command of the *Daedalus,* would your reaction have been quite so forgiving?"

Dumont stiffened, but didn't seem to have an answer.

The director nodded. "I thought not."

He glanced at his fleet captains, who remained unmoved by the onlookers' reaction to their decision. He had hoped the six of them might work together efficiently someday, maybe even learn to tolerate one another as people. But this . . .

This was something Abute had never imagined in his wildest dreams.

Turning to the officials who had been invited to this occasion, he assumed a more military posture—for the sake of those who cared about such things. "I hereby turn over command of this proud new vessel, the *U.S.S. Daedalus . . .* to the brave and capable *captains* of Starfleet. May they always bring glory to their ships and to their crews."

Everyone present nodded to show their approval. That is, with the notable exception of Big Ed Walker. But that, Abute reflected, was a battle they would fight another day.

Look for STAR TREK fiction from Pocket Books

Star Trek®: The Original Series

Star Trek: The Next Generation®

Star Trek: Deep Space Nine®

Star Trek: Voyager®

STAR TREK
THE EXPERIENCE
LAS VEGAS HILTON

Be a part of the most exciting deep space adventure in the galaxy as you beam aboard the U.S.S. Enterprise. Explore the evolution of Star Trek® from television to movies in the "History of the Future Museum," the planet's largest collection of authentic Star Trek memorabilia. Then, visit distant galaxies on the "Voyage Through Space." This 22-minute action packed adventure will capture your senses with the latest in motion simulator technology. After your mission, shop in the Deep Space Nine Promenade and enjoy 24th Century cuisine in Quark's Bar & Restaurant.

- -

Save up to $30

Present this coupon at the STAR TREK: The Experience ticket office at the Las Vegas Hilton and save $6 off each attraction admission (limit 5).

Not valid in conjunction with any other offer or promotional discount. Management reserves all rights. No cash value.
For more information, call 1-888-GOBOLDLY
or visit **www.startrekexp.com**.
Private Parties Available.